THE
MEMORY
TRAP

BY
DONNA JOPPIE

Printed in the United States of America

Hardcover ISBN: 978-1-961624-43-6
Paperback ISBN: 978-1-961624-44-3
ebook ISBN: 978-1-961624-45-0
Library of Congress Control Number: 2024912117

DartFrog Plus is the hybrid publishing imprint of DartFrog Books, LLC.

301 S. McDowell St.
Suite 125-1625
Charlotte, NC 28204
www.DartFrogBooks.com

To my husband, Rick, for putting up with years of me
hiding away to write.

"A great writer is an emotion recycler.
No experience of pain, love, loss, joy, or grief is forgotten.
Each is used and infused into the lives of their characters."
—Donna Joppie

CHAPTER ONE

Spring 1962

Rob Chambers pushed certified copies of the document he had just found into his briefcase and rushed up the staircase into the sweltering 104-degree temperature. The still air did little to clear his lungs of dust and fibers from hours of searching through the decaying files of people long dead. This type of work was expected, fresh out of law school. Every young lawyer had to endure something like this.

He entered the hotel where he and two long-term associates from the Tolland Law Firm were staying. Andrew Rider was standing in the lobby. "Mr. Rider. Do you have a moment?" Rob said.

The short, stocky, middle-aged man took a handkerchief from his pocket and blotted his face as Rob approached. "So this is Brownsville, Texas," he said. "How do people who live here survive this heat?"

Rob smiled. "I think they're probably accustomed to it."

"Did you find the heirs to plat 287?"

"I did. But while I was looking, I came across a document that may change the leasing on 345."

Andrew raised a hand. "Stop right there. Anything connected to the Ortega lease goes through Horton. That's the most sought-after plat we're leasing, and Horton's very protective of it."

"I understand the plat's significance to Mexicana Oil, Mr. Rider. That's why Mr. Horton needs to see this document before he signs a lease."

"You'd better be sure about this, Rob. You're a new associate, and Horton is not one to be questioned."

"I wouldn't bother him if I didn't think it was important."

"Then I'll ask him to call you. But please keep me out of it."

"Sure. If that's what you want."

"Now, please excuse me. I'm ready to get out of this suit and relax. I hope they get Red Skelton on the channels down here. I never miss his shows."

"I'm sure they do."

"I suggest you stay close to your phone tonight. You don't want to miss Horton's call."

"Yes, sir. I will."

Rider took the elevator, and Rob used the stairs. He got to his room, ordered room service, and then took the documents from his briefcase and laid them on the bed. There was no need to review them. Every word was embedded in his memory.

Eidetic imagery, photographic memory, whatever you called it, Rob preferred to keep quiet about the fact that he possessed it. The only people at the firm who knew were Wanda Snow and the firm's owner, Gary Tolland.

Room service came, and hours passed. He was about to put the document back in his briefcase when his phone finally rang.

"I heard you wanted to speak to me?" senior associate James Horton said.

"Yes, sir, I did. I found something important today."

"I'm listening."

"In my research for plat 287, I discovered a codicil that appears connected to plat 345. If I'm right, the Ortega daughters aren't the rightful heirs of the mineral rights to that section of land you are about to lease." He waited for a response but heard nothing. "Mr. Horton, are you there?"

"How long have you been with the firm, Chambers?"

"Since being your intern? Only a few weeks."

"Correct, and I've been the firm's senior associate for the last fifteen years. Mexicana Oil is not only our largest client, but I was also the one who brought them to the firm. Securing these rights is worth millions to Mexicana Oil. They entrusted us to sign ironclad contracts for these plats before another company snatches them away."

"Yes, sir. I'm well aware of how important our work is. That's why I brought this to you."

"I spent over a year investigating the Ortega holdings. I dare you to question my work."

A large lump lodged in Rob's throat. "I--I apologize, sir. That was never my intent."

"Well, that's exactly how it sounds. Are there any other insulting remarks you wish to make before you listen?"

"No, sir."

"Good. As I recall, you and Carlos Rojas struck up a friendship during your time as interns."

"Yes, sir. We did."

"I just received word that he will join us in Juárez as our interpreter. I insist you handle yourself professionally. You must never forget his father owns Mexicana Oil."

"You have nothing to worry about, sir."

"See that I don't. We leave for the airport at six o'clock tomorrow morning. Don't be late."

The line hummed, and Rob hung up the phone, exhaling audibly. He glanced at the copies of the codicil, then picked up the phone and made a long-distance call, grinning when he heard Wanda's voice. "Hi, there. Sorry for calling so late."

"It's never too late. How is it going?"

He'd never had much time for the girls he had met at the University of Texas. Once they learned you were studying law or premed, you were high on their target list as a husband. But Wanda wasn't made in that mold. That was the first thing that had attracted him to her. It wasn't the last. "I found something today that could change the ownership of mineral rights on our key plat."

"The Ortega estate?"

"How did you know?"

"I did a lot of research for Horton. From everything I saw, the daughters were his only heirs."

"That's what Horton said. But, according to the codicil, Ortega gave his son the mineral rights to that section of land."

She paused. "I never saw anything that mentioned a codicil or a son."

"The codicil's testator was Ortega del Rio Lafuenta, and the son's name is Victor Munez Ortega del Rio Lafuenta."

"Rob, there was nothing about anyone named Munez."

"That's because Munez is Victor's mother's name."

"If you are certain this is related to Ortega, that codicil must be validated as soon as possible."

"I realize that. But I'm a new associate, and Horton refuses to look at it."

Wanda paused a moment. "That has nothing to do with it, Rob. Horton resents you."

"Why? I haven't been with the firm long enough to offend anyone."

Wanda's pause this time was longer. "Look. I'm going to say something, but you can't share a word of this with anyone."

"Of course not."

"Horton took over hiring and overseeing all staff and associates years ago. As I understand it, Tolland offered you the associate's position weeks before he told Horton. By the time Horton found out, he had promised your position to the son of one of his former classmates."

"Then why was I hired?"

"Tolland made Horton recant his offer."

Rob took a deep breath. "And he blames me."

"I'm afraid so, and Mr. Tolland's obvious fondness for you doesn't help."

"Okay. Now I understand why Horton dislikes me. But that shouldn't keep him from protecting the firm. If I'm right, and we sign the Ortega daughters instead of the son, it could be catastrophic--not only to the firm, but also to Mexicana Oil."

"I agree. This could seriously damage the firm's reputation. What are you going to do?"

He rose and paced as far as the cord would stretch. "If Horton doesn't validate the codicil, then I have to do it. The document says the son was born in Ciudad Juárez, Mexico. Maybe while we're there, I can locate Victor's birth records."

Wanda hummed low in her throat. "How are you going to do that without Horton finding out?"

"I don't know, but it's the only way to get him to take it seriously."

"Be careful. If Horton discovers you're doing this behind his back, he will move heaven and earth to terminate you."

"Wanda, I can't stand by and see Tolland hurt."

"Horton won't see it that way."

"And if I do nothing, and it turns out I'm right?"

"It could destroy everything Mr. Tolland has spent years building."

"Exactly."

"I think you're going to be a wonderful lawyer."

God, I love her. "Until I met you, it's all I wanted." He heard her laugh. "Damn, I wish I was there."

"Me too," she said through a yawn. "Sorry, it's been a long day."

He let himself growl. "I like how you sound when you're warm and cozy."

She laughed. "Stop it. Keep talking like that, and neither of us will sleep. Call when you can. I'm anxious to hear what you find."

"I will. Good night, sweetheart." He hung up, returned the codicil to his briefcase, and went to bed.

*   *   *

The Tolland team's plane landed at a small airport near Corsicana, Texas, the following morning. Rob looked out the window as they taxied to a group of hangars. Carlos was waiting for them beside a large, black Lincoln Continental, ready to greet the men as they exited the plane.

"Welcome, gentlemen. My father sends his greetings."

Horton looked past the young man. "Carlos. I thought I requested a second car for our luggage."

"Do not be concerned, señor," Carlos said as a red Ford Econoline van appeared. "You see, everything is under control. My driver will take us and your boxes to the office, and your luggage will be taken to the hotel by the van."

Carlos turned to Rob. "Roberto, my friend. I am pleased you are here."

"It's great to see you, Carlos."

The conversation ended when Horton stepped between the two young men. "We have work to do, Chambers. You can visit later."

The younger men exchanged a glance before getting into the car. A short time later, the sedan stopped in front of a three-story building on Corsicana's main street. Carlos escorted the team up an open staircase through the hallways to a conference room. "Please. Make yourselves comfortable. My father will be here soon."

They didn't have to wait long before three men entered the room.

"Señor Horton, welcome." Enrico Rojas, a man in his early sixties, extended one hand to Horton and gestured for Carlos to step aside with the other. "May I introduce our legal counselor, Héctor Díaz? He will be assisting you while you are here." Rojas turned to the younger man. "You must meet my firstborn and appointed heir to my position, Arturo Rojas."

Horton reached for the young man's hand. "I heard much about you during our last visit. As I recall, you were away on business."

"*Sí*, señor. It is a pleasure to meet you."

Rojas approached Rob. "I hear congratulations are in order, Roberto. I understand you are now a member of the Tolland Law Firm."

"Yes, sir." Rob shook the elder Rojas's hand.

Horton took a step forward. "A diploma doesn't make one a lawyer, señor. He still has to pass the bar."

"A minor detail, I am certain," said Héctor Díaz.

Rojas waved a hand toward the table. "Come, we have much to discuss."

As the men were taking their seats, Arturo turned to his brother. "Not you, Carlos. Have you forgotten? Luis is arriving from university today."

"I know. I have asked my secretary to let us know when he arrives."

Rojas turned to Carlos. "Absolutely not. You will meet Luis and bring him to me at once. Arturo and I will handle the business."

Carlos glanced at Rob before pushing back his chair. "*Con su permiso*, gentlemen. It seems I have duties elsewhere."

Rob winced as Carlos left the room. He'd witnessed a few exchanges between them during his first trip, but nothing so public and embarrassing as this.

Rojas waited for Carlos to leave the room before speaking. "Gentlemen. I understand you require our assistance to complete the agreements."

"That's correct," Horton replied. "Our goal is to have all leasing documents signed as quickly as possible so you can plan your drilling schedule."

"None of it will matter without securing the largest plat," Rojas added.

"Of course," Horton replied. "That is my primary focus."

"Where should we start?" Díaz asked.

Horton took a yellow pad from his folder and slid it down to Rob. "Take notes, and don't leave out a single detail."

*   *   *

Hours later, Rojas, Díaz, and Arturo remained in the conference room as the Tolland team was shown to an office by Carlos's secretary.

Horton surveyed the room and turned to the secretary. "Where are our files?"

"Sorry, sir. I don't know."

"Where is Carlos?"

"Mr. Rojas is in the lobby awaiting the arrival of his brother."

"Chambers, find Carlos and locate our files."

"Yes, sir."

Rob left the room and went to the lobby. He saw Carlos embracing a younger man with dark hair and similar features. They were speaking Spanish as Rob descended the staircase. Carlos switched to English when he saw him. "Roberto, I am glad you are here. Come meet my little brother. Luis, this is my friend Roberto Chambers from Dallas."

Rob extended his hand. "It's a pleasure to meet you, Luis."

"You as well, Roberto. My brother has spoken of you many times."

Carlos struck his younger brother lightly on his forearm. "The last time I saw this one, he was a boy. Now, look at him. He is so tall."

"I haven't grown, Carlos. You have shrunk."

Carlos placed his arm around his younger brother's shoulders. "Careful, *hermanito*. I can still take you down."

Carlos's expression changed when two men entered the foyer.

"Luis, why are these two with you?" Carlos asked his brother.

"I did not bring them, Carlos. They were at the airport in México City."

The men approached, and Carlos lowered his voice. "I made it clear we would meet at the end of the week."

"There are matters that could not wait."

"Forgive me, Roberto. These unwelcome guests are old university brothers, Diego, and Alejandro."

Rob shook hands, then turned to Carlos. "Sorry for intruding, but we're having difficulty locating the file boxes. If you tell me where they are, I will leave you with your brother and friends."

"You are my guest, I will show you. In fact, we will all go. Diego, Alejandro, this is Roberto Chambers. He has just joined the Tolland Law Firm."

Alejandro focused his attention on Rob. "We have heard much about you, Roberto."

"Enough, Alejandro," Carlos ordered. "Roberto doesn't have time to hear you chatter.""

The men followed Carlos to an office where the boxes of files were stacked on a table next to a desk.

Rob surveyed the room. "Carlos, may I use this space?"

"Yes, of course. It is all yours." He turned to his brother. "Before I take you to Papá, have you been a good son and taken care of our mamá?"

Luis threw up his hands. "I try to counsel her, Carlos, but she is stubborn, and her reasoning confuses me."

The men laughed. Carlos placed a hand on his shoulder. "I have news for you, brother. All women are confusing. Now we must go. Our father will grow angry if I keep you from him a moment longer."

Luis crossed his arms and shook his head. "Carlos, I wanted to spend time with you. I hate him and Arturo for how they treat you."

Carlos glanced apologetically at Rob, then grasped his brother's shoulders. "Luis, you must not hate Papá. Our love for you is the one thing we have in common." The words were barely out of Carlos's mouth when Arturo entered the room.

"Carlos, you were told to bring Luis to us as soon as he arrived."

"No one detained me, Arturo. My flight was delayed."

Carlos locked eyes with their older brother as he spoke. "You are wasting your time, brother. Arturo takes great joy in insulting me every chance he gets."

"Come, Luis," Arturo said. "Papá is waiting. Make yourself useful, Carlos, and see to our brother's luggage. Papá and I are eager to hear about Luis's semester at the university."

Carlos was silent after they left, then turned and displayed a false grin to the men in the room. "Sorry for the interruption, Roberto. My secretary will assist you with your needs while I'm away."

"I think I can handle it from here, Carlos. Thanks for your help."

The grin on Carlos's face vanished when he addressed his unexpected visitors. "Diego, you and Alejandro wait for me until I return. We have much to discuss concerning your untimely arrival."

When Carlos had left the room, Rob turned to the men. "If you will excuse me, I must let the other team members know where the files are being kept."

"Do not be concerned with us," Diego said. "Alejandro and I must secure a car to take us to the hotel."

"It was good to meet you both." Rob walked out and met Andrew Rider in the hallway.

"Please tell me you have our files," Rider said, twisting his hands.

"They're in the office behind me."

"Thank goodness. Horton wants the files in plat order."

"When does he need them?"

"Right away. I better get back before he comes looking for me." Rider turned and hurried down the hallway.

Rob returned to the workroom and discovered Alejandro going through one of their boxes, but he stepped away as soon as he saw him.

"Is there something I can help you with?" Rob said.

"Sorry. I've been told I have an inquisitive mind."

Who is this guy, and why is he going through our files? "Do you work in the oil industry?"

Alejandro laughed. "I know nothing of the petroleum business, and neither does Diego. His family has owned coffee plantations in Colombia for generations. Diego is to take over the operations when his father retires."

"Sounds like a daunting task. What about you?"

"My father and older brother are thoracic surgeons in México, but that is not my path. The sight of blood makes me ill." He smiled. Oh, at least his mouth moved in a way that, in someone else, could have been a smile. "To save my family's dignity, I was *encouraged* to enter the medical research field. So, I became a chemist."

Alejandro walked over to the desk. "Diego and I are friends of Carlos, but his relationship with you is different from ours. He considers you a true friend."

"We are."

"That is good because he needs one. His relationships with his father and older brother are difficult ones. Do you know why?"

"No, and it's not my place to ask."

"If you are true friends, you should know. Have you seen *As the World Turns*? I love that show."

"As I said, it's none of my business."

Alejandro took a chair next to the desk. "Doesn't matter. I will tell you anyway."

Rob shook his head and began sorting files as he tried to avoid listening.

"I will start from the beginning," Alejandro said. "Señor Rojas married Carlos's mamá just before México's government took ownership of all minerals in México. Are you aware of this?"

Rob didn't answer.

"Roberto, do you know about the Mexican government claiming all minerals?"

"Oh, sorry. I do if you are referring to the government's 1930s claim to all oil, gas, gold, silver, and other precious metals."

"That law took away Rojas's career, and he found himself with nothing to do but manage the family's ranches and business holdings. Rojas despised it, so after Arturo was born, he came to Corsicana and started Mexicana Oil. He dedicated himself to building his business in Texas while his beautiful wife and young Arturo remained in México. He did not return to them for almost a year, and as the story goes, his beautiful wife grew lonely, and a former suitor started calling." Alejandro raised his eyebrows. "Do you understand my meaning?"

"I think it's time to stop this conversation."

"But this is the good part. After being away for so long, Rojas returned to México and discovered his wife was expecting a child. As you can imagine, he was furious."

Rob looked up from his box. "Are you saying Rojas isn't Carlos's father?"

Alejandro nodded. "That is precisely what I am saying."

"If Rojas was so angry, why didn't he leave her?"

"He could not. Without her family's name, money, and connections, no one in México would have trusted him. He needed those connections to lease oil-producing land in Texas, Arizona, and California. Her wealth and credibility are vital to the success of his business."

"So, Arturo and Luis are Carlos's half-brothers?"

"Sí, but as you saw, Luis idolizes Carlos, and their mamá also favors him. That is why Rojas pours all his attention on his other two sons and his anger on Carlos. Unfortunately, Rojas's hatred blinds him to Carlos's genius. All his university professors referred to him as *El Cerebro*."

"Sorry. I don't speak Spanish."

"It means 'the brain.'"

"It sounds like Carlos has been through a lot."

"He has, and now Rojas plans to give Arturo his position as head of Mexicana Oil when he retires. Unfortunately, Arturo is not smart enough to run water, much less a company."

"That's too bad. Maybe Rojas will have a change of heart and give it to Carlos."

"Not possible. Carlos has done everything possible to earn his father's approval, but nothing has worked."

"Alejandro," Diego shouted, entering the room. "I could hear you gossiping from the hallway. If Carlos hears of this, he will not be pleased. Come. I have a car waiting to take us to the hotel."

Alejandro turned to Rob. "I am sure we will meet again, Roberto," he said, leaving with Diego.

Rob stood, looking at the open door. He couldn't pinpoint it, but something about those two didn't seem right.

CHAPTER TWO

After three days in Corsicana, the team took Mexicana Oil's private plane to Juárez, where Carlos was to join them. They were standing at the hotel desk, checking in, when Carlos arrived.

"Good afternoon, gentlemen. Was your trip pleasant?"

"As much as traveling can be," Horton scoffed. "I hope you have completed your business because I need your full attention."

Carlos gave a slight bow. "I'm at your service."

"Perfect. Give me an hour to settle, and we'll meet in the lobby to discuss scheduling."

"I will be waiting." After Horton and Rider walked away, Carlos turned to Rob.

"I have arranged for a couple of beautiful ladies to join us for dinner and to amuse us tonight."

Rob shook his head. "Yes to the dinner, *no* to the ladies."

Carlos clasped Rob's face in his hands. "What is wrong with you?"

Rob brushed his hands away. "I told you about Wanda when I was here last summer."

"Yes, but we are in México. She will never know."

"I will know, Carlos. And that's enough."

Carlos shook his head. "You disappoint me, my friend."

Rob grinned as he picked up his bags. "Sorry, pal, but that's how it is."

*   *   *

Horton's "short" meeting ran for over two hours before he checked his watch. "I think we covered enough to realize the necessity of starting early each day in order to see everyone within the two days I have allotted for this. That will require our first meetings to start at 8:00 a.m."

"Señor, this is México. No one accepts visitors at that time of day. Business is always discussed in the afternoon or evening."

"I am aware of that. I'm relaying on you to convince them how important it is to meet with us before we leave."

"I understand, señor. Unfortunately, the people you wish to see will not."

Horton sank back into his chair and crossed his arms. "You're right. This means we will have to stay for several more days."

"Yes, but having a favorable outcome will make it worthwhile. That will not happen if you force people to break Mexican tradition."

Horton unlocked his arms and started drumming his fingers on the arm of the chair. "Chambers, contact the firm and let them know of our change of plans."

"Yes sir. And after Carlos has confirmed the meetings. I'll also prepare the files in the order of our appointments." Horton's expression soured.

"On second thought, Rider will notify the office and arrange the files," he said.

"Then what else can I do to prepare for our meetings?"

"Nothing, because you aren't going, Chambers."

It would have been good to know why, but that wasn't something Rob could ask. He wasn't eager to be humiliated in front of everyone like the way Carlos had been by his father.

Horton turned to Carlos. "Set the meetings. Rider and I will meet you here at 10:00 a.m.," he said, then turned and headed towards the elevators.

Rider stepped next to Rob and whispered, "Sorry."

"Rider," Horton called. Rider gave Rob a nod and hurried to the elevator.

Rob and Carlos stood silently as the two men left the lobby, then Carlos shook his head. "I was hoping to work alongside you, my friend."

"So was I, but maybe it's for the best. This gives me time to check into something."

"What is that?"

"Birth records. I need to find churches or missions dating back at least forty years in and around Juárez."

"You should start at the *Catedral de Nuestra Señora de Guadalupe.* Speak to the priest. He will have records of every church or mission in the area. Do you need a car?"

"I'll manage."

"Don't be ridiculous. I will have a car waiting for you in the morning. After I make the appointments, we will go to dinner. Then you can explain why I am wasting my time with you instead of two beautiful ladies."

"I don't think anything I say will make you understand my reasons for being faithful to Wanda."

"Perhaps you are right. Until later, my friend."

*   *   *

The following day, Rob was in the lobby when Horton and Rider exited the elevator. "What are you doing here?" Horton asked. "I thought I made it clear you weren't going."

"I wanted to know if there was anything you needed me to do while you're away."

"Yes. Stay out of trouble."

Carlos came through the doors of the hotel and joined the men. "Our car is here."

"Perfect," Horton said and proceeded out the door with Rider trailing behind.

Carlos handed Rob a set of keys. "There is a pale blue '55 DeSoto Fireflite in the parking lot. It was the best I could do on short notice."

Rob slid the keys into his pocket. "It's perfect. Thanks."

"Enjoy your day, my friend. I'm sure mine will not be as pleasant," Carlos said, and hurried to join the other men.

*   *   *

It was late afternoon when Rob returned to his room and left his briefcase before going downstairs. He had just entered the lobby when Horton and Rider came in. "How were the meetings?" Horton ignored him and went straight to the elevator.

"Long but successful," Rider said. "And we have another full day tomorrow. I'm exhausted."

Rob watched the man enter the elevator before running up the stairs to his room. He could think of a thousand things he'd rather do than follow Horton to his room, but waiting wouldn't make this any easier. He took the documents from his briefcase, and went to Horton's floor. He paused outside the door and took several deep breaths, then knocked. The door opened, and Horton rolled his eyes.

"What do you want, Chambers? I'm busy."

"This won't take long, Mr. Horton." Rob handed him the large folder.

"What's this?"

"The documents verifying the information in the Brownsville codicil to plat 345."

Horton glared at him. "You have some nerve, young man. I've already told you that codicil was nothing."

"Yes, sir, you did. But since you didn't need me today, I had time to look into it further, and it was good that I did. These documents confirm that the person named in the codicil is Ortega's son and *heir* to the mineral rights of plat 345. If you agree with the finding, you will save the firm from a major financial disaster."

"Don't patronize me, boy. I don't consider your so-called research valid unless it was verified."

"Yes, sir, I understand. As you can see, I had the authenticity of these documents certified."

Horton thumbed through the pages, glared at him again, and closed the door in Rob's face. Rob shook his head and went down the staircase to the lobby where Carlos was waiting. "Thanks for the car," he said, handing him the keys.

"Did you find what you were searching for?"

"I did. I just gave it to Horton."

"Then why do you look so troubled?"

"Horton doesn't consider it relevant. When we return to Dallas, he'll shove it in a file and forget it exists."

"Then we should go. I have something I wish to discuss with you." Carlos tucked a leather folder under his arm and pointed to the door.

"You're right. I need to think about something other than Horton for a while."

They left the hotel and headed to a nearby cantina. Carlos placed the leather folder on the chair next to him when a woman came to take their order.

"How was it today?" Rob asked.

"It went well. Your James Horton is a knowledgeable attorney despite his disdain for you. I was impressed."

"I'm sure he is. I was hoping to see him work."

"Perhaps you will, my friend."

They chatted through the meal until the waitress removed their plates.

"What did you want to talk to me about?" Rob asked.

Carlos leaned forward. "I have a favor to ask."

"Sure. What is it?"

"I need you to purchase something for me at a supply company in Chihuahua. If you leave early, you will return before Horton knows you have gone."

"I will be happy to, but I need to check to be sure I'm not needed."

"There was no mention of you, Roberto."

"If that's the case, what am I buying?"

Carlos paused for a moment. "Laboratory equipment."

"Lab equipment. Why does Mexicana Oil need lab equipment?"

"This is not for my father's company, Roberto. It is a purchase for a friend."

Rob thought about the men he met in Corsicana. "Alejandro is a chemist. Is he the friend?"

"That is not important. I helped you today. It's your time to return the favor."

Rob tried to hide the shock he felt at his friend's response. "I'm not arguing with you, Carlos. I'll be happy to pick up your order."

Carlos paused a moment, then reached for the leather folder. He took a stack of pages out and placed them on the table.

Rob picked up the pages and began looking through them. "Carlos, this is enough equipment for a full lab. What is your friend going to do with this?"

"That question is best not answered."

"Then why aren't you handling this yourself?"

"I can't. Our families are well known in México. Neither he nor I can be seen making the purchase."

"So, you are involved?"

Carlos took a moment. "It's nothing to be concerned about, Roberto. It is only a hobby."

Rob glanced down at the stack of pages. "Carlos, this much equipment is far more than a hobby."

"You disappoint me, Roberto. I thought our friendship was such that you would do this without it becoming uncomfortable."

"What are you talking about?"

"How important is Mexicana Oil to the Tolland Firm?"

"Very important. Why?"

"And are you not an associate of the firm?"

"You know I am."

"Do you not agree that having a Rojas family member in your debt is good for your firm's best interest?"

Rob peered into Carlos's eyes. "Is that a threat?"

"Of course not. But I am concerned it may not go well for you or your firm if my father hears of your team disrespecting our countrymen."

"But you just said you were impressed with Horton."

"Did I? I don't recall."

Rob saw a look in Carlos's eyes he had not noticed before. "How will I explain a list like this to the authorities if I'm stopped?"

"That will not be a problem because you will memorize it."

"There are at least a dozen pages here."

"Roberto. I know your secret. I saw evidence of your memory last summer, but to be certain, I had my people make inquiries."

"You had me investigated?"

"I prefer to call it research." Carlos leaned back and entwined his fingers around his glass. "Do not be concerned, Roberto. We only use the equipment to make small amounts for personal amusement."

"This hobby can get you and your friend into serious trouble."

Carlos held up his glass of tequila. "It is only a matter of time before our amusement becomes as commonplace as this drink. We are just ahead of the times."

Rob glanced at the list and thought about all Gary Tolland had done for him over the past two years. There was no way he could let him lose his most profitable client. "What am I to do?"

"I will notify the store manager you are coming. All you have to do is duplicate the list when you arrive."

Rob gathered up the pages. "I'll place your order, Carlos, but don't ask me to do anything like this again."

Carlos leaned forward and tapped the stack of pages. "Let me see you memorize the list."

"Here?"

"If you are so worried about the authorities, why risk taking it?"

Rob held Carlos's gaze, then took the pages and read each page word for word. When he was done, he handed them back to Carlos.

"Is that it?"

"That's how it works."

"Amazing. A suitcase containing the payment will be in the car's trunk, waiting for you in the morning," Carlos said as he placed the pages back into the leather folder.

"A suitcase?" Rob lowered his voice and looked around. "I'm paying for this in cash?"

"Relax, my friend. That is how it is done."

"Are you certain you can trust these people?"

"That is not your problem. Just do as instructed and tell no one about this."

"Don't worry. I won't." Rob got to his feet. "I need to get back to the hotel."

"Of course. I will meet you in the lobby tomorrow before we leave. Get some rest, my friend. Tomorrow will be a busy day."

*   *   *

Rob was waiting in the lobby when Carlos arrived the following morning. He handed him the keys just as Horton and Rider joined them.

Rob pocketed the keys and approached Horton. "Is there anything I can do while you're out?" Rob prayed there was.

"Definitely not. You've already proved you don't listen." Horton directed his attention to Carlos. "We need to go." He headed out the door with Rider on his heels.

After the two men left, Carlos stepped closer to Rob. "I look forward to hearing about your trip when I return."

Rob waited until Carlos, Horton, and Rider left before going to the car. His gut twisted into knots when he got behind the wheel and turned the key.

*   *   *

Four hours later, Rob parked beside the supply company in Chihuahua and gripped the steering wheel as his heart pounded. His gut screamed at him to not to do this, but his memory kept repeating Carlos's threat. He scanned the area and saw people going into shops and others milling about. Nothing unusual. He had to get this over with and get out of here as fast as possible.

Rob glanced around him as he took the suitcase from the trunk. He had barely cleared the door of the building when a man in a button-down shirt and khakis approached him. "I am the manager. Come with me."

Rob followed him through displays of glass beakers, scales, and other items he didn't recognize. They passed a young woman with brown skin and long braided hair sitting at a desk, taking notes as she spoke in Spanish over the phone. She looked up at him briefly with large, dark eyes before returning to her order-taking.

They entered an office, and the manager closed the door. Rob saw the man glance at the suitcase and would swear he'd licked his lips.

"Excuse me," Rob said. "I didn't catch your name."

"Santos, and yours?"

Rob wasn't expecting that. "My name isn't important. I'm here to place an order."

The manager grinned and displayed his cigarette-stained teeth. "Where is the list?"

"I have to write it out for you."

"But I was told it was a large order."

"It is. Give me some paper."

Santos opened a drawer on his desk, took out a pen and a paper tablet, and placed them on the desk. "You can sit here."

Rob started writing. As the list grew, the manager inched closer until Rob could smell his cigarette breath. After completing all fourteen pages, he handed them to the manager.

"How is this possible?"

"That's not important. You have the order and the delivery instructions. Let's get this done."

The manager pointed to the suitcase. "Nothing will happen until I'm paid."

Rob placed the suitcase on the desk. "You'll get your payment after I get a receipt."

The manager began to laugh. "This is not Sears and Roebuck, *gringo*. We don't give receipts."

"I'm not giving you anything until you give me something to prove I was here."

The manager opened a drawer on his desk, removed a pistol, then ripped a page from the company's invoice tablet and handed it to Rob.

"Now, you have something. Give me the case."

Rob set the suitcase on the desk, and the manager opened it. There were multiple rows of American bills in different amounts. The man took each bundle and fanned through it.

"All seems to be in order. Tell your people the equipment will be shipped." Santos closed the case. "You should leave."

"I couldn't agree more." Rob tucked the paper into his pocket and walked past the young woman and out to the car. He wasted no time getting out of town.

It was late afternoon when Rob returned to the hotel and waited near the lobby door for his team and Carlos to return.

"Welcome back," Rob said when they came in.

Horton ignored him once again and went to the hotel desk. Rider paused and took Rob aside.

"What's going on?" Rob asked.

"We've had a change of plans. Carlos called his office and was told the Ortega sisters' adviser had called and canceled their meeting."

"What does that mean?" Rob said as Carlos joined them.

"It means we're going home sooner than expected," Rider said.

Their conversation ended when Horton joined them. "Carlos, since we're not meeting the Ortega sisters, I want you to move our last appointment as early in the day as possible so we can fly back to Dallas as soon as we're done."

"I will change the appointment and have the company plane on standby."

"Call me as soon as you have it scheduled." Horton started for the elevator and stopped. "Rider, stop talking. We have much to do before we leave tomorrow."

"Yes, yes, coming." He hurried away as fast as his short legs could carry him.

When the two men were gone, Rob reached into his pocket and handed Carlos the keys and the slip of paper.

Carlos unfolded the invoice. "I see you met the manager."

"I insisted he give me something to prove I delivered the order and the suitcase."

"I never doubted you, Roberto." He placed the note and the keys in his pocket. "Let's have dinner and enjoy ourselves before you go."

Rob shook his head. "No, thanks. Not hungry."

"Don't be upset, my friend. It was only a favor."

"Friends don't blackmail friends, Carlos. Whatever we were is over."

"Roberto, wait. Don't leave like this. We need to talk."

Rob never looked back.

CHAPTER THREE

Carlos drove through the gate to his villa, and one of his guards opened his door, saying something. Carlos was lost in thought and had to ask the man to repeat himself.

"Your friends have arrived and are waiting for you," the guard said.

"They are only business associates." Carlos paused a moment. "A word of advice. Never invest yourself in friendships. They weaken you when they end."

"Sí, señor. I will remember that."

Carlos entered the house and paused a moment before joining the men.

Diego looked up as Carlos entered. "Did Roberto pass the test?"

Carlos went to the bar, poured a drink, swallowed it, then poured another. "He took some convincing, but he did it."

"He memorized the whole list?" Alejandro asked.

"In one reading. It was amazing."

"You were right," Alejandro continued, nodding. "He is perfect. When can you get him to join us?"

Carlos held up a hand. "It may take some time."

"Why?" Diego asked. "He is a lawyer with a reputable American firm. His memory will help to conceal documents from the authorities. Your friendship will make this less complicated."

"I think his opinion of me has changed after I forced him into making the purchase. 'Friendship' may be too strong a word now."

"Carlos, the authorities were there to arrest us."

"I realize that."

"You were right to send Roberto. Things would be different if you had not."

"True, but as I said, I think persuading Roberto to join us will take time."

Diego cursed as he threw his empty glass into the fireplace, shattering it. "We don't have time, Carlos. I have told you this before. Our profits are growing too fast for me to hide much longer."

"Then perhaps it is time I find someone who will."

Alejandro stepped between the men, "Carlos, please. We should be celebrating, not fighting."

Diego and Carlos stood glaring at each other for a long moment before Diego dropped his gaze.

"If Roberto is as smart and honest as you say, he is a perfect choice. All we have to do is convince him."

Carlos stepped away from Diego. "And if he refuses?"

Diego glanced at Alejandro before looking at Carlos. "You know the answer to that."

"I hope it does not come to that," Carlos said. "We'll never find anyone else with Roberto's gift."

"Then make him an offer he can't refuse."

"You know him better than anyone," Alejandro added. "Everyone has a price. It is your job to find out what it is."

Carlos shoved his finger in Alejandro's face. "I do not need to be told my job, Alejandro. Roberto is my decision, not yours."

"We understand, Carlos," Diego said. "No one will touch Roberto until you give the order. However, having our people monitor him until you are ready could be wise."

Carlos lowered his hand. "I agree. See that it's done. Enough about Roberto. Now, give me an update on the construction of the cookhouses? This new equipment does no good unless we have the facility and the people to work it."

*   *   *

The plane landed in Dallas, leaving behind Rob's concerns of pursuing the codicil. There was no need to bring it up after the Ortega daughters canceled their meeting. All Rob wanted to do was put Carlos out of his mind and find Wanda.

A car and van met them at the airport. Once everything was loaded, they were taken to the office where Rob oversaw unloading the files and luggage. As he hurried past Tolland's office, Gary Tolland called out to him.

"Rob. Come in."

When Rob walked in, he found Horton and Rider sitting at a table in his office. "Gary, we don't need the boy for this," Horton grumbled.

"Calm down, James. We'll get back to the review in a moment." Gary got up from the table and shook Rob's hand. "Welcome back. How was your first trip as an associate?"

Rob glanced at Horton before answering. "Truthfully, it's about the same as being your intern. But I'm new at this."

"Yes, but there will be more opportunities like this to learn."

"I'm looking forward to it, Mr. Tolland."

"Rob, you're an associate. It's time to stop the formality and call each of us by our first names."

"That might be rushing it a bit, Gary," Horton grumbled. "The boy's been here less than a month and hasn't even taken his bar exam. He hasn't earned the right to use first names."

"Nonsense, Rob will pass the bar on his first try." Gary turned back to Rob. "Before I forget, you're expected at dinner tonight." Rob started to speak, but Gary raised a hand. "Don't even think of refusing. That order came from my wife and daughter. They haven't seen you since you got back."

"Thank you, sir. I look forward to seeing them. I'm sure Sissy is excited about attending college this fall."

"She'd better be. I've already paid a fortune for clothes and tuition. Have you found a place to live?"

"Yes, sir. I just rented a garage apartment on Mockingbird Lane. My friend is helping get my things out of storage in Austin and move into my apartment."

"That's great. I just wanted to say hello before I get too deeply involved with James and Andrew."

"Yes, sir. I won't keep you."

As Rob left, Gary's secretary, stopped him. "Rob, close the door to Mr. Tolland's office."

"Yes, ma'am."

"How was your trip?"

"It was . . . interesting."

"I'm sure it was. Mr. Tolland has great plans for you, young man. Don't mess it up."

"I'll do my best to keep that from happening."

"I understand your bar exam is scheduled."

"Yes, ma'am. I'm taking it next week."

"If you don't make it this time, you can repeat it. It's happened to several of our new associates."

"I hope that doesn't happen."

"Just letting you know. You'd better go. I'm sure you have lots to do."

"Yes, ma'am. Thank you."

Rob rushed down the hallway. When he didn't find Wanda in her office, he went to the research library. She looked up from behind a desk stacked high with law books. "Well, hello. I wasn't expecting you until tomorrow."

He came around the desk to kiss her, but she pushed him away. "Rob, someone might see us."

"I don't care." When he reached for her again, she slipped out of the chair. "I do. I could lose my job."

"That's ridiculous. The firm values you too much."

"It may be 1962, but you would think we still live in the early '50s. You'll get a slap on the wrist, but I'll be shown the door if we get caught."

"He can't dictate relationships."

"Oh, yes, he can. That man's so uptight, I'm not sure he even fraternizes with his wife."

He shook his head. "Thanks. Now I have that image in my head. But I just got here. I need a few minutes to be alone with you."

"It's too risky. We'll have to wait until we are together after work."

Rob shook his head. "It's going to be longer than that. I'm invited to dinner at the Tollands' tonight. Maybe I can get out of it."

"You have to go. Every associate here would jump at dining at the Tollands' home." She wagged a finger at him. "Just remember to keep your distance from Sissy."

"Sissy? Why?"

"Rob Chambers, surely you know Sissy Tolland has a huge crush on you? Everyone else does."

"That's ridiculous. She's like a little sister to me."

"Oh, she definitely doesn't think of you as a brother. You are a tall, handsome man, Rob. Every woman here drooled over you the first day you walked into this office."

"I was too busy looking at you to notice." He tried again to kiss her.

"Rob, no."

"Then where?"

"Meet me on the third level of the parking garage. No one from the firm parks there."

"Make it quick, or I'm coming back and kissing you in front of everyone."

She laughed and pointed to the door.

Rob went to the third level of the parking garage and waited by the door. A few minutes later, Wanda came up the staircase. He led her to a secluded spot and kissed her. "I hated being away from you so long," he whispered.

"I don't like it either, but this is nothing compared to all those years you were in law school."

He pulled back and lifted her chin. "I know, but it didn't stop me from missing you. I love you."

"And I love you. I can't wait for you to finally have a place to call home."

"Neither can I. It's hard to sleep with my feet hanging off the end of Joey's couch."

"What happened with Horton and the codicil?"

"Nothing. The Ortega daughters canceled their appointment, so I didn't need to bring it up."

"Good. At least you didn't have to confront Horton with your proof."

"Too late. I'd already given Horton my research before I heard the appointment was canceled. All I can do now is hope he gets over it."

"Not likely. He's resentful of your relationship with Mr. Tolland and his family."

"But why?" Rob asked. "He's senior associate, and I've only been here a few weeks."

"That's true, but I'm only telling you what I hear."

"Glad to know you're watching my back."

"We should get back."

"I know." He held her and whispered, "Can I come by your apartment after dinner?"

"You'd better." She wrapped her arm in his as they walked to the staircase.

CHAPTER FOUR

Rob went to his office, which was barely large enough to hold a desk, a filing cabinet, and a couple of chairs. He removed his hat and coat and had just settled in when one secretary after another came in with work folders and placed them on his desk. He wondered if he'd be considered an intern until he passed the bar. Sighing, Rob picked up the first folder and got to work. He didn't look up until hours later, when he realized he'd be late for dinner if he didn't leave immediately. He grabbed his coat, hurried out the door, and nearly collided with Horton.

"Careful, Chambers." Horton looked at his watch. "Leaving already?"

"Yes, sir. I-I'm having dinner at the Tollands.'"

Horton glared at him for a moment. "Oh, yes, Gary's golden boy." Horton stepped closer to him. "I'm watching you, Chambers. You're out of here the first time you mess up," Horton said, then waved him off and walked away.

Rob shook his head and went in the opposite direction to the parking garage.

His childhood memories flooded back as he drove to Tolland's home. Born and raised in Dallas, he'd only moved away to attend the University of Texas. He and Joey had spent hours riding bikes through dirt roads to play ball on the open field that was now part of Love Field Airport, and pretending to be Johnny Weissmuller, out-swimming crocodiles in the Tarzan films they loved.

Those thoughts ended when he turned his '53 Oldsmobile Fiesta into the Preston Hollow neighborhood. The beauty of the Tollands' property wasn't its architecture or manicured lawn. It was the people who lived here. Gary, Helen, and Sissy Tolland had treated him like family during his two years as an intern.

High heels clicked on the wood floor as soon as Rob knocked. "Rob, you know better than to knock," Helen Tolland said as she opened the door. "Come in." Helen Tolland looked years younger than her age. Her wavy brown hair was pinned into a Grace Kelly French twist, and pearls draped her slender neck. Helen's southern drawl was her trademark.

"How are you, Mrs. Tolland?"

"Just perfect, but if you call me Mrs. Tolland again, I'm sending you to your room." She gave him a warm hug and closed the door. "Gary, Sissy—he's here."

Rob removed his coat, folded it, and placed it on the back of the sofa, as he had done many times before. Sissy came rushing in from the hallway and hugged him. He gave her a quick embrace and released her. "Sorry, I missed your graduation, Sissy."

"It wasn't much. Just kids' stuff."

Gary appeared from the kitchen with a tray of drinks. "Not true, little girl. Graduating from high school at the top of your class is an important milestone."

Sissy took hold of Rob's arm. "There are more important things than high school, aren't there, Rob?"

He held up his hands. "Your dad's my boss, Sissy. I'm staying out of this."

"Sissy, stop hanging on him."

She pulled away and crossed her arms in a huff.

"She's fine," Rob said. "Aren't you, little sister?"

"Little sister." Sissy threw up her hands and stormed into the kitchen.

Helen glanced at her husband. "I should check on her."

"She's pouting, Helen. Let her be." Gary turned his attention to Rob. "You said something about going to Austin this weekend to pack."

"I'm leaving right after work tomorrow night."

"Nonsense. You just got back from a long trip. Take tomorrow off, get moved, and be ready to work Monday morning."

"Thanks, Gary. I'll call Mr. Horton and let him know I won't be in."

"It's James, Rob. Stop calling him Mr. Horton. I'll tell him tomorrow. You just get settled."

Gary reached for Helen's hand. "With your permission, Miss Scarlett, I think it's time to eat. I'm starving."

*　　*　　*

After dinner, Rob drove across town to Wanda's apartment. He saw her lights were on and rushed up the staircase. She wore fluffy pink slippers and a robe over blue pajamas and when she opened the door, he stepped in, kissed her, and pushed the door closed with his foot. "I've needed that all day."

"Me too," she said as they went to the couch. "How was dinner?"

"Dinner was great. Before it started, Gary called Sissy down for being overly friendly with me, but I think she got over it."

"I wouldn't be too sure about that."

The front door opened, and an attractive woman came in. She was wearing a dark blue suit and dragging a suitcase.

"Hello, Shelly," Rob said, getting to his feet. "Let me take that to your room."

"Thanks, Rob." Shelly removed her cap.

"How was your flight?" Wanda asked.

"It's been three long days, and I'm exhausted."

"So much for the glamorous life of an airline stewardess," Rob added.

"True. Good to see you, Rob. What's it like living in Dallas again?"

"Too soon to know." Rob took Wanda's hand. "I should go. You ladies need to get some rest."

"Don't leave on my account," Shelly said as she untied her neck scarf. "I'm going to bed. Good night."

Wanda put her arms around Rob's neck. "See you tomorrow."

"I'm not coming in. Gary gave me the day off to get moved."

"All by yourself?"

"Joey's helping me move."

"Don't wear yourself out."

"I'll be fine." He pulled her close and kissed her. "Good night, sweetheart."

Rob drove to Lewisville, parked his Fiesta in front of Joey's tiny white wood-framed home, took the key under the doormat, and let himself in. The only light in the room was a lamp next to the Zenith TV. The ceiling fan was on, making the squares of aluminum foil wrapped around the TV's rabbit-ear antennas flutter in the breeze. A quilt and pillow were placed on one end of the sofa with a note in Joey's scribble.

Keep it down. Baby hasn't been sleeping. We're tuckered out. See you in the morning.

He switched off the lamp, stripped down to his boxers, and stretched out on the sofa. Just as he drifted off to sleep, the cry of a newborn infant pierced the silence.

*   *   *

Three sleep-deprived adults sat at the small kitchen table the following morning. Joey yawned and took a sip from his coffee cup. "Sorry the baby kept you up. Apparently, she got her mother's eyes and my lungs."

Rob chuckled. "It's amazing how something so little can make so much noise."

"Laugh now," Joey's wife, said. "One day, you'll have one of your own." She rose and took her empty cup to the sink before returning and kissing Joey on the forehead. "If you guys don't mind, I'm going back to bed."

Joey took her hand and kissed it. "Get some rest, honey."

"When will you get back from Austin?"

"Probably not till tomorrow night."

"Sorry about taking your husband," Rob said.

"Don't be. Now I don't have to cook." She went to their bedroom and closed the door.

"I want to show you something." Rob reached into his pocket and handed Joey a small box. "I've been carrying this around for months."

"Damn, this looks like an engagement ring."

"Do you think Wanda will like it?"

"Hell, I'd like it." He removed it and slipped it on his little finger. "How does it look?"

Rob reached across the table and took the ring from him. "Like crap on you."

"Why haven't you asked her?"

"I was waiting until I knew I'd passed the bar."

"You know she's gonna say yes." Joey got out of his chair. "Let's go. It's time to get you off my couch before you destroy it."

*　*　*

Carlos was at his desk in Corsicana when his private line rang. "Can you talk?" Diego asked.

"Let me close my door." When he returned, he picked up the phone. "This had better be important, Diego. You were told never to call me here."

"I just sent off the largest shipment we have ever done. It will make us at least seven million this week."

"I know the numbers, Diego."

"We should celebrate."

"No celebration until we have the money."

"You are wealthy, Carlos. Why do you insist on working for a man who hates you?"

"I do not need to explain myself to you."

"No, you don't, but now it is time to discuss Roberto."

"I will decide when it is time, Diego. Not you. Now get back to work, and don't call here again." Carlos hung up the phone. "*Burro*," he said with disgust.

*   *   *

Rob was at work early Monday morning after his move. He wanted to finish as many files as possible before leaving for the bar exam. Wednesday afternoon, he took the few files he had not completed to Gary's secretary.

She looked up at him. "Is this it?"

"It is. I placed a detailed note on the first page of each file regarding the information still needed. If you prefer, I could finish and leave late tonight."

"Don't even think about it," Gary said from the doorway of his office. "Are you packed?"

"My suitcase is in the car. I was planning on leaving after work."

"Taking the bar is work. You should leave now to get a good night's rest before you start the exam. I want this behind you so I can put you to work."

"Thank you. I'm ready."

"Then get out of here." Gary shook his hand and returned to his office.

"Well, you heard the man," the secretary said. "Go and pass that thing."

"I'll do my best."

Rob left her office, went down the hall to the research room, and found Wanda hovering over several legal books. She looked up when he closed the door.

"Leave it open. We can't be in here with the door closed."

"If you insist," he said and pushed it partly closed. "I'm leaving for Austin, and I couldn't go without seeing you."

She got up from the desk, took him to the far side of the room, and cupped his face with her hands. "You have worked a long time for this, Rob Chambers. You can do it."

He looked into her eyes. "Passing the bar is only half the dream, Wanda."

She tilted her head. "And what is the second?"

"I will tell you when I get the test results."

"Not fair. Tell me now."

"Nope, you're going to have to wait." He took her into his arms and was about to kiss her when the door opened. They quickly parted, and Wanda grabbed a book from the shelf.

"This may answer that question."

Rob took the book. "I think you're right. Thanks for checking."

Horton stood for a long moment looking at them. "What are you doing here, Chambers? I was told you had left."

"I was, then I thought of something that might come up on the test. I came to ask Wanda's help locating the answer."

"I see. Well, take your book and go. Wanda and I have work to discuss."

Rob turned to her. "Thanks again," and walked out. He went to his office, put the book in his desk drawer, and went to his car. He wanted to call her to find out if Horton had said something but knew it was risky. He waited until he was in Austin and made a long distance call to her that evening. "Did Horton see us?"

"I don't think so. We discussed a project I was working on, and he left."

"I wanted to call earlier but thought it better to wait until you were home."

"Stop worrying about me. These next two days will be tough, even for someone with your memory. I don't want you to call or think about anything here until the testing is over."

"Yes, ma'am."

"You can do this, Rob. I'll be waiting right here Friday evening, anxious to hear how it went."

"It's a promise."

Rob blew out a rush of air in relief. They had been lucky this time but couldn't risk it happening again. He unpacked and readied himself for the next two days.

CHAPTER FIVE

Rob left his last exam and went straight to a pay phone. Despite Wanda's insistence to wait, he called her direct line at the office, but she didn't answer. He knew not to contact the main number, so he drove back to Dallas.

It was about 3:00 p.m. when he hit the city limits. He knew Wanda would still be at work, so he went to his apartment, unpacked, and freshened up before going to her place. When he arrived, he was shocked to find her car was there. Rob rushed to her door and knocked. The smile on his face faded as soon as he saw her.

"Wanda, what's wrong?"

She stepped back as he closed the door.

"I was fired."

"Fired? Why? Because of us?"

She nodded. "Horton must have heard or seen enough to know we're together." She went to the sofa and sat.

Rob sat next to her and wrapped her in his arms. "I'm so sorry, sweetheart. This is all my fault."

"It's both our faults." She started to cry. "Horton will use this against you, Rob."

"I'm sure he will, but we were together long before he made up this stupid rule."

"It doesn't matter. We knew the rules and broke them. Now I have to leave Dallas."

"That's ridiculous. Firms will be fighting for you once they know you're available."

She shook her head. "Horton said I couldn't work for any firm we were in litigation against. If I do, he said I would never work in a Dallas firm again."

"He can't do that." He paused a moment. "Did you sign a noncompete?"

"No."

"Then you can work anyplace you like."

"Rob, he's done it before."

"I can't believe Gary would allow that."

"It's his company, Rob. Tolland must have known what Horton was going to say."

"This is a big city. There must be firms we aren't working against."

Tears ran down her cheeks. "The firm has twenty-seven associates. Each of those associates has several litigation cases. That means we're up against almost every firm in Dallas. I have no place to go."

"Horton can't do this to you. You're the best research assistant I've ever seen."

"I'm the only research assistant you've ever seen."

"I'm not letting him do this without a fight."

Wanda grabbed his arm. "Rob, don't. I can't let you get fired over this."

"That's a risk I'm willing to take." He kissed her forehead and went out her door.

Rob arrived at the firm and went straight to Horton's office. His secretary was about to leave when he walked in. "I need to talk to Horton."

"He's meeting with Mr. Tolland and Mr. Rider in the conference room. Would you like to leave a message?"

"No, this has to be done in person." Rob left her and went down the hallway to the conference room. He was about to enter when he heard Gary's secretary call his name.

"Rob, what are you doing here? We weren't expecting you back until Monday."

"I have to speak with Horton."

"You need to wait until after their meeting."

"This can't wait."

"Rob, come in," Gary called from the conference room. "How did you do?"

Rob went in. "It went well, thank you for asking."

"I've seen others be confident," Horton scoffed, "and they failed."

Rob fought the urge to punch the man. "I need to speak to you in private, Mr. Horton."

Horton glanced at Gary, then back to Rob. "Can't you see I'm busy? Whatever it is you want to say, do it now. We need to get back to work."

"Rob, what's going on?" Gary asked.

"Wanda was fired because she and I broke your new rule. We take responsibility for that, but it doesn't give you the right to keep her from working in this city with any firm she chooses."

"Oh dear," Rider exclaimed.

"James, what is he talking about?" Gary asked. "We need her. You should have told me before you fired her."

"I was going to bring it up after our meeting, but since Chambers has interrupted us, we can discuss it now. Yes, I fired Wanda. She and Rob broke the rule of staff and associates forming a relationship." He turned his attention to Rob. "This is your fault, Chambers. You should never have gotten involved with her."

Rob fought to contain his anger. "We have been together for two years. That's at least a year and a half before you implemented this. I love Wanda, and no rule will change that."

"Then you and she must accept the consequences. If I make an exception for her, I must make it for everyone." Horton turned to Tolland. "This is a perfect example of conflict created by office romances. It jeopardizes the quality of our work. This policy must stand, or situations like this will continue."

Gary removed his glasses and looked from man to man. "I'm sorry this happened, Rob, but I have to agree with James. The integrity of this firm is vital to our success. Your relationship with Wanda started before this rule was introduced. I accept that. And you've done a very good job of keeping it quiet because I knew nothing about it," he said. "Nevertheless, the rule is there, and I'm afraid you and she will have to abide by it. Wanda is a talented research assistant, and I'm happy to help her find a new job. We'll give her a glowing reference, and I will contact any firm she chooses with my personal report of her abilities."

"I appreciate that, Gary, but Horton told Wanda she couldn't work for any firm we are in litigation with. If she did, he would have her banned from ever working in Dallas again."

Gary rounded on Horton. "You said what?"

"We can't risk her giving our opposition information."

"Wanda would never do that. If I hear something has been said or done to prevent her from finding a job in Dallas, she won't be the only person looking for a job. Do I make myself clear?"

Horton glared at Rob, but he nodded his agreement.

"Rob," Gary said, "please tell Wanda a courier will deliver my letter of recommendation to her first thing Monday morning. And have her call my secretary with the firms she has selected. I'll make my calls to them about how qualified she is."

"Thank you, Gary. She . . . we appreciate that." Rob turned to leave.

"Wait. Take a seat. You need to be in this meeting."

"What on earth for?" Horton sputtered. "He has nothing to do with this."

"He's going with you, James. And this time I expect you to treat him as an associate, not an intern."

"That's preposterous. Chambers doesn't know anything."

A rare grin crossed Gary's lips. "Then teach him. It's time the two of you learned to work together."

Horton started to protest, but Gary held up his hand. "Have a seat, Rob. There's a lot for you to get caught up on."

Rob sat down. A glance at Horton's face told him the man was seething. To make things worse, Gary gave him a wink that was by no means surreptitious.

Gary positioned his glasses. "I have the plat sheet and completed Black Pond leasing files. Where are the summaries?"

"They're in my office," Horton said, struggling to maintain his composure. "Before Black Pond purchased Mexicana Oil, I put everything we did in plat categories."

Rob reached for a legal pad and pen. "When was Mexicana Oil purchased by Black Pond?"

"It was finalized a few days ago," Gary answered.

"That's why our trip was cut short," Rider added.

"I thought we left because the Ortega daughters canceled their appointment."

"That was part of the reason," Gary said. "Rojas wanted as many leases signed as possible before closing the Black Pond sale. We were told they are using the Corsicana offices as their Texas headquarters, and we were contracted to complete the work we started when it was Mexicana Oil."

"Who's in charge now?"

"Rojas. Black Pond made him division president because of his connections with the Mexican families who owned land and mineral rights in Texas, New Mexico, Arizona, and California. The pressure is on to get the last mineral owners signed as quickly as possible."

"When did we know the company was being sold?" Rob questioned.

Horton shifted in his seat. "I was told the day before we returned from our trip."

Rob remembered the codicil he'd found in vivid detail. Now that they were in charge of leasing, Horton must have reviewed it with Gary.

"We're on a deadline, gentlemen," Gary added. "Black Pond wants these leases signed by the end of September. Their plan is to start drilling by March of next year."

"That doesn't give us much time," Rob said.

"That's why we have to be sure we get this right. We don't have time to clean up mistakes. I've contacted Rojas. He's agreed to have his legal adviser, Héctor Díaz, as our mediator on this trip. We will need his credibility with the families in Mexico."

Rob was relieved to hear Carlos wasn't mentioned.

"I should be ready to go as soon as I move a few clients around," Horton said. "I'll get back to you Monday morning with a date I'm available for the trip."

"That won't be necessary," Gary said, reaching for his glasses. "Black Pond's plane is picking you up tomorrow afternoon."

"Saturday? I can't possibly go that soon."

Gary looked over his glasses. "Yes, you can. Some of your appointments have been rescheduled. Other associates will handle the rest. Everything will be returned to you as soon as you are back."

"Don't I have a say in this?" Horton protested.

Gary closed the file. "Yes, you do, but this is Black Pond's timetable, not ours. They are too large a corporation to ask them to wait for you to clear your calendar. If you aren't interested in going, I'll send someone else."

"Of course, I'm going."

"Good. We don't have much time. I suggest you go to your offices and pull every file we have on these plats. I will meet with you in the morning before you leave." Gary motioned for Rob to sit as the men were leaving the table.

Horton turned back. "Should I stay?"

"No, I can handle this."

Horton gave Rob a stern look, then ordered Rider to follow him.

When they were alone, Gary gestured for Rob to sit. "I'm sorry about this, Rob. I had no idea you and Wanda were together."

"We thought it best to keep it private. I appreciate your offer to help her."

"There's no reason she should have to leave Dallas. She's a talented researcher and will be an asset to any firm that hires her." Gary paused before continuing. "Whatever this is between James and you has to stop. I'm sending you on this trip so you can learn to work together."

"I'll do everything possible to make that happen. I certainly don't want trouble."

"Good. Now go get ready for the trip."

"Thank you, Gary." He left the conference room and entered his office as his private line rang.

Before Rob could say hello, Joey blurted, "Did she say yes?"

"I haven't asked her, Joey. Results won't be sent out for weeks."

"Buddy, you know you passed. Stop stalling and ask her."

The image of Wanda sobbing flashed in his mind. "This isn't the time."

"You love her. Stop dragging your feet."

"You're right. I'll ask her as soon as I get back."

"Where the heck are you going now?"

"Corsicana. I leave tomorrow."

"How long will you be gone?"

"Only a few days." The thought of leaving Wanda now troubled him. "Do me a favor and check on her while I'm away. She's dealing with something right now."

"Sure. What's wrong?"

"Work stuff."

"You got it, buddy. We'll take good care of Wanda. See ya when you get back."

Rob ended the call and dialed Wanda's number. She gasped when he told her the news. "I can't believe Mr. Tolland is doing this."

"He's trying to help all he can. Changing the rules for us would put him in a difficult place. The only good coming out of this is we no longer have to keep our relationship a secret. You should have seen Horton's face when Gary told him I was going on this trip."

"Trip? What trip?"

"I'm accompanying Horton and Rider to Corsicana to finish the mineral leasing we started with Mexicana Oil."

"How long will you be gone?"

"Two, maybe three days at the most." He paused for a moment. "I'm sorry to be away while you deal with this."

"Don't be. I'll be busy looking for a job."

At that point, Horton entered Rob's office and slammed the door. Rob said, "I need to call you back. Someone just walked in." He hung up. "What can I do for you, Mr. Horton?"

"You could quit, but since that isn't going to happen, I'm here to set the boundaries for this trip. You are to do as you're told and stay out of my way. Is that clear?"

"How can I do that and learn from you? You and Mr. Rider have years of oil and gas experience, Mr. Horton."

Horton crossed his arms and scoffed. "I'm on to you, Chambers. That approach may work with Gary, but it doesn't with me." Horton spun on his heels and went out the door.

Rob shook his head. So much for putting conflict behind them.

CHAPTER SIX

Rob didn't see Horton again until the meeting Saturday morning. "Are you sure you have everything?" Gary asked Horton.

"Andrew and I spent most of the night reviewing every leased plat and section Black Pond wants us to lease. We have all the files boxed and ready for pickup."

Rob wanted to ask if that included the codicil, but after yesterday's confrontation, he didn't dare question Horton about it. It was a decision he would come to regret.

Gary's secretary entered the office. "The files and luggage just left for the airport. I have a car downstairs waiting to take the team when you're ready."

"Thank you. Tell the driver they're on their way." Gary stood, and the team followed. "James, I expect a daily report on your progress."

"I will keep you informed."

"Learn all you can on this trip, Rob. You'll need it when you head a team of your own."

Rob sensed Horton's glare without even looking. "Thank you, Gary."

*　　*　　*

Horton and Rider sat beside each other during the flight. Rob could hear their conversation from where he was seated. When the Ortega lease came up, he moved to the seat across from them.

"Excuse me. I heard you mention plat 345."

"Go back to your seat, Chambers. This doesn't concern you."

"I won't keep you. I wanted to ask about the codicil documents. Did you get a chance to look them over?"

"Andrew," Horton said. "Have we missed any documents connected to this trip?"

Rider glanced from man to man, then began to stutter. "N-none. I checked that file three times to make sure."

Horton glared at Rob. "Now, may Andrew and I get back to work?"

Something about that response didn't feel right.

On landing, they taxied to the same private hangar as before. Rob glanced out the window and groaned inwardly when he saw Carlos get out of a waiting car.

Horton turned to Rob as they exited the plane. "You stay here and ensure every file box and piece of our luggage is off this plane. The last thing I need is to be delayed because you overlooked something." He walked away with Rider a few steps behind him.

Rob welcomed the task. Anything to put space between him and Carlos. A van pulled up next to the plane, and two men got out and took over the unloading of the aircraft. It was done in minutes, and Rob had no choice but to join his group.

As he approached the car, Carlos left Horton and Rider. He advanced as if intending to embrace Rob, but Rob stepped back and extended his hand. Carlos paused a moment before taking it. "I see you are still upset, my friend."

"You used threats to get me to help you, Carlos. And you deceived me. You knew your father's company was being sold."

"Nothing had been finalized. In a purchase that size, either party could walk away at any moment."

"That's not what you implied."

"Chambers," Horton called from the car. "Stop talking. We need to get to the office."

"This is probably the first time Horton and I agree," Rob said.

Carlos kept pace with him all the way to the car. "You must give me a chance to make this right, Roberto."

"I'm not sure that's possible."

"I apologize for the delay, Señor Horton," Carlos said as they neared the car. "I was the one keeping Roberto."

"Doesn't matter," Horton said. "We need to go."

As they drove, Rob listened to the three men in the back seat discussing the sale to Black Pond. They arrived at the newly named building and entered the foyer. Carlos said, "The same offices you used before have been prepared for you."

"Thank you, Carlos," said Horton. "What about our luggage?"

"My driver will take your bags to the hotel after the files are delivered here."

"Chambers, stay back and ensure every box is unloaded," Horton ordered. "Andrew and I are meeting with Señor Rojas."

"Señor, my father is also expecting Roberto. I assure you, every box will be unloaded."

"He's not needed, Carlos.

Carlos glanced back at Rob before escorting Horton and Rider up the staircase.

Rob made sure every box was unloaded and delivered to his workroom. When that was done, he removed his jacket and got to work. He had already unpacked two boxes when Horton entered the room.

"What do you think you're doing?"

"I'm sorting files into plats."

"Repack them and take them to my office. I don't want them in here with you." Horton turned and left the room.

Rob returned the files to the boxes and made the first of several trips to Horton and Rider's office. When he returned with the last boxes, he found Rider pulling files. "Can I help you with that?"

"Yes. Thanks. I have to collect all the files of heirs requiring a translator and get them to Horton before Rojas leaves and we go to the hotel."

When the two of them had finally finished, Rider picked up the files. "I will let you know when we're ready to go to the hotel."

"Thanks. I'll be in my workroom."

Rider nodded and walked out the door.

Rob returned to his office and sat behind the desk. Two hours passed without a word from anyone. He slipped on his jacket, picked up his briefcase, and went down the hallway to find Rider. He saw Carlos instead.

"Roberto, what are you doing here? I thought you had gone with the rest of your team."

"They left?"

"Yes, almost an hour ago. Come, I will drive you to your hotel."

"I appreciate the offer, but I'll just call a cab."

"Don't be ridiculous. I will have you at the hotel long before a taxi arrives."

"Thanks. It's been a long day."

"That it has, my friend."

The first thing Rob saw when they exited the building was a new 1962 red Corvette so shiny it seemed to glow. An admiring whistle escaped his lips. "Is this your car?"

"Do you like it?"

"You have to be joking. I'm still driving the same '53 Oldsmobile Fiesta I purchased secondhand in law school."

"You will be able to afford one of your own now that you are an associate."

"That will take a while."

Rob settled into the soft leather of the passenger's seat as Carlos slipped behind the wheel. He felt the engine come to life and surge as Carlos pressed the accelerator.

Carlos turned to him and grinned. "I must admit, there are times I am torn about which is more enjoyable--driving this new car or a beautiful woman."

"It depends on the woman."

"Well said, my friend. Why don't you drive and decide yourself?"

"Maybe another time."

"Then we will go."

Several blocks later, they stopped at a traffic light, and Carlos looked over at Rob. "How is your Wanda, Roberto? Are you still together?"

"Why do you want to know?"

"I am just inquiring. I mean no offense."

"She is well, and yes, we are together."

"That is good. When are you taking your bar exam?"

"I already have."

"Congratulations." Carlos kept his eyes on Rob.

"Why are you asking all these questions?"

"I want to end this conflict between us, Roberto. Your friendship is important to me." A car horn behind them sounded, and Carlos pressed the accelerator.

"You coerced me into buying your drug equipment, Carlos. It will take some time to get over that."

"I apologize, Roberto. I should never have gotten you involved in my personal matters." Carlos pulled in front of the hotel and stopped. "How can I make it up to you?"

"I'm not sure that's possible. I can't be friends with anyone I can't trust." He got out and went into the hotel.

*   *   *

Carlos heard his phone ringing as he unlocked his apartment door and rushed to answer.

"Señor Carlos Rojas?"

"This is he."

"Señor Diego Martínez on the line. Go ahead, señor."

"Carlos, I have news. We have expanded to the north."

"How far north?"

"The border."

"How is that possible? What happened to those who claimed it?"

"Let's just say the opposing groups are in a state of confusion without their leaders."

"Excellent news. This means we can expand our operation much faster than expected. Well done, Diego."

"It is time, Carlos. Do I have your permission to collect your friend?"

"As it turns out, he is here."

"This is good. We need Roberto to start as soon as possible."

"I know what we need, Diego."

"I was not questioning you. I am only concerned."

"You handle your responsibilities, and I will take care of mine. Tell Alejandro I will meet with both of you in a few days."

*   *   *

Rob didn't say a word to the two men about being left the following day as they were driven to the office. Horton was already giving orders to Rider by the time they arrived at the building.

"Andrew, collect the data for the first sections we discussed and be quick about it. I need them for this meeting with Díaz," Horton said, then left Rider and Rob and went to the conference room.

"Do you need help?" Rob asked as they entered Horton's office.

Rider took a sheet of paper from his briefcase and handed it to Rob. "I need the files attached to these names. You take half the list, and I'll work on the other. Then I will put them in order."

Rob read the list and handed it back to Rider. "To make this go faster, let me pull the files, and you put them in order."

"Good idea," Rider said. "You'll need the list of names."

"I don't need it," Rob said as he pulled a file. "I have it memorized."

"That's not possible. There are at least a dozen names."

"It's just something I do," Rob said, not wanting to get into it.

Rider shook his head. "One day, you'll have to teach me that trick. I can barely remember my own name some days."

Rob laid the last file on the stack as Rider tried to pick them up. The pile of files was about to topple over when Rob steadied them and took them from Rider's hands.

"Let me carry these for you."

"Good idea."

Rob followed Rider into the conference room, where Díaz, Rojas, Arturo, and Horton were waiting. He placed the files on the conference table and started to leave.

"Roberto," Rojas said. "Where are you going? You are part of this meeting."

"I didn't know I was needed."

"Of course you are. Sit. We have much to discuss."

Rob saw the frown on Horton's face as he reached for a yellow pad and sat. He listened intently as the schedule was discussed and Díaz was asked to contact families for appointments. Rojas suggested that Díaz accompany the team to Mexico to engender trust with the families and interpret when needed.

They worked through lunch and into the late afternoon. When Rojas and Arturo left, Horton looked at Rob and pointed to the door. Rob was gathering his notes when Díaz touched his shoulder.

"Our meeting is not over, Roberto. We still have much to discuss." Rob ignored Horton's disapproving glare and sat.

"Gentlemen, I received a message before you arrived that the daughters have contacted the families of the 825,000-acre ranch adjoining their land and are demanding the same royalty they received from their company lease."

"How will this affect the other sections we are contracting?" Horton asked.

"Not well. If we match that offer, the families of the smaller leases we've already signed will be greatly offended and they will demand the same percentage."

Rob looked at Horton, then at Díaz. "Excuse me, señor. Are you referring to the daughters of Don Ortega del Rio Lafuenta?"

"Sí, Roberto. Plat 345 is the most important lease we are to acquire."

Horton jumped to his feet. "Chambers, it's time for you to leave."

Rob knew what he was about to do would result in confrontation, but it was time. "Señor Díaz, forgive my interrupting, but we should review something before meeting with the Ortega sisters."

"And what is that?"

"Chambers," Horton shouted. "Stop talking and get out of here."

So now Rob knew. Horton had dismissed the codicil and the supporting documents without looking at them. But how could he do that? Was he trying to ruin the firm? Whatever it was, Rob knew he had to find those documents before a lease was signed. He left the meeting and went to Horton's office and searched every box for the file. It wasn't there. *Horton left the file in Dallas on purpose. Now I have to recreate the entire file and force him to read it.* He went to Díaz's office and found his secretary. "I'm sorry to bother you."

"It's no problem. How can I help you?"

"I need a typewriter, paper, and several boxes of carbons."

"I have them delivered to your office momentarily."

She was as good as her word, and Rob got started by sandwiching a carbon sheet between two sheets of paper. He put them in the typewriter and rolled them under the bar, closed his eyes, envisioned the contents of the codicil, opened his eyes, and started to type.

He worked the rest of the day and through the night.

The sun had been up for only a couple hours when Rob separated the last carbon copies from the original and placed them on the stacks. He was surprised when a man dressed in coveralls entered his office.

"Sorry, sir. I didn't know anyone was here."

"That's all right. What do you need?"

"I am here to take the Dallas team's boxes to the car."

"Has the Tolland team left the hotel?"

"No, sir. I'm supposed to pick them up at the hotel after we've loaded the boxes."

Relief filled him. He still had time. "You want the office next to Mr. Díaz's."

"Thank you, sir."

After the man had gone, Rob placed the carbon copies into one folder and the originals in another. He put both folders into his briefcase, grabbed his hat and coat, and rushed out. As he was going to the stairs, Díaz's secretary was coming up the staircase.

"I'm surprised to see you here so early, Mr. Chambers."

"I never left. Could you please have someone drive me to the hotel? I must speak to Mr. Horton before they leave."

"Of course. Wait at the door, and I'll have someone take you."

Rob rushed down the staircase, and minutes later, a car arrived. He got to the hotel and ran into the lobby just as Horton and Rider appeared with a bellman and their luggage.

"You look terrible," Rider said.

Horton glared into his face. "Chambers. I'm insisting you be fired when we return to Dallas."

Rob reached into the briefcase and took out the carbon file. "If you lease to the Ortega daughters without reading this, it won't be me who's fired."

"What's this?"

"A copy of the file you left behind, stating that the rights were given to a son, not the daughters."

Rider gasped. "What?" He stepped closer to look as Horton flipped through the pages. A third of the way through, he stopped and shoved the folder into Rob's hands.

"Chambers. This is all carbon copies and can't be certified."

Rob's blood boiled. "The originals I gave you *were* certified."

Horton leaned in and poked Rob in the chest with his finger. "Doesn't matter. There was not one shred of documentation to indicate Ortega had a son. The daughters are his only heirs. If I had the time,

I would rip this to shreds like I did your first file. Now get out of my way." He pushed past Rob and went to the door.

Rider stepped next to Rob. "Did he just say he destroyed a file?"

"He did."

"Andrew, we're leaving," Horton shouted.

"I can't believe he did that. Not good," Rider said, and rushed out the door.

Rob followed them to the door and watched them drive away. "Damn you, Horton," he whispered. "You aren't doing this to Gary without a fight."

CHAPTER SEVEN

Rob went to his room to freshen up and change before returning to Black Pond. He raced up the staircase to his office, closed the door, took a deep breath, and picked up the phone.

"I need to make a long-distance call."

*   *   *

Gary was at his desk when his intercom buzzed.

"Mr. Tolland. Rob is on line two," his secretary said.

"Why is Rob calling?"

"He didn't say. Shall I ask?"

Gary reached for his phone. "No, I'll take it." He hit the button. "Rob, has something happened? Where's James?"

"Horton is the reason I'm calling."

"Be careful, Rob. This is no way for you and James to build trust."

"I know that, sir, but he's about to do something that could damage the firm."

"What?"

"He is about to sign a lease agreement with the Ortega daughters for the rights to plat 345."

"Rob, that's the reason you're there."

"I found a codicil to the Ortega will stating he left the land to his daughters and all mineral rights for 345 to *his son*."

There was a long pause. "That's ridiculous. James would never miss something like that. Get him on the line."

"I can't. Horton left this morning with Mr. Rider and Héctor Díaz."

"Rob, you're mistaken about this. James would never make that kind of a mistake."

"I wish I were, Mr. Tolland, but I'm not. You sent us here to build a relationship with the Black Pond Corporation. What do you think they'll do when they find out we had evidence we knew the rights belonged to someone else and intentionally signed the wrong heirs?"

"Stop. Go back. What do you mean *we've known?*"

"I stumbled across the codicil during our last trip to Brownsville. After we left Brownsville, we went to Juárez to locate the families we are now contracting with for mineral rights in South Texas."

"Yes, I recall. What did you find?"

"I was searching for a Maurice Múñez in the Brownsville courthouse when I came across a document under Victor Munez Ortega del Rio Lafuenta. I knew there had to be a connection, so I kept digging. What I found led to Victor being Ortega's son."

"I admit the name would cause concern, but it doesn't prove they're connected. Why wasn't this codicil attached to Ortega's will?"

"It was filed in Brownsville on December 18, 1939, under Luisa de Luna Munez, Victor's mother. There was also a reference to the fact that he was born in Juárez."

"I don't recall that Luisa was the wife's name."

"It wasn't. I'm guessing Luisa was Ortega's mistress."

"Rob, that doesn't prove the codicil belongs to Ortega. We need more proof."

"During one of our meetings with Héctor Díaz, Manuel Ybarra Esquivel was mentioned as a lifelong friend of Ortega's. The codicil was witnessed by Esquivel."

"Are you sure about that?"

"Very sure. I located the mission and found the records of Victor's birth and baptism during our trip to Juárez."

"Did it list the father?"

"It was Ortega del Rio Lafuenta." There was a long pause on the line.

"We need to find Manuel Esquivel."

Rob took a deep breath. "I agree. Héctor Díaz said Esquivel lives in Mexico City. His confirmation of the codicil will prove the son's ownership."

"If you had all this, why didn't you give it to James?"

"I did, along with the certified electrofax copies of every document."

"Then why haven't I seen it?"

"Horton destroyed it."

"Are you sure about that?"

"He told Mr. Rider and me this morning before he left. I spent last night retyping the file from memory. Everything is documented word for word, except for the certification."

"You what? Oh, right, your memory."

"I tried to give James a copy this morning, but he refused. That's when he said he'd destroyed the originals."

"Damn it . . . I need to see that copy. How quickly can you get it to me?"

"Let me ask."

"Wait. Find out how we can contact James and Andrew."

"I'll be right back." Rob put the call on hold, grabbed the file, and raced out the door. He passed one office after another without seeing a secretary. Rob went around the corner and saw Carlos leaving his father's office. He was the last person Rob wanted to ask for help, but he was short on time.

"Carlos," Rob said, rushing up to him. "How quickly can I get this file couriered to Gary Tolland's office in Dallas?"

"I can have it done within the hour."

"Perfect. It has to get there, Carlos."

"Consider it done."

"Is there a way for Mr. Tolland to reach Horton?"

"Let me check Señor Díaz's schedule. We may be able to reach them at their first appointment. As soon as I know, I'll come to your office and tell you."

"Thanks, Carlos. I appreciate this." Rob gave him the document, hurried back to the workroom, and took Gary off hold.

"Sir, Carlos Rojas is arranging to courier the document to you. He assures me you will have the document before the end of today."

"Good. I'm not leaving here until I get it. Did Carlos know how to contact James and Andrew?"

"He is checking on that now."

"Rob, you realize if you're wrong about this, James will have every right to insist I fire you."

"If I'm wrong, I *should* be fired. But I've watched you for two years, Gary, and seen what you've created. I knew there was no way I could let one stupid mistake destroy everything you've built."

"I appreciate that, but if you're wrong, it's out of my hands."

Rob took a breath. "Remember when we first met? You asked me why I wanted to be a lawyer? I said it was because I wanted the life it would offer."

"And I said that's not enough. You had to want to be a lawyer because you wanted to uphold the law regardless of what it cost you. Anything less, and it's too easy to become one of the bad guys."

"That's not the path I want to take."

Rob looked up when Carlos entered the room. "Gary, Carlos is here. I'm putting you on speaker."

Carlos stood next to the desk. "Señor Tolland. I have been assured you will have the document by seven tonight."

"Perfect. Is there a way for me to contact Horton?"

"I had Señor Díaz's secretary call their first appointment to relay your message to have Señor Horton call you. Is there anything else I can do?"

"Actually, there is. I need Rob to get certified copies of a codicil in Brownsville and baptismal records from Juárez. Can you arrange a car for him?"

A grin crossed Carlos's lips. "I have business in Juárez myself. I will drive Roberto there after we visit Brownsville."

"How quickly can you leave?"

"Within the hour."

"Excellent. Thank you, Carlos. Rob, call me as soon as you have the information."

"Yes, sir."

"Thank you, Carlos."

"I am happy to be of service."

Rob hung up the phone and exhaled. "Thanks, Carlos."

"I am honored you are allowing me to help."

"I'm sorry to take you away from your obligations here."

"I will not be missed. As I said, I have business in Juárez."

"Oh. I assumed your meeting was company business."

"We have no time to talk, Roberto. We must get on the road if we are to get to Brownsville before the courthouse closes. When you are done, we will cross the border and drive until we reach Juárez."

Rob grabbed his jacket. "Thanks for doing this, Carlos."

"I am pleased to help, Roberto. I will do anything to rebuild our friendship."

"This will be a great start."

*   *   *

It was late afternoon when Gary's intercom buzzed. "Sir, Mr. Horton is on line three."

"Hold my calls." Gary removed his glasses and hit the button. "Where are you?"

"We just finished our first appointment in El Paso. We will cross the border tomorrow and finish up there. I'll have everything done in two or three days. My plan is for us to fly back Friday evening after the Ortega daughters' meeting."

"I want that appointment canceled."

"Canceled? Gary, that lease is the primary reason we're here."

"James, I heard we may be negotiating with the wrong parties. I don't want you doing anything until we know who owns those mineral rights."

"Chambers called you, didn't he?"

"The boy has a convincing argument, James. One you should have taken seriously."

"Damn it, Gary. I've been with you longer than any associate at the firm. You should trust me, not some kid just out of law school."

"During your last trip, Rob gave you certified copies of a codicil and supporting documents concerning the rights to plat 345. Why haven't I seen those documents?"

"I spent a year reviewing every document attached to 345. All the research I saw said Ortega left everything to the daughters. A son was never mentioned, so I destroyed Chambers' worthless documents. I insist he be fired for going to you behind my back."

"I'm not doing anything until I get the whole story. I've sent him to Brownsville and Juárez to secure new certified copies of everything you destroyed. Until I have those, I'll start with Rob's typed copy, which I should have any minute. Until we get this sorted out, no one is meeting with the Ortega daughters."

"What do you expect me to do while Chambers is on this ridiculous mission?"

Tolland's mouth tightened. "Your job. Sign the smaller leases, then find a person named Manuel Ybarra Esquivel. Rob said he witnessed the codicil."

"How do you expect me to do that?"

"Ask Díaz. I'm told he knows of him."

"So now I'm Chambers' assistant."

"Stop arguing. Find Esquivel, and leave the Ortega daughters alone until we have confirmed they are the heirs to the mineral rights." Gary hung up and sat back in his chair. A frown creased his face.

*　　*　　*

It was late when the Corvette stopped in front of the largest hotel in Juárez. Rob and Carlos, weary from the drive, exited the car as bellmen ran out to retrieve their luggage.

Carlos strolled up to the desk and presented his card.

"Señor Rojas. We are honored to see you again." The man snapped his fingers. "*Rápido, rápido.*"

A young boy dressed in a white jacket came running across the room. He took the keys from the desk clerk, gave Carlos a short bow, then led them down the hallway.

When they got to their suite, a flurry of staff scurried about fluffing pillows and delivering flowers and a food tray.

"I take it you've stayed here before," Rob said.

Carlos grinned as he tipped the staff. "Many times."

Finally, the suite cleared, and Carlos muffled a yawn. "Good night, Roberto." He gave a half-hearted wave and went to his room.

Rob did the same.

It felt like he had just closed his eyes when he heard pounding on their door. He glanced at the clock and was surprised to see it was after 10:30 a.m. The door flew open as soon as he released the lock.

"Hola," Diego said as he and Alejandro entered. "Where is Carlos?" Rob pointed, and the two men went to his door.

Alejandro knocked. "Carlos, get out of bed. We have much to do."

The door opened, and Carlos came out with matted hair, wearing only his underwear. "Why are you here so early?"

"Early? It is almost eleven."

Carlos started to curse. "I will meet you at Cantina Alegre in an hour. Tell our guest I was detained." He turned and slammed his door.

The men left.

Rob dressed, went down to the lobby, and asked the clerk at the desk to call him a taxi. When it arrived, the taxi was so old and dilapidated that Rob was concerned it wouldn't survive the rough road. It wasn't air-conditioned, either, so all the windows were down and dust clouds filled the car as they drove to the old mission where the records of Victor's baptism were kept.

When Rob returned to the hotel, it was dark. He was exhausted and covered in dust, but everything he needed was in his briefcase. All he wanted to do now was shower and sleep, but right after he entered his bedroom, someone knocked at the door. Rob put his case on the dresser and went to the door.

"Where is Carlos?" Diego asked as he and Alejandro entered.

"I don't know."

"What should we do?" Alejandro asked.

Diego shrugged his shoulders and slumped into a chair. "We wait. Alejandro, make Roberto and me a drink."

"Not for me," Rob said. "I need a shower."

"Take your time, Roberto. We may be here a while."

The two men spoke to each other in Spanish as Rob went into the bathroom and turned on the shower.

*　*　*

Diego got out of the chair and joined Alejandro at the room's small bar. "Do you have your new sample?" he asked in a low voice.

"Sí. Why do you ask?"

"Pour some in the gringo's drink."

"That is not a good idea, Diego. I have not perfected the formula."

"You worry too much. It will be amusing to see how Roberto reacts."

"Carlos would not approve."

"Let me see the formula."

Alejandro took a small vial from his pocket, and Diego tried to snatch it from his hand.

"No," Alejandro said as he pulled away. "The drops must be measured."

"Then do it."

"This is not a good idea, Diego. Much can go wrong."

"Shut up and do it."

Rob walked in wearing clean clothes and smelling of soap.

Diego took the glass from Alejandro and offered it to Rob.

"What's this?"

"A little tequila to wash the day's dust from your throat. You look weary, Roberto. Take a seat," Diego said.

"No thanks. I'm not much of a drinker," Rob said as he settled in a chair.

Diego carried the drink to Rob. "Come now, Roberto. It is impolite to allow your guests to drink alone."

"All right, but just this one." Rob took the glass and sipped the liquid.

"How long will you be in our country?" Alejandro asked.

"That depends on Carlos. I need to get back to Corsicana as soon as possible."

Rob took another sip as the two men talked. When he finished, he tried to set his glass on a nearby tabletop, but the table kept moving. He looked down and saw the lower half of his body had melted into the chair. Rob opened his mouth to ask for help and saw his tongue roll down his chest to his lap.

CHAPTER EIGHT

A bolt of pain flashed between Rob's ears, shocking him into consciousness. He rolled to his side and was overcome with nausea, vomiting the contents of his stomach before being immediately engulfed in cold water. He tumbled from the bed and tried to stand, but he was hit with water again.

"Stop!" he yelled as he fought the water spray. "Stop." The rush of water ended, and he staggered forward, unable to see. He collided with something hard and grabbed hold to steady himself.

Someone laughed, and Rob rubbed his eyes.

"What the hell?" He was behind bars. Someone laughed again, and he squinted to see a short, fat Mexican dressed in a sweat-stained khaki shirt, baggy pants held up by a belt with keys, and handcuffs dangling down to his knees. He was holding a large water hose.

"Why am I here?" Rob shouted, but the little Mexican only grinned in reply. "I have to speak to whoever's in charge here. There's been a mistake. I haven't done anything." The man ignored him and started rolling the hose up while walking away. "Wait! This is a mistake. I don't belong here," Rob yelled, but the man kept walking. Rob heard something slam shut, then silence. "Hey. Is anyone here?" He ran his hands through his dripping hair and yelped when his fingers found a large bump on his scalp. He looked down at his soaked clothing and pulled his shirt from his skin. *How did I get here?*

Rob pushed away from the bars and sat on the soiled, wet cot. An overwhelming odor burned his nostrils, and he looked for the source.

There was a stained porcelain sink attached to the wall of his cell with a chunk missing from its edge, and next to it was a seatless toilet. Rob stood to get a better look and the sight and smell of human waste made him gag.

Rob heard men's voices and rushed to the bars. Three khaki-uniformed men were coming his way.

When the men reached his cell, they glared at him through the bars. Rob's breath caught in his throat when he saw they were holding clubs. One of the men, with a row of ribbons pinned to his chest, grunted in Spanish, and the round little guard unlocked his cell.

Rob stepped away from the bars when the guard and a larger man entered his cell. The big man grabbed him, spun him around, and pushed him against the wall.

"Stop," Rob said. "I'm not fighting you." He was handcuffed, dragged from the cell, and presented to the officer with the ribbons. Rob could feel the contempt radiating from the officer's eyes, even before he spat in Rob's face.

"*Ándale*, gringo."

Rob was spun around and pushed forward through an iron gate the guard hurried to open. He was led to a small room, where an enormous wave of relief washed over him.

"Thank God you're here." Rob started towards Carlos but was grabbed and shoved into a chair. "Please tell these people there's been a mistake. I haven't done anything."

Carlos sat across the table from him and looked at him for a moment. "But, Roberto, you did."

"What are you talking about? I didn't do anything. Ask Diego and Alejandro. They were in the hotel room with me."

Carlos shook his head. "You were alone."

"What are you talking about?"

"You don't remember because you were drunk."

Rob pushed back in his chair. "That's impossible. I only had one small drink."

"That is not true. Diego and Alejandro said you had been drinking before they arrived and continued drinking until they left."

"They're lying, Carlos. I didn't want a drink, but Diego insisted. One is all I had."

"No one blacks out from one drink, Roberto."

Rob shook his head. "What are they saying I did?"

Carlos took a breath before answering. "You assaulted a young woman, Roberto."

"That's crazy, Carlos. There was never a woman in our suite."

"Yes, there was. I was detained and called the hotel to request a message be sent to our suite to let you know. The manager's teenage daughter delivered this message."

Rob's eyes glazed over as something sparked a memory. "The angel was on fire."

"Sí. The police said you were shouting fire and angel." Carlos shook his head. "The girl was wearing a red dress when she came to the room. Perhaps that is what you saw."

Rob closed his eyes and swallowed hard. "What . . . what did I do to her?"

"She was found naked and unconscious in your bed. Her red dress was ripped to shreds on the floor."

Rob's insides heaved, and his voice cracked when he spoke. "Was she . . . did I?"

"She was not raped, Roberto. The girl told her papá she thinks she struck her head when you jerked her through the door. That was her only injury."

Rob released a deep sigh. "Thank God." He dropped his head and was silent for a moment. "I'm never getting out of here, am I?"

Carlos leaned in, ignoring the guard's protest as he did. "This charge is serious, Roberto. I assure you, Diego, Alejandro, and I will do all we can to free you, but it could take time."

"I don't have time, Carlos. Once Horton learns I'm here, my career is over."

"I give you my word. I will do everything possible to keep that from happening." Carlos glanced up at the guards and then back to Rob. "Listen closely, my friend. Do not offend these men. People disappear on far lesser charges than this."

"Are you saying I could be *killed?*"

"Exactly. The Juárez chief of police is the girl's uncle. It will not take much for him to take revenge."

Rob recalled the officer with the ribbons. "I met him."

Before Carlos could respond, Rob was jerked from the chair and dragged out of the room.

*   *   *

Carlos drove to a cantina and parked his Corvette. A scruffy-looking man in tattered clothing walked up to him and held out his hand. Carlos took a hundred pesos from his money clip and handed it to him and said, "I will have your head if anyone touches this car."

The man pocketed the money and showed a weathered baseball bat in his calloused hand. "Sí, señor. I guard it with my life."

When Carlos entered the cantina, a young woman wrapped her arms around him and pressed her body against his. He looked into her dark eyes and whispered, "Not now, María."

Her ruby red lips formed a pout as Carlos joined Diego and Alejandro at a table in the corner of the cantina. Diego poured a shot of tequila for him as he sat. "How is our friend?" Diego asked.

Carlos leaned forward. "I should have the two of you flogged for giving him drugs."

"We meant him no harm," Diego said. "I was curious as to how he would react."

"If his firm learns of this, he will lose his position and possibly his career," Carlos said, then tossed back his shot. "And if he is killed, I will do the same to you."

Alejandro shrugged his shoulders. "What he did is not our fault, Carlos. We thought he was sleeping."

Carlos raised his fist and shook it. "Idiota. You should never have left him."

Diego held up his hands in surrender. "Okay, okay. We made a mistake. So let's use it to our advantage."

Carlos looked at him through half-closed eyelids. "There is no advantage."

"Oh, but there is. Without our help, Roberto is doomed. I think we should let him stay in jail for a while and pay the jailers to make every second he is there as miserable as possible. When he thinks all is lost, we offer him the opportunity of great wealth and freedom if he works for us."

"And if he refuses?" Carlos asked.

"Then let him rot in there. That way, he tells no one about us, and his death is not on our hands."

"I do not wish to have Roberto killed."

"Then hope it does not come to that."

Carlos tapped his empty glass on the surface of the table. "Money will not entice Roberto. But I know of something else that will."

"Tell us," Alejandro asked.

The corners of Carlos's lips broke into a sly smile. "He will do anything to save a certain woman, and I know who she is."

"*Excelente,*" Diego said and raised his glass.

*   *   *

Rob spent two days pacing his cell, seeing no one, not even the guards. He peered through the bars and wondered if he would ever see Wanda again.

"Hey!" he yelled, desperate to hear a voice, even his own. He heard the gate creak, followed by muffled voices and saw four men. When they got to his cell, they started rolling up their sleeves, their eyes boring into him. The short, stocky guard's lips turned into a wicked grin as he put the key in the lock. Rob stepped away from the bars, frantically looking for something to defend himself with, but there was nothing.

"*Espera!*" a voice called down the hallway.

Rob didn't know much Spanish, but knew the word for "wait." All heads turned in the direction of the voice. Moments later, the police chief appeared and pointed to the lock. The guard turned the key and pushed the door open.

Rob took another step back and balled his fist. "I'm sorry about your niece," he said. "I never meant to harm her."

Three of the men rushed in. Two grabbed him by the arms and held him as the third approached, his leather-wrapped knuckles raised. Rob was hit in the face and stomach, the blows causing his legs to buckle, but the men lifted him back to his feet.

As they did, Rob mustered up all of his strength to kick the leather-fisted guard between the legs, sending him to the floor. Rob lunged at the man on his right, knocking him off balance. With his now-free arm, Rob swung at the guard on his left, but missed. The guard on his right recovered and got behind Rob, pinning his arms to his sides.

The man with the leather bands slowly got to his feet, grinned at Rob, and beat him until he was unconscious.

*   *   *

Faint moaning sounds roused Rob from the darkness. As they grew louder, he realized they were coming from him. He tried to open his eyes, but they were swollen shut, and all he could see were slivers of light. He shifted his weight, and every cell in his body screamed in protest. The pain was excruciating as he pushed himself up into a sitting position, and he was certain every rib was broken.

Rob heard the iron gate open and shut and forced himself to stand, leaning against the wall for support. He could barely make out the two men on the other side of the bars.

"Only two of you?" he said through his cut, swollen lips. "You're going to need more than that to kill me." He balled up his fist as best he could and braced himself.

The door to the cell opened. The men grabbed Rob, who cried out in pain as his hands were pulled behind his back and cuffed. The men dragged him from the cell by his arms.

"Stop," he yelled. "I can walk."

The men ignored him and continued to drag him down the hallway to a room, where they forced him into a chair. Rob weaved in and out of consciousness from the pain until he heard Carlos's voice.

"My friend. What have they done to you?"

"They punished me," Rob mumbled.

"If this happens again, you will need an undertaker."

"I won't get out of here alive anyway."

"But you can." Carlos paused for a moment. "If I offered you a way to walk out of here, would you take it?"

Rob tried to force his eyelids open. "What way?"

"If you agree to work for me, you are free."

"Tolland already works with you."

"I am not speaking of Black Pond, Roberto. I am talking about my organization. It is profitable, and I can make you very rich."

"What organization?"

"I lied when I said the equipment you purchased was for a hobby, Roberto. We have become the largest drug organization in México. I am telling you this because we need your help expanding our operations into the States. We have exhausted our ability to conceal our wealth in México, and with this expansion, it is imperative to have someone like you to help us."

Rob leaned back in his chair. "You had me drugged."

"It was not me, Roberto. Diego and Alejandro did it as a joke."

"That joke destroyed my life."

"Not destroyed, Roberto. It merely opened the door to an opportunity. Your respected position with the firm is perfect for our operation. And your gift of memory will prevent a paper trail that could lead back to us. Join me, Roberto, and we will no longer be friends but brothers."

"No." Rob tried to stand but was shoved back into his chair. Carlos held up a hand, and the guard backed away. "I'd rather stay here than handle your dirty money," he told Carlos.

Carlos closed his eyes and shook his head. "Roberto . . . Roberto . . . If your own life means nothing to you, perhaps the life of your Wanda will."

Rob lurched forward, and Carlos scrambled out of his reach. The officer grabbed Rob and pulled him back.

"I'll rip you apart," Rob snarled through clenched teeth.

Carlos smiled back at him. "I anticipated this response, Roberto, so I sent some men to Dallas. Since you have refused my offer, I will call them and have them visit your lady. What will happen to you is nothing compared to what my men will do to her." Carlos leaned back in his chair and crossed his arms. "But because we are friends, I will give you a little more time to think it over before I make that call." Carlos nodded to the guards, and Rob was jerked from the chair.

"Leave her alone!" Rob yelled. He was still shouting when the guards threw him back into his cell.

CHAPTER NINE

Gary pressed the button on his intercom. "Have you heard anything from Rob?" he asked his secretary.

"No, sir. Should I contact Corsicana?"

"He's not in Corsicana. He's with Carlos Rojas working on something. I told him to keep me posted."

"Sir, I'm sure one of them will."

"I hope you're right." He let go of the button. "Damn it, boy. Where are you?"

$*$ $*$ $*$

Carlos's voice mingled with the pain in Rob's head for hours, filling him with rage. Carlos and his worthless friends had trapped him, but he would die trying to protect Wanda, no matter what.

He forced himself off the cot and made his way to the bars of his cell. "Guard! Guard!" Rob yelled until he finally saw the little officer coming up the hallway. "I need to speak to Carlos Rojas. *Comprende?* Get Señor Rojas in here." The little man walked away without speaking. "Get Carlos Rojas!"

Hours passed before he heard footsteps. Rob rushed to the bars, hoping it was Carlos, but it was the little officer. "Where is Carlos?"

The little officer unlocked the cell and walked away. Rob opened the door and stepped out, and the little officer signaled for him to follow. On the other side of the gate, Carlos stood with two officers behind him.

"I'm pleased to see your common sense has prevailed, Roberto."

"I will work for you if you leave Wanda alone."

He could see Carlos trying to keep the grin off his face. He failed. "Wise choice, Roberto. No harm will come to Wanda unless you force me to punish you. Is that clear?"

"Yes."

"Good. I think you will enjoy working with me when I make you a wealthy man."

"I'll handle your money, but don't expect me to enjoy it."

Carlos wrinkled his nose and took a step back. "We will address that another time. Now I insist you wash and discard those filthy clothes before you ride in my car. I do not wish to replace my leather seats."

Carlos spoke to the guards in Spanish, and the guard who'd beaten him grabbed Rob's arm.

"Touch me again, and I'll break your neck," Rob said, jerking his arm free of his grasp.

"Calm down, Roberto. He was only directing you to a shower." Carlos snapped his fingers, and one of the guards handed Rob his suitcase.

"Where is my briefcase?" Rob said, ignoring the pain in his arm as he lifted his suitcase.

"It's in the car. Now go."

Rob was taken to a private bathroom where he discarded his clothing and stepped into the shower. The warm water was like a caress on his bruised and battered ribs, and he carefully scrubbed himself with the soap to remove the filth and stench from his body. He could feel his muscles relaxing as the water rushed over him. He dressed after shaving and left his soiled clothing in a heap on the floor, then picked up his suitcase and opened the door. A guard was waiting.

"Much better," Carlos said as he approached. "Come, there is something we must do before we return to Corsicana."

Rob lowered his sore body into the seat next to Carlos, and they sped away. He had no doubt the hell he'd endured in that cell was nothing compared to what lay ahead.

The Corvette maneuvered through the streets of Juárez to an area where large homes were encircled with walls, many with guards posted at their gates. Carlos stopped at an ornate iron gate guarded by two armed men, who opened the gate and closed it when the car was inside. Carlos parked in a large open area before a spectacular home, and a man opened his door. He said something in Spanish as Carlos got out.

Rob marveled at the beautiful home as he pulled himself out of the car, wincing from the pain in his ribs, but kept his thoughts to himself.

"Come," said Carlos. "I am told everyone is here."

Rob followed him through the massive doors, stepping gingerly onto the Persian rug in the entry hall that probably cost more than he made in a year. They entered an exquisitely decorated room with hand-carved furnishings, tapestries on the walls, and drapes from ceiling to floor, framing large glass doors that led to a patio. A gentle breeze wafted through the open doors, carrying the heady scent of Mexican flowers. Diego and Alejandro were standing near the large fireplace. "I see you survived," Diego said.

"No thanks to either of you."

A woman came into the room. Carlos spoke to her in Spanish, and she left. Carlos said, "We will eat on the patio. From the looks of Roberto, he has missed many meals."

"Don't bother. I've lost my appetite."

"That was not an invitation, my friend. You need to regain your strength. You have much to do once you return to Dallas."

Alejandro stepped forward and offered Rob a glass. "Welcome to the organization, Roberto."

Rob looked at the glass. "No thanks, I prefer to pour my own." The three men laughed as Rob picked up a fresh glass and poured himself a small shot of tequila, hoping it would take away some of the soreness in his body.

The woman returned and spoke quietly to Carlos, who turned to the men and said, "Our food is ready."

If Carlos had intended to show Rob the material rewards that awaited him, he could not have arranged it better. A large round table set with fine china waited for them on the patio, and trays of food began arriving as soon as the men were seated. Rob watched as Carlos, Diego, and Alejandro filled their plates.

Carlos looked across the table. "Eat, Roberto, or I will have my men force it down your throat. You are no good to us if you are sick."

Rob hesitated, then filled his plate with the softest foods available, hoping he could eat without too much pain. When the four men had finished, the woman cleared the table and refilled their glasses before leaving.

Carlos motioned to someone in the doorway, and a young man stepped onto the patio and handed Carlos a folder.

"What's this?" Rob asked as Carlos handed each man a sheet of paper.

"It's the money we need you to move in the next two weeks."

Rob looked at the page. "Carlos, there is no way I can conceal ten million dollars in two weeks. I haven't even passed the bar yet. There is no way I can keep this amount hidden from the firm."

Carlos leaned forward. "Then figure it out. This small amount is merely a test."

"Ten million isn't a small amount, Carlos. Research has to be done, accounts opened, and procedures put in place before I can move a dime of your money." He gave the page back to Carlos. "Not to mention the authorities will flag an amount this size if it comes in outside the proper channels."

Carlos addressed his partners in Spanish. After a lengthy back-and-forth, he turned back to Rob. "How long before you are licensed?"

"It could be weeks, maybe months, before it's official. That's assuming I passed."

"You have six weeks, Roberto. I suggest you complete your research, open accounts, and do whatever else is needed while you wait. We need this done."

"Until I know I have perfected a system, the money you give me must be broken down into smaller amounts."

Rob was silent as the three men again conversed in Spanish. Diego seemed agitated, but Carlos had the last word and the discussion ended. "We will do as you suggest for now, Roberto, but soon, you must handle the amounts we give you. Is that clear?"

"Yes. I will keep you informed of my progress."

"No, you will not. Contact will only be initiated by me."

"Whatever you say."

Diego tapped the table. "Roberto. Why do you think you were chosen to purchase the lab equipment?"

"I wasn't chosen. I was blackmailed."

"That was your reason for going, not ours for sending you. There was an informant at the lab equipment company. The authorities were waiting, and we would have been arrested the moment we walked through the door."

"So, now the authorities are looking for me."

"You are safe, gringo," Diego scoffed. "I took care of the girl before she knew who you were."

"Girl? Are you talking about the young woman answering the phone?"

"She was working with the authorities."

"You killed her?"

"We must make examples of those who try to destroy us," said Carlos.

"What the hell has happened to you, Carlos? You weren't like this before."

"You saw what I allowed you to see," he said, and shrugged. "We tell you this so you will understand this is not a game."

Diego tapped his forehead. "Use your memory to set this up, Roberto. Anything on paper will be traced back to us."

"Businesses and banking systems don't work that way, Diego. They use contracts and forms."

"Do what you must, as long as we are protected. If you don't, you will wish we had left you to rot in that jail." He opened his arms to their surroundings. "Do it well, and your efforts will be richly rewarded."

Carlos got to his feet. "I must make a call before we return to Texas."

Alejandro glanced at the door as Carlos entered the house. "Carlos is not a patient man, Roberto. You should never question his decisions. I have seen what he does to those who do."

Rob thought about that until Carlos returned.

"Come, Roberto, we have many miles to travel."

The reality of their expectations felt like a boulder pressing down on Rob as he and Carlos drove back to Texas. He didn't even know where to begin with setting up what the Mexicans wanted, but he knew he'd better learn fast, or Wanda would pay the price.

As they approached the border, Carlos pointed to the glove box. "Your billfold and passport are there. Get them and say as little as possible. Tell them you have been in México on holiday and fell off a scooter, that is why your face is bruised. Smile, Roberto."

The exchange with the border patrol was brief, and they passed through.

"How am I going to explain my absence to Horton and Rider?" Rob asked finally, breaking the silence as they neared El Paso.

"No need to. They have not returned. I called Señor Díaz from my villa and told him your situation was resolved, and we were leaving Juárez."

"So he's working with you."

"He knows of your incarceration, but nothing of my organization. Señor Díaz was my mother's loyal friend and advisor long before he worked for my father."

They arrived in Corsicana after midnight. Rob got out, took his suitcase and briefcase from behind the seat, and was about to walk away when Carlos stopped him.

"Tomorrow, your associates will return. Mention nothing of our agreement or your stay in jail. If you do, it will not go well for Wanda or you."

"I know, Carlos. I remember every word you've said."

"I'm sure you do. As I've said, that is the reason you were chosen."

Rob glared at him, then walked away.

That night, his mind in turmoil, Rob lowered himself gingerly onto his bed, grateful to lie on clean, dry sheets for the first time in a week.

CHAPTER TEN

The following morning, just getting out of bed was a painful process. When he tried to dress, the pain was so intense that Rob struggled to avoid blacking out. Just bending over to put on socks was grueling. When he finally stood in front of a mirror to knot his tie, the face looking back at him had various shades of purple blotches and deep dark circles under his eyes. His lips were a maze of cuts, and every word he'd uttered to Carlos and his cronies had only made them worse. How on earth was he going to explain this, he wondered, loading his suitcase and briefcase into the cab that was taking him to Black Pond. When he entered the building and saw the staircase, he groaned. Rob took one step at a time, but still had to pause halfway up to keep from passing out.

When he reached his office, he slid his coat carefully from his shoulders and set it aside. He saw the typewriter and carbon boxes on his desk and knew he had to remove them before Horton returned, or it would only remind him of the codicil and enrage him all over again. His cracked ribs wouldn't allow him to carry them, so he placed the typewriter on the seat of his rolling desk chair, stacked the remaining supplies on top of that, and then pushed the chair out the door and up the hallway, nearly colliding with Señor Rojas and Carlos, who were coming out of an office.

Señor Rojas looked at Rob, then turned to Carlos. "This is your fault. Roberto should never have been allowed on the streets without security." He turned back to Rob. "Please accept my apology, Roberto. This should never have happened to you."

"Sir, this was not your fault." Rob's eyes shifted to Carlos, then back to Rojas.

"Carlos tells me your injuries were the reason for your prolonged stay in Juárez."

"Yes, sir. I was a prisoner to my bed for many days."

"At least you had the comforts of the hotel."

"Papá," Carlos said. "I will have someone assist Roberto. You have a meeting to attend."

"Stop rushing me. Can't you see I'm speaking?" Rojas turned back to Rob. "You must be more careful the next time you visit México."

"I assure you, sir, I will constantly be on guard wherever I go after this." His eyes shifted to Carlos.

"Good. Take care, Roberto." Rojas took a step. "Stop lagging, Carlos. You are making me late for my meeting."

Rob watched them go down the hall. As they turned the corner, Carlos looked back and gave him a wink.

Rob looked at his cargo. There was no time to wait for help. He continued down the hallway to Díaz's office and gave the supplies to his secretary. Pushing his chair back to his office, he saw Señor Díaz approaching. "It is good to see you, Roberto," Díaz said.

"Yes, sir. Thank you for detaining my associates in Mexico."

"Carlos explained the situation and I was pleased I could help."

Rob looked into the older man's eyes. "Sir, it's important that you know I would never have harmed that girl." Díaz motioned for him to stop speaking.

Rob turned and saw Horton and Rider walking up behind him.

Horton's eyes narrowed. "What girl? Chambers, what did you do?"

Díaz stepped forward. "Roberto had an unfortunate encounter with a group of unruly men while we were away. An innocent girl was accidentally injured during the altercation, but she is fine, and all is well. Nothing for you to be concerned about, señor."

"That looks painful," Rider said, peering at Rob's face.

"I'll recover," Rob replied.

"Why do I feel there is more to this?" Horton said.

"Carlos informed me about the altercation, señor. You should be grateful Roberto is alive," Díaz answered.

"That's debatable," Horton said. "We'll discuss this later, Chambers. Come, Andrew, we have things to do before we fly home." He started down the hallway with Rider at his side.

"Señor Horton is a complicated man," Díaz said as the two men walked away.

"Complicated is a description that is much too kind. I had better get back to work before he returns."

"I agree. Take care, Roberto."

"Thank you, sir."

The two men parted. Rob returned to his workroom with the chair and found the files Horton had carried with them on his desk. Just as he was about to open one of the boxes, Horton entered the room. "You are one disaster after another."

"I was attacked."

"I'm not talking about your little bruises, Chambers. I'm talking about going over my head."

"This could have been avoided if you'd read those first documents I gave you."

"I'm not going to explain my actions to a new associate that hasn't passed the bar."

"It's about the firm, Horton. Not you or me."

"Don't question my loyalty. I've spent half of my career building the Tolland Firm. But you overstepped, and I will see you're fired for this. We are leaving for the airport in an hour. Make sure these boxes are on that plane."

*   *   *

The black Lincoln and a van stopped a few yards from the waiting plane. Horton got out and motioned to the van. "See to those boxes, Chambers, and hurry. The sooner we're in Dallas, the better."

"James," Andrew Rider said, "Rob can barely walk. He's in no condition to carry our boxes and luggage."

"Not my concern."

"There is no need, señor," Carlos said. "My men will load your files and luggage."

Carlos went to the van and spoke to the men in Spanish, then returned to the Tolland group.

"I'm glad the trip was a success, señor," he said to Horton.

"It wasn't, Carlos," James scowled. "Thanks to Chambers, the Ortega plat was never signed. But I'll rectify that once he is fired."

"I am sorry to hear that, señor. My father and I are fond of Roberto."

"Yes, well. Good-bye."

Rider rushed to shake Carlos's hand, then hurried to catch up with Horton.

Rob started for the plane, but Carlos caught up with him.

"Horton is planning to have you fired, Roberto. We can't let that happen. Either you resolve this, or I will handle it."

Rob looked at him. "I'll take care of it."

"See that you do. Remember, my men are in Dallas."

"Chambers, we're leaving," Horton shouted. "Get on board or find your own way to Dallas."

Rob glanced at Carlos. "I need to go."

"Do not think you will be free of me because you are returning to Texas."

"So you keep reminding me." Rob limped to the plane and climbed in.

When they reached cruising altitude, James unbuckled his seat belt, crossed the aisle, took hold of Rob's shoulder, and pointed a finger in his face.

"Enjoy your flight, Chambers. This is the last one you'll take for the firm."

Rob pushed Horton's hand away. "I suggest you get back to your seat. I've had enough of bullies this week."

"You arrogant pup. There is no way Gary will save you from this."

Rob unclipped his seat belt and pushed himself to standing. He let the anger on his face speak for him.

"Gary's going to hear about this, Chambers," Horton said, stumbling back to his seat.

Rider snickered, and Horton turned on him, berating him until the chubby associate was cowering in his seat. Rob pressed his head against the back of the seat and closed his eyes, staying out of it. Diego's voice replayed in his head. They had killed the girl at the lab company. They would do the same to Wanda if he crossed them.

When they landed, Rider told Rob not to worry about the boxes, that the firm had sent a car and a van. Rob got to his feet, relieved, and walked with Rider to the car.

"I was beginning to think we were never getting back," Rider said, sliding in beside Horton.

"Strange how a new automobile suddenly developed a carburetor problem that took almost a week to repair," Horton said. "What do you think about that, Chambers?"

"I wouldn't know."

When they reached the firm's parking garage, Rob waited for the van to be unloaded and followed the files into the building, then went to Tolland's secretary's office.

"You look awful," she said. "Sit down."

"I can't. I have something I need to give to Mr. Tolland."

"This isn't the time."

The door swung open, and Rider rushed out, looking red-faced and frazzled. He flew past them, and Gary's voice boomed from the adjoining office. "James, I don't care what you think you heard. I spoke with Hector Díaz at Black Pond this morning, and he told me everything. He said the witness to the codicil confirmed the mineral rights were given to Ortega's son, Victor. That boy you're insisting I fire saved this firm from a major disaster. I suggest you go to your office before you lose your job."

Seconds later, Horton appeared in the doorway and saw Rob. "This isn't over, Chambers. One way or another, you're going to pay for this."

The intercom on the secretary's desk buzzed. "Ask Rob to come to my office," Gary said.

Horton glared at Rob. "What are you waiting for? Go get your gold star," he said and stormed out.

"Díaz told me about the beating," Gary said, gesturing to Rob's face as he entered the office. "Do you know if they caught the guys who attacked you?"

"The police know who they are. I'm just grateful I'm back."

"Were you able to get the certified copies?"

Rob opened his briefcase, removed a large folder, and handed it to Gary.

"Take a seat before you fall down." Gary positioned his glasses on his nose and reviewed the documents.

Several minutes passed. Finally, Gary removed his glasses and looked at Rob. "You were right. We need these to validate James's deposition with Manuel Esquivel. Rob, you saved this firm from making a horrible mistake."

"Are we going after this lease, or will Black Pond?"

"That's Black Pond's decision. The trick will be to find Victor."

"Can I borrow your pen and a sheet of paper?"

"What are you doing?"

Rob finished writing and handed the paper to Gary. "Those are Victor's business and home addresses. Those are his phone numbers."

Gary looked at the page, then back to him. "How did you get this?"

"After I found the codicil, I visited the courthouse tax office. I asked if they had a record of a Victor Munez Ortega del Rio Lafuenta. The girl handed me the Brownsville phone book. He and his mother moved there just after his birth and never left."

The intercom buzzed on Gary's desk. "Mr. Tolland, Black Pond is on line one." Rob got to his feet, but Gary motioned for him to stay.

"I'll be right with them." He looked up at Rob. "I sent Wanda my recommendation letter but haven't heard from her. Please have her call with the names of the firms she's considering."

Rob's heart ached at the mention of her name. "I will."

"Now, see a doctor and take some time off to heal."

Rob nodded and walked out as Gary answered Black Pond's call.

"Wait," Gary's secretary said as he passed her desk. "I had the receptionist give me your messages." She handed him several pink slips of paper. "They are all from Joey Evans. He's very persistent."

"Sounds like Joey. Thank you. I'll give him a call."

Her intercom buzzed. She lifted the receiver, listened, then hung up. "Mr. Tolland asked me to make an appointment for you with his doctor."

"That's not necessary. I'll handle it. But thanks."

Rob went to his office, trashed the slips, and picked up the phone. "Hey, Joey, it's me."

"Dang, man. It's about time you called. Wanda's been a wreck. What happened to you?"

"It's a long story."

"So, start talking."

"Can't. Too much to do."

"Then when?"

"Not sure. I'll get back to you when I can."

"Soon, buddy, or I'm coming to you."

Rob hung up and dropped his face into his hands. He had been thinking about this since they left Corsicana, and as far as he could tell, there was only one way to save Wanda. He had to end their relationship. If Carlos thought she meant nothing to him, he might leave her alone.

He forced himself out of his chair and left, making the drive to Wanda's apartment, where he parked and sat looking up at her door. After a time, he got out and started up the staircase. The pain of climbing the stairs was nothing compared to his heart being ripped to shreds. He squeezed his eyes shut and put his head against her door. He could do this. He had to. There was no other way to save her. He raised his head and balled his fist.

He tapped the door with his knuckles, and the door was flung open.

"Oh, my God! What happened to you?"

"I need to sit down," he said, pressing a hand to his side.

"No. I'm taking you to the hospital."

"We need to talk." He allowed Wanda to lead him to the sofa, flinching as he sat.

"You're hurt. We can talk later."

"Damn it, Wanda."

"You're scaring me," she said as she sat beside him. "What's this about?"

He closed his eyes and forced his mouth to open. "A lot became clear while I was away. I have to spend every minute focused on nothing but work."

"That's true of all new associates. I will support you in every way I can."

"You're not listening to me, Wanda. I don't need your support. I'm saying I don't have time for you anymore."

She tried to reach for his hand, but he pulled away.

"You're a lawyer, Rob. Not a monk. I love you, and you love me. You told me so a hundred times." Her face was a mask of pain.

"I thought I did, but not any longer. I want what Gary has, and you will only slow me down." The words were acid on his tongue.

Tears welled in her eyes. "Don't do this, Rob. We can make this work."

He got to his feet. The sight of her beautiful, tear-stained face was more than he could bear. His voice cracked as he spoke. "Good-bye, Wanda," he said and walked out.

"Rob, don't do this," she cried as she followed him onto the landing. "I love you. I love you."

Her words felt like an ice pick plunging into his chest. He took hold of the railing and descended the stairs, trying not to crumble as she cried out to him. He managed to drive away, but his resolve evaporated into an onslaught of tears as soon as he lost sight of her building.

CHAPTER ELEVEN

After an agonizing night, Rob couldn't stand the emptiness of his apartment any longer and went to work. As soon as he entered, every eye in the associate's meeting locked onto his battered face. He pretended not to notice and sat at the back of the room, remaining silent as each associate reviewed their current cases and addressed any concerns. The meeting was about over when Horton looked at Rob and got to his feet. "One more thing before we go," Horton said, unable to suppress the sly grin on his face. "As you know, we are currently short a research assistant. I'm assigning that duty to Chambers until further notice."

Every person in the room shifted their eyes to Rob. After the miserable night he'd experienced, he didn't trust himself to respond, so he simply sat mutely until the meeting ended. He was about to leave when Gary called out, "Rob, I need you to stay."

Rob waited until everyone else had left before approaching Gary.

"What are you doing here?" Gary asked.

"I'm fine. Work is the best medicine for me right now."

"I know what you mean. But let me know if you're not up to handling the research requests."

"It's all right, Gary. This is just Horton's way of reprimanding me."

"Well, that will stop once you pass the bar. I just got word that Black Pond signed the contract on plat 345 with Victor. They heard that another company signed a contract with the daughters, and now there will be a legal battle with the sisters to get their money back. Black Pond is so pleased we found the rightful heir that they asked us to represent their whole company. I have you to thank for that."

"I'm happy it worked out."

"So am I. Look, go home if working gets to be too much for you."

"Thanks. I'll be fine."

Rob went to his office and found his inbox filled with research requests. He picked up several of them, went to Wanda's former office, and settled into her chair. The faint aroma of her perfume filled the air, and his mind flashed back to the ugly scene the night before.

"I had to do it, sweetheart," he whispered, wiping tears from his eyes. "It's the only way to protect you." He took a deep breath and reached for the first folder.

He spent the rest of the day going back and forth from his office to Wanda's. It was late in the evening before everyone else left the office and Rob could put the research requests aside and started working on a plan to handle Carlos's money. After making a list of ideas, he went to Wanda's library and researched incorporation laws. He needed to know which states were the most flexible with regulations.

Night after night, the routine was the same. After everyone left, Rob worked on hiding Carlos's money, then went home to his apartment, where he was tormented by dreams of Wanda. By Saturday, he was exhausted and had to clear his head. Rob was taking his swim bag from the closet when his phone rang.

"Have you come up with a plan?"

"It's coming together, Carlos."

"Make it fast, Roberto. I expect to hear you have an answer the next time I call."

Rob picked up his swim bag and went to the YMCA. It felt good to get back in the water, but after a few strokes, he realized he had to take it slow. After several leisurely trips from one end of the pool to the other, he was ready to ease into his usual work-out and try to outswim the thoughts in his head.

Hours later, he pulled himself from the pool and sat on the edge. Exhaustion he could handle. A shattered heart and a drug lord were other matters.

*   *   *

Carlos heard his father's angry voice. "Answer me, Carlos," Rojas yelled. "I know you are here."

"Papá," Carlos said, rising to stand in the doorway of his office. "It's Saturday. Why are you at the office?"

Rojas came to stand mere inches from his son's nose. "You ungrateful little bastard. I raised you like a son, and this is how you repay me?"

"Calm down, Papá." Carlos reached for Rojas's arm, but he jerked away.

"Don't touch me." Rojas shook his balled fist in Carlos's face. "How dare you poison Luis against me?"

"What are you talking about?"

"Luis told me he wants nothing to do with me or my company. He said he is to work with you."

"Luis is a grown man. Let him choose the path he will take."

Rojas punched his finger into Carlos's chest. "Never. I decide what is best for my sons. I demand you stop whatever foolishness you are up to and focus on the job that has put food in your mouth and clothes on your back. If you don't, I will crush you like the worm you are."

Carlos pushed his hand away. "All my life, old man, I have endured your insults and rejection. Today, it stops." He turned and walked back to his desk.

"Remember who you are speaking to, foolish *hijo*."

"I know exactly who you are, and it repulses me. You would have none of this without my mother," Carlos said, waving his arm.

"Get out. Get out," Rojas shouted, pointing to the door. "You will never get another peso from me or your mother even if you starve."

"I have no need of your money. I make more in an hour than you make in a year. The only reason I put up with you was to fulfill my mother's wishes for us to be a family."

"How do you think she will feel when I tell her you are taking Luis from her?"

Carlos straightened his back, put his hands on his hips, and laughed in his father's face. "Nothing you can say will change Mamá's love for Luis. Or for me."

Rojas curled his lip as if repelling an odor. "I should have thrown you to the dogs the minute you were born."

Carlos's shoulders slumped, but he quickly recovered. "I'm grateful my mother took another man to her bed. Grateful it is his blood and not yours that runs in my veins."

Rojas shoved Carlos against his desk and pointed his finger in his face. "Get out and never show your face here again."

Carlos smiled. "Leaving you is a gift, old man. My years of concealing my hatred for you are over. From this moment on, I will never think of you again." Carlos walked out the door, leaving Rojas to curse his back as he walked away.

Once he was home, Carlos placed a phone call, pacing angrily until it was answered. "Diego, I want you to build four cookhouses instead of two. Tell Alejandro to find twice the number of workers for every house so we can produce around the clock. Once he's trained the new people, keep doubling the houses and the number of people until I tell you to stop."

"Carlos, I can't supply enough crops to handle that much new growth."

"How soon will you harvest the fields in Colombia?"

"Two months, possibly three, but that won't be enough to supply that many cookhouses. We will need at least thirty or forty more fields."

"Then do it. If we don't have what we need when our cookhouses are built, take it from other growers."

"They will fight back."

"Then kill them before they get a chance. I expect you to have a plan when we meet at my villa in seven days."

"We can meet sooner. I know what has to be done."

"I cannot. First, I must visit my mother and Luis."

"Carlos, this much growth will require you to spend more time here. How will you explain your absence to your father?"

"I have no father. Now, get to work." Carlos ended the call.

*　　*　　*

Rob was at his desk Monday morning when the intercom buzzed. "Mr. Chambers, Joey Evans is here to see you."

"Damn, buddy," Joey said, when Rob found him chatting with the receptionist. "You look horrible."

Rob turned to the receptionist. "I'll be back in a few minutes."

The two men walked to a nearby coffee shop. After the waitress left, Rob said, "What brings you in from Lewisville?"

"You never called. What's going on?"

"I've had a lot on my mind."

"I tried to call Wanda, and her roommate told me she moved out. Said you broke up with her."

"Moved? Where did she go?"

"I hoped you would know. What happened, buddy?"

"I don't really want to talk about it."

"Tough. I'm your best friend."

Rob paused a moment. "The firm is keeping me working night and day. I don't have time for a girlfriend."

"Girlfriend? Hell, you bought an engagement ring."

"Things changed."

"Stop being a jerk and go after her."

Rob closed his eyes and shook his head. "I can't."

"Yes, you can. I'll help you find her."

"Stay out of this, Joey."

"I'm not going to sit by and let you mess up your life."

"I have to get back to work," Rob said, getting to his feet. He took several bills from his pocket and placed them on the table. "I appreciate you coming, though."

"If you don't fix this, buddy, I will," Joey muttered as Rob walked away.

Rob turned around. "What did you say?"

Joey gave his two-finger salute. "I said, see you later, old buddy."

CHAPTER TWELVE

When the receptionist handed Rob his mail, he thanked her absentmindedly and started to set the stack of letters aside, but a return address caught his eye. The Texas Bar Association. He stared at the envelope for a while, getting up the nerve to open it. He took a deep breath, opened his briefcase, took out a ring box, and held the sparkling diamond ring in his hand. Then he put it and the briefcase back under his desk and ripped the envelope open. He sat motionless for some time, then returned the letter to the envelope and set it aside. He worked for several more hours before making a call. "Hey, Joey. It's me."

"What's up?"

"I passed the bar."

"That's great! So why do you sound like somebody died?"

"I didn't have anyone else to tell, I guess."

"Gee, thanks."

"I didn't mean it like that. It's just--"

"I get it. You were going to ask Wanda to marry you. Why don't you have dinner with us tonight to celebrate?"

"Maybe some other time."

"Look, I know something that might cheer you up. I found Wanda."

"Damn it, Joey. I asked you to stay out of this."

"I know. But I remembered Wanda's parents lived in Tyler, so I went to see them."

"You spoke to her parents?"

"Yep, and it's a good thing I did. There's another guy in the picture."

Rob felt like he had been punched in the gut. "Another guy? It's only been five weeks and three days."

"You don't care about the woman, but you know exactly how long she's been gone?"

Rob closed his eyes. "Thirty-eight days and seven hours, if you want to be precise. But it doesn't matter."

"You love her, stupid. According to her parents, she dated this guy for years before she met you, but she broke it off after she moved to Dallas."

"You shouldn't have done this, Joey."

"I beg to differ. I told them I was in town on business, and my wife had asked me to look Wanda up. They even fixed me lemonade."

"Was she there?"

"Kind of. I saw her get in the car with some guy when I got to the house."

"How is she?"

"From what I saw, not good. She's got the same sad look as you. But the guy was smiling like he just won *The Price is Right*."

"He did if he's with her."

"Yeah, well, I'm not sure this guy is her idea."

"What?"

"I listened to her parents talk about how great this dude is for an hour. I think they are in love with him."

Rob sank into the chair. "Doesn't matter. It's over."

"You never give up on anything. Why this?"

"Joey, I left her."

"Buddy, you got to do something fast. This guy's a doctor."

"Please stop."

"Get off your ass and get her back before it's too late. You two belong together."

"Not anymore."

"Okay." Joey exhaled audibly. "When you see the old Rob," he said, "tell him to call me." Then he hung up.

Rob returned the receiver to its cradle and picked up a letter and several research reports and dropped them off on his way to see Gary's secretary. When he went into her office, Horton was at her desk.

"What can I do for you, Rob?" the secretary said.

"This came today." He placed the envelope in her hand. A smile lit her face as she read the letter.

"Congratulations." She turned to Horton. "Rob passed the bar on his first try. Isn't that wonderful?"

"If you say so," Horton said and walked out.

"Don't mind him. Mr. Tolland is going to be thrilled. I'll hold on to this so he can see it when he returns from court." She placed the letter in her top drawer. "This is an important day," she said. "We always let our associates take the day off after receiving their letter, so go celebrate!" She shooed him away like a small child.

Rob was in no mood to celebrate. All he wanted to do was see Wanda. Two and a half hours later, he pulled up across the street from Wanda's parents' home. He had no right to be there, but if Joey had found her, so could Carlos. She was safer with him than on her own.

Rob sat in his car, watching the house for hours. He didn't realize it was dark until the front porch light flicked on, and the front door opened. He got out of his car when he saw Wanda's father walking down the driveway.

"What are you doing here, Rob?"

He dropped his head. "I'm here to tell Wanda I'm sorry and ask her forgiveness."

"It's too late. I suggest you go before I call the police."

"Sir, I'm not here to make trouble."

"Son, you've already done that."

"I'm so sorry. Could I at least speak to Wanda before I go?"

"She and her mother are in Shreveport. But even if she were here, I wouldn't let you see her. You broke her heart, young man. It took us a week to get her out of bed. She wouldn't eat or sleep. All she did was cry. She loved you, Rob, and lost a job she cherished because of you.

Then you tossed her away. What kind of man are you?" He squeezed his eyes shut for a moment. "You have no idea how hard it is to see your child in such pain."

Rob wanted to tell him why but couldn't. "Sir, I know I have no right to say this, but I love her."

"You gave her up. I had a visit today from a wonderful man asking for permission to marry her. There's no way I'm allowing you to destroy her chance for happiness."

A large lump lodged in Rob's throat. "But we just broke up."

"She was in love with Peter before you. Had she not moved to Dallas, they would have been married. Her mother and I always hoped this day would come, and now it has. Peter is a good man, and he loves her. He's always loved her. He would never dream of hurting her."

"Is she in love with him?"

Wanda's father stepped closer. "Go back to Dallas, Rob. There's nothing for you here anymore."

Rob watched him go back to the house. The porch light went off a moment later. Rob got into his car and allowed himself one final look before driving away.

It was late when he unlocked the door to his apartment. The phone was ringing and he hesitated a moment before picking it up.

"Hello, Carlos."

"It is time to start moving money."

"I'm still waiting for confirmation of incorporation requests."

"How many do you have now?"

"Only a couple. I've been layering businesses on top of the corporations I've established to hide the money source. Once I get the letters of incorporation for more corporations, I will open more businesses and bank accounts to handle the transactions. Then I'll keep adding business accounts as needed."

"Excellent plan, Roberto, but how much can you handle now?"

"Three, possibly four million this week."

"We need to move eight times that much."

"I can't dump that much money into these few accounts. It will draw too much attention."

"When will you be ready?"

"Hopefully next week."

"You have one week. You know the consequences if you fail."

"Wanda and I are no longer together, Carlos. I'm surprised you didn't know. I heard she is about to be engaged."

There was a pause at the end of the line.

"When did this happen?"

"Weeks ago. She means nothing to me."

"You are a terrible liar," Carlos said, laughing. "I know you are still deeply in love with her, same as when you refused my offer of female companionship in Juárez. I also know she is not the only one you care about. I know of your attachment to the Tolland family."

"I'm doing what you ask, Carlos. There's no need to bring them into this."

"You are, but not fast enough."

The call ended.

Rob shoved the phone off the table. Some day of celebration. He had to find a way to stop this before anyone got hurt.

CHAPTER THIRTEEN

Rob was at his desk when his intercom buzzed and Gary Tolland's secretary summoned him.

"Take a seat," Gary said as Rob settled into a chair. "I told you as soon as you passed the bar, I was putting you to work, and today's that day." Gary handed him a sheet of paper.

Rob glanced at the name and phone number on the page. "I don't understand. Who is this?"

"That, son, is your first case. It's a small dispute between a landowner and an upstart oil company."

"Do we have the rest of the file?"

"That's for you to build."

"Why me?"

"I think it's a perfect case for you to get your feet wet."

"Thanks, Gary. I'm honored. I'll call them now."

"Good, and if anyone tries to dump their research request on you, send them to me. I'll make sure it never happens again."

Rob rushed back to his office and set an appointment with the client. He was thrilled to have a new client, for a couple of reasons.

Rob had already opened more accounts in Dallas than he was comfortable with. He needed to leave the city to open more, but that was impossible without a reason, and Carlos was already wiring more money than the types of businesses he created could ever justify. With one or two large clients with offices out of state, he would have an excuse to be away from the office. This new client was a start, but he needed more.

Rob started attending every Chamber of Commerce, Rotary Club, and oil and gas-related gathering he could find. When Tolland's secretary asked him to attend a fundraiser at the Dallas Petroleum Club and represent the firm, he was delighted. He shook hands and introduced himself to as many people as he could. When he was talking to a group of men from an equipment service company, one of them mentioned a place called The Club. "What is The Club?" Rob asked.

The man laughed. "I thought you said you work for an oil and gas law firm?"

"I do, but I'm new there."

"The Club is the favorite gathering place for oil and gas executives. More deals are done there than in boardrooms." He elbowed the man standing next to him. "We've made a few deals there ourselves."

"Interesting. Where is this club?"

"Commerce Street."

"Thanks for the tip."

After the event, Rob drove to Commerce Street to locate the establishment. The next night, he met Jack, the owner. He returned several times over the next few weeks, and during one of his visits, Jack came to his table and took a seat. "Rob, I make it my business to know everyone and everything happening in my city. I've been checking up on you and your firm and heard good things."

"I'm not sure who you've been talking to, but thanks."

"Your firm handles a lot of oil and gas legal work, is that right?"

"We do."

Jack leaned back in his chair and puffed out his chest. "I'm a problem-solver. I put people together. Hubert Oil is talking about dropping their current law firm. You interested?"

"You're damn right I am."

"Then I'll introduce you to Wendell Stern, the VP, next time he's in." Jack rose from his chair.

"That's great. Thank you."

"Give me your card. I expect you to come when I call. That's the only way this works."

Rob's pulse began to pound as he reached into his pocket for a card and a pen. He did his best to conceal his excitement as he wrote his home phone number on the back of his card before handing it to Jack. "I've added my home phone number, so call anytime."

Jack tucked the card into his pocket and went to greet a group that had just come in.

Days passed without a call, and then Rob's private line rang one evening at the office.

"Hey, it's Jack. The Hubert Oil VP and several of his top people are here. Get here fast if you want to meet them."

"On my way."

Rob shoved Carlos's files into his briefcase and ran to the elevator. Jack was waiting near the door when he arrived after speeding across town.

As Rob and Jack approached a table of several men, the group stopped talking.

Jack launched into such a flattering introduction that Rob wasn't sure if they would laugh or dismiss him, but to his relief, Wendell Stern invited Rob to join them. The Hubert Oil group was more than willing to talk about their dissatisfaction with their current legal team and listen to what Rob had to say.

"I like what I'm hearing, Chambers. Let me talk to a few key people, and I'll get back to you by the end of the week," Stern said, and Rob took his cue to shake hands all around and leave.

The following day, Rob researched Hubert Oil's current and past legal cases and their locations across the country. This account alone would give him plenty of reasons to travel in and out of state. The trick would be to get Hubert Oil as a client without Horton hearing about it and trying to step in.

His intercom buzzed. Joey was calling.

"Joey, I need to call you back. I'm in the middle of something."

"His name is Peter Lawrence. He's with the Highland Hills Cardiology medical practice here in Dallas, and they're engaged."

"Joey, stop."

"She's *engaged*, Rob! If you don't do something soon, you'll lose her forever."

"It's too late. And I have to go." Rob hung up the phone and closed his eyes. The thought of Wanda marrying someone else made him sick, but he knew he had to let her go if this guy was who she wanted. Rob shook off the thought and forced himself to focus on the problem before him: Carlos was sending a deposit so large that it would surely draw attention. Rob had no choice but to break Carlos's rule and contact him, in the hopes of making Carlos understand why it couldn't happen.

"Just open more accounts," Carlos said when Rob called him later that night.

"I've already set up accounts with every bank in and around Dallas. Opening any more in this area is too risky."

"Then go somewhere else."

"It's not that easy, Carlos. It will take me at least a week of traveling to surrounding states to open enough accounts to handle all the money you expect me to hide."

"You need a reason, then I will give you one. I want you to purchase a business for Luis."

"Your brother? I thought he was working with your father."

"Luis is working with me. He will be in charge of our expansion into the States."

Hearing those words sent chills up his spine. "What . . . what type of business are you looking for?"

"One that will enable us to have our people in and out at all hours of the day and night without causing suspicion. It must be near the Gulf of Mexico so we can transport our people and product as needed."

"We need to hide this purchase, Carlos. It shouldn't be linked to you or Luis."

"You are right, but find it soon, Roberto. Every day waiting on you puts millions in danger."

"Carlos, you don't understand. I need a billable client to justify leaving the office to find your business."

"Then I will be your client. We have outgrown México, Roberto. Our future lies in the States. After I set this up with Tolland, I expect results."

Rob dropped into his chair and hung up the phone. Up to now, he'd been able to be willfully naive. But if he did what Carlos wanted, he would be helping to poison America with drugs. Rob got to his feet and started pacing.

The next morning, Gary summoned Rob to his office.

"Yes, sir?"

"Have a seat. I just got off the phone with Carlos Rojas. He told me he inherited a large sum from an aunt and wants you to represent him in his upcoming business negotiations."

"I'm surprised he's not using Héctor Díaz with Black Pond. He has represented Carlos's mother for years."

"I suspect it's because of your friendship."

Rob considered what this so-called friendship had cost him. "You may be right."

Gary handed Rob a page from his notepad. "This is his new contact information. I told him you would be calling within the hour. Congratulations, Rob. This could be your first big account."

"Thank you, Gary." Rob returned to his office, closed the door, and made the call. It was answered before the second ring.

"You spoke to Tolland."

"Is this a one-time number, or can I use it to contact you?"

"It is only for messages. Now, what else do you need to get started?"

"I need a retainer fee, and since your primary residence is Mexico, I will need to prepare a power of attorney document so I can work on your behalf."

"Whatever you need, do it. I've done my part. You do yours."

Rob got to work on the documents and left Carlos a message regarding the retainer fee. The money was wired a few days later, and a power of attorney document was couriered back to him. Rob met with Gary and requested several days out of the office to work with Carlos, which was the truth and a lie rolled into one. Whatever it was, it didn't sit well with him. He packed a suitcase and a box with the documents he would need to establish new accounts and put them into the trunk of his car, drove out of Dallas, and spent the next day and a half opening accounts in every town he passed through on his way to the Gulf Coast. When he got to Houston, he spent a day opening accounts across the city before looking for a suitable business to buy for Luis. Then he spent several days in Corpus Christi, Port Lavaca, and Galveston. Once he reached Port Arthur, the new accounts were piling up, but he still hadn't found a business that met Carlos's demands.

Rob searched Port Arthur for possible businesses after the banks closed, then decided to call it a night. He found a small hotel, pulled into the parking lot, and almost laughed when he saw all of the people entering and leaving the lobby. Why hadn't he thought of hotels? This was the perfect business. And then the reality of it all hit him like a ton of bricks. It was bad enough that he was opening accounts and laundering money. But if he bought a business for Luis, he would be actively betraying his country, his career, and his principles, and putting the woman he still loved in even more danger.

Rob started the engine and drove east into Louisiana. Driving down back roads in the middle of nowhere, he found a small grocery store with a pay phone near the front door. He dropped a coin into the slot and dialed the operator.

"Please connect me to the main office of the FBI."

"That will be a dollar and five cents," the woman said in a monotone.

Rob dropped coins into the slots and questioned his sanity when the call was answered. "Bureau," said the woman on the other end. "How may I direct your call?"

"I need to speak to someone about a drug organization."

"Please hold."

Rob was about to hang up when he heard a man's voice.

"Senior Agent Schneider speaking. Your name, please."

Rob took a deep breath. "I can't give you that. People's lives are at risk."

"Sir, without a name, your information is less credible."

"A large drug operation is moving into the States from Mexico. Are you interested in stopping them or not?"

"How did you come by this information?"

"I have personal knowledge of the people involved."

"Personal as in being one of them or observing from afar?"

"I would rather not answer that."

"So, who are we talking about?"

"The head of the organization is Carlos Rojas. The two others involved are Diego Fernando Martínez and Juan Alejandro Suárez. They are extremely dangerous and well organized. If they aren't stopped, Texas, Louisiana, and other states will soon be overrun with their people and drugs."

"How did you come by this information?"

"I can't answer that. It could cost the lives of people I care about."

"People or you?"

"I'm included in that list."

"Where are these men?"

"Mexico, I suspect, but they could be anywhere. They already have people in Dallas."

"Has any of these people committed a crime in the US?"

"Not yet, but they must be stopped."

"Stop them from what?"

Rob shook his head. "So, you're telling me you won't do anything until they pour drugs into this country and start killing people here?"

"I'm not wasting my time or the Bureau's money on some story from an anonymous caller concerning people out of our jurisdiction."

The surge of hope Rob had experienced collapsed. He was alone in this. "Forget it. I'll figure this out on my own." He hung up and drove straight through to Dallas.

CHAPTER FOURTEEN

When he returned to Dallas, Rob contacted commercial real estate offices along the Gulf Coast. He found a few hotel properties available, but the one that stood out was a small chain with several hotels scattered around the Gulf Coast. He called the number Carlos gave him and left a message. As he was hanging up, his intercom buzzed.

"Someone is calling from Mr. Stern's office," his secretary said.

"Great, put it through."

"Mr. Chambers, this is Barbara, Mr. Stern's secretary. Mr. Stern requests a meeting with you today at 4:00 p.m. He is preparing for a trip and wants to meet as soon as possible."

"I will be happy to meet him."

"Good. See you then."

He had just hung up when his private line rang. Rob sighed and answered. "What do you have for me, Roberto?"

"I think a small hotel chain would be a good business for Luis." There was a long pause. "Carlos, are you there?"

"Where are the locations?"

"Destin, Florida; Baton Rouge, Louisiana; and Corpus Christi, Texas."

Another long silence.

"How quickly can we take ownership?"

"You haven't even looked at the buildings. They could need major repairs."

"Does not matter. Money fixes anything. Buy it. I want to take ownership as soon as possible."

"I'll make a cash offer without contingencies and demand a short closing date. That should get this done quickly."

"Do it."

"I will purchase it under one of the established corporations."

"Good. Make sure I get those hotels. Luis needs to be in the States as quickly as possible."

Rob hung up and glanced at his watch. If he hurried, he could get Luis's offer out and still have time to prepare for the Hubert Oil meeting with Mr. Stern.

Stern's secretary greeted Rob as he rushed in and took him right away to the small boardroom where three men were waiting. Stern extended his hand. "Thank you for coming on such short notice. I've asked Mike Rodale, field operations manager, and Dennis Moore, our senior financial advisor, to sit in with us."

"It's a pleasure to meet you."

Stern pulled out a chair. "Let's get started."

Rob handed documents around the table and said, "Based on our previous conversations, I've presented similar situations the Tolland Firm has addressed, along with their outcomes."

Rob waited as the men reviewed the documents and conferred between themselves. After many questions and answers, the two men with Stern gave him a nod.

"Well done, Chambers," Stern said. "This answered several of our questions. Before we go any further, I want to meet with you and the head of your firm as soon as possible. I'm leaving the country in a few days, and I want this decision made before I go."

"That shouldn't be a problem. I'll meet with Mr. Tolland in the morning and give you a call."

Stern got to his feet and shook Rob's hand. "Perfect. Sorry to cut this short, but I have another meeting. My secretary will show you out."

The office was almost empty when Rob returned, but his day was far from over.

The next morning, Rob walked into the weekly associates' meeting with files in hand. He sat at the back of the room and waited as each associate reviewed their current cases with Gary and the group. As usual, Horton called on him last.

Rob gave a short overview of his cases, then stood and passed a set of documents to the head of the table.

"What's this?" Horton asked as he opened the folder.

"It's a contract proposal for the Hubert Oil Company."

All eyes in the room went to Rob.

Gary reached for the file and scanned the pages. "Rob, this is incredible. How did you get Hubert Oil to consider us?"

"I attended several functions around town and introduced myself. One of those functions led me to someone who knew Hubert Oil was unhappy with their current legal counsel, and he introduced me."

A low murmur rose from the men around the table.

"Quiet," Gary ordered. "This is important. Continue, Rob."

"I met with the senior vice president of Hubert Oil, Wendell Stern, and his team yesterday. Mr. Stern is leaving the country soon and wants to meet with you as soon as possible."

Gary got to his feet. "Gentlemen, this is how you bring the big ones in. James, finish the meeting. Rob and I have a call to make."

"I'll come with you," Horton said. "We can finish with the associates tomorrow."

"That's not necessary. Finish up here, and I'll fill you in. We are just making an appointment, not signing a contract."

Rob could feel Horton's eyes drilling holes in his head as he left the room. When they got to Gary's office, they called Stern's secretary and set the meeting for the following day.

"Bring me everything you have on Hubert Oil, and meet me in the conference room," Gary said. "We have work to do."

Rob had just returned to his office when his door flew open, and Horton burst in.

"How dare you? You know the rules. I evaluate every new client before Gary sees a proposal. This is the second time you've gone behind my back, Chambers. You won't survive a third." He walked out, slamming the door behind him.

Rob shook his head, gathered his Hubert Oil file, and went to the conference room. Gary, Horton, and Rob worked the rest of the day and half of the night to prepare the presentation. After a few hours of rest, Rob arrived early the next morning and went to check with Gary's secretary if the proposal packets were done. He was surprised to see the light on in Gary's office. He was about to step in when he heard Horton's voice and stopped in the doorway.

"Gary, that boy's too inexperienced to be in this meeting," Horton said.

Rob caught Gary's eye as Horton continued his protest. "He's brash and outspoken. He'll destroy our chance of getting this contract."

"I agree he lacks experience, James, but I've also seen how well he's handling the cases you've given him."

"Those cases were so trivial my wife could handle them, and she can't even balance her checkbook."

"He brought us Hubert Oil, James. Rob's earned the right."

Gary motioned for Rob to enter. "Come in. We were just talking about you."

"Sorry to interrupt. I'm here to pick up our presentation copies."

"James and I were just going over the meeting protocol."

"Has there been a change?"

Gary looked from man to man. "Only one. James, your role in this meeting is to take notes."

Horton looked like he had been slapped. "We have secretaries for that."

"I don't want anyone except us and the client in the room. Is that a problem?"

"As you wish. I'll be in my office." Horton glared at Rob as he left the room.

"James is a great lawyer, despite his need to control things," Gary said. "But, for some reason, you seem to bring out the worst in him." Gary reached for his glasses. "I'll finish here while you check the conference room. I want everything ready when they arrive."

A few minutes later, Rob escorted the Hubert Oil group to the conference room. "Welcome, gentlemen," Gary said, extending his hand as each man entered the room. Rob made the introductions, and everyone sat. For the next two hours, Gary and Rob answered questions about the firm and addressed potential cases that a company the size of Hubert Oil might encounter.

Stern looked at his two directors. "Do either of you have any more questions?"

"They answered my questions," one said.

"And mine," said the other. "I think we're good."

"Well, I have one," Stern added. "Will Chambers lead our account?"

Gary saw Horton open his mouth to speak. He raised his hand, and Horton sat back in his seat, mouth shut.

"That will depend on the case," Gary said. "The Tolland Firm has a broad range of experts. Surface damage and wrongful death accidents require a different level of expertise. We can handle whatever is needed."

Stern reached into his briefcase, took out a folder, and slid it to Gary. "You can start with this. Where do I sign?"

Rob could almost smell the adrenaline in the room as contracts were signed and hands were shaken. He escorted Stern and his team to the elevator. When the doors closed, Rob went straight to Gary's office. He hesitated in the doorway when he saw Horton standing beside Gary, sporting a smug grin.

"Excellent job, Rob," Gary said, pointing to a chair. "I'm proud of you. There is something we need to discuss."

Rob didn't like the sound of this.

"I'm giving this first case to James."

Rob went cold. "This one, or all of them?"

"As I told Stern, I'll evaluate each case as it arrives. If we don't handle this case right, there won't be a second one."

"You aren't ready to handle a wrongful death suit," Horton said.

"Can I sit in?"

"Absolutely not," Horton blurted.

"That's enough, James. Rob will partner or take the lead on every case Hubert Oil gives us. Is that clear?"

Horton's smug grin disappeared. "Understood."

"Good, now both of you get out of here."

Rob knew Gary was right. Horton did have more experience in this type of case. But knowing that didn't make accepting it any easier.

*   *   *

The red Corvette skidded to a halt in a remote area north of Mexico City, scattering grit and dust over several men holding rifles. Diego stepped out of a weather-worn building as Carlos emerged from the vehicle. "You look out of place in your clean linen shirt, jeans, and custom boots. Aren't you afraid you will get them dirty?"

Carlos surveyed his surroundings before approaching Diego. "I am not here to discuss my clothing, Diego. How much have you produced?"

"Come take a look."

The guards inside, who were leaning on doorframes and window sills, got quickly to their feet when Carlos entered the building. The workers paused momentarily, then resumed sorting dried plants and packing them into bundles. Carlos noted the pallets of product covering the floor of the remainder of the building. "When will this go out?"

"Before dark. It will be in the hands of our distributors by midnight."

"Good. I have just returned from Salina Cruz, Jalapa, and Tampico. I am pleased with your progress, Diego."

"Have you spoken to Alejandro?"

"He has just trained six new crews for our cookhouses."

"Then we are on schedule."

"Is there a place we can talk?"

"Sí, follow me." Diego led him to the back of the building and ordered the guards to move further out so they could speak.

"I have instructed Alejandro to expand our product lines," Carlos said. "He is to produce more of the drops you gave Roberto."

"That is a new product, Carlos. Are you sure Alejandro has perfected it?"

"You know what it did to Roberto."

"Exactly. That is why we can charge more for small quantities. Can Roberto handle it?"

"He must. We will start moving into the States and selling our products ourselves as soon as Luis is established."

"What about the existing drug brokers? Luis will find himself in a war if they are not handled."

"Then take care of it, but do it quickly. I won't tolerate delays."

The man rubbed his hands together. "We all have our gifts, Carlos. Yours is business. Eliminating problems is mine."

CHAPTER FIFTEEN

Rob didn't have time to be upset over the Hubert Oil case. He had to get the hotel chain purchased before someone else did. As he worked, his private line rang. "Congratulations, Rob. I just heard you got Hubert Oil," Jack said. "Looks like my introduction worked."

"It wouldn't have happened without your help. I hope, one day, to return the favor."

"As it turns out, you can. One of my customers has gotten himself in a huge bind, and I thought you might be able to help."

"What kind of bind?"

"Have you heard of Sam Gaston?"

"Gaston? Isn't he the contractor for the LBJ Freeway?"

"He is. Sam's wife of twenty-two years walked in on him with his secretary. Now she's bent on cleaning him out, and he desperately needs to dispose of some Dallas property. Quietly, if you get my drift."

"Jack, I want to help, but I'm not a real estate broker."

"I know, but after hearing how well you handled Hubert Oil, I thought you might have a few ideas for him."

"What are we talking about?"

"He owns a couple of properties. One's a small strip center on the east side of Dallas, and the other is a five-story building near the heart of the city. They were purchased through one of his side corporations. If he uses the traditional process to sell them, his wife, her attorneys, and taxes will take more than half of what he gets. He needs the money to survive the divorce, but stipulations exist."

"Tell me?"

"He needs an all-cash deal with as little paperwork as possible. He's desperate, Rob. The sooner you can make this happen, the better the price. And of course, I'll get a commission on the side."

Rob thought for a moment. "Ask him to call me tonight around seven."

"Thanks. I appreciate this."

It was almost 7:00 p.m. when Rob finally got to his apartment. He tossed his briefcase onto the sofa and removed his jacket as his phone rang. "Right on time," Rob said, but the voice on the other end wasn't the one he was expecting.

"On time for what?" Joey said. "We have to meet. It's important."

"What's going on?"

"I can't do this over the phone."

"Where are you? I'll come to you."

"Not right now. Meet me at Metro Café on Harry Hines Boulevard at noon tomorrow. It's across the street from the Dallas Medical District. Go to the booths at the back of the café."

"Joey, if you're in trouble, we can do this now."

"Has to be tomorrow. You'll understand when you get there." The line buzzed.

Rob hung up and sat on the sofa, wondering what Joey had gotten himself into. The phone rang again and he snatched the receiver up.

"It's Jack. Can you meet me tomorrow morning at my club around nine? Sam prefers I show you the properties instead of him."

"Sure, but I have a meeting at noon, so we'll need to be done by then."

"We'll go in two cars, then. Thanks for doing this."

The next morning Rob and Jack toured the shopping center and building. Rob asked Jack for title documentation on the properties. If they were clean, he would present them to Carlos. Then he hurried across town to Harry Hines Boulevard. But when he got to the Metro Café, Joey's pickup wasn't in the parking lot.

The café was full of customers. Rob made his way to the last booth, then froze. "Wanda. What-- are you doing here?"

She grabbed her purse and scooted out of the booth.

"Please, don't go!" His words came out much louder than Rob intended. Wanda tried to step past him, but he blocked her. "Please. We need to talk."

She looked past him. "People are watching."

"Are you going, sweetie?" the waitress asked as she approached. "I already mixed you up a Cherry Coke."

Wanda flashed a strained smile and sat down. "Oh. Thank you."

"Your order will be out in a minute." The waitress turned to Rob. "What can I get you?"

"I'll have what she's having."

"You sure? You don't look like a salad man to me."

"Today I am."

The woman tucked the pencil behind her ear. "Then salad it is," she said and walked away.

"How did you know I was here?"

"I didn't. I thought I was meeting Joey. I should have known he was up to something. Did he call you too?"

"No. I come here all the time. I volunteer at the hospital's children's wing across the street."

"How are you?"

"I'm okay," Wanda said, averting her eyes from his.

"Wanda, I made a horrible mistake. I'm so sorry. I was out of my mind to do that to you."

Wanda looked down at her hands as he spoke. When she lifted her head, she had tears running down her cheeks. "Why, Rob? Why did you do it?"

"I thought I had to, but I was wrong. I love you, Wanda. Please forgive me."

"If that's true, why haven't you come to tell me?"

"I did, but your father told me about Peter. He told me to stay out of your life and let Peter make you happy." He swallowed back the lump in his throat. "And I want you to be happy. But with me."

Wanda wiped the tears from her face. "It's too late. I'm engaged. My parents have spent a small fortune on this wedding and have mailed out a hundred invitations."

"You can't marry him for your parents, Wanda."

She gathered her things.

"Please don't go. You haven't eaten."

"I've lost my appetite." She slipped out of the booth.

"Wait," he said. He grabbed the pen from his pocket and wrote the number to his direct line at work on a napkin, folded it, and placed it in her hand. "Please call, even if it's to yell at me. I just need to hear your voice."

She looked at the folded napkin, then at Rob. "Peter can't know anything about this." She left him and walked away.

Rob sat and stared at where she had been long after she'd gone. When the two salads arrived, he shook himself, said, "Thank you very much," dropped too much money on the table, and left.

Back at the office, Rob worked on finalizing the hotel deal. When the documents arrived for the properties owned by Jack's friend, everything checked out, so he called Jack and made an offer for both properties that would have been an insult under normal circumstances. "I realize it's low, but he won't pay commissions on either side of the sale. That's a substantial sum, and my buyer is paying cash with a ten-day close."

"Sounds good to me," Jack said. "Let me see if I can get Gaston to take it."

Later that day, Rob closed Luis's hotel chain deal, called Carlos's number, and asked for a return call. As he was hanging up the phone, his intercom buzzed.

"Mr. Tolland would like to see you," Gary's secretary said.

"I'll be right there."

"Take a seat," Gary said when Rob arrived in his office. "We need to discuss Hubert Oil."

"Has something happened to their case?"

"Hasn't James been keeping you updated?"

"Last I heard, he was preparing depositions."

"So he didn't tell you about today's meeting."

"What meeting?"

"Stern gave us another case. An accountant in another company's division has embezzled a substantial sum of their money. They want us to handle it. I'm giving this one to Cameron. He has more experience in this type of criminal case."

"I see."

"You're the reason we have this account, though, and I think it's time you got something in return. I'm giving you the Bridwell account."

Rob leaned forward. "But James has been handling their cases. Are you sure you want to do this?"

Gary grinned. "I'm sure he'll make our lives miserable, but Bridwell is a house account. I gave it to James, and now I'm giving it to you. It's only fair that you have something of value in return for the Hubert cases I've given away. I think you've earned this."

"I don't know what to say."

"This isn't a favor, Rob. Most of Bridwell's cases are surface damage suits, and those are difficult. Historically, oil companies have lost those suits. Your responsibility will be to minimize the losses. Can you handle it?"

Rob got to his feet. "I know I can. Thank you, Gary." He sighed. "Do I break the news to Horton, or will you?"

Gary shook his head. "That's one of the pains of being the boss." He reached for his glasses. "I'll see that you have all the files by the end of the day."

Rob went to his office and sat at his desk, wishing he could tell Wanda this news. Less than an hour later, his door flew open.

"I hear you are stealing my account," Horton said, glaring at him.

"I had nothing to do with the Bridwell decision."

"I don't believe that." He leaned over the desk, uncomfortably close to Rob's face. "I know exactly what you're doing, Chambers. You're trying to weasel yourself into a partner position. It won't happen after I tell Gary what you did in Mexico."

"What are you talking about?"

"Díaz tried to cover for you, but I heard enough to know you hurt that girl, and it was no accident." He pointed his finger at Rob. "Watch yourself, Chambers. You cross me again, and I'll drag Díaz here and force him to tell Gary the truth." He spun on his heels and left his office as Rob's private line rang.

"Do we have the hotels?"

"You will have them by the middle of the week, Carlos."

"Excellent. I can expedite my plans."

"There's something else. I've put in offers on two properties in Dallas."

"What is the reason?"

"It establishes you as a client."

"So, what am I buying?"

"One is a small shopping center."

"How is that beneficial?"

"Currently, the center is generating income. If that changes, I suggest we close it and level it. The land is more valuable than the structure."

"And the other?"

"A five-story office building in the heart of downtown Dallas. I'm uncomfortable with records showing it's in your name, so I suggest we buy it under one of the corporations I established."

"I agree. How soon will we know if we have the properties?"

"It shouldn't be long. The owner is anxious to sell."

"I can see many advantages to owning a building, Roberto. I may have you keep an office for my use. That way, I can closely monitor you and my money."

Rob didn't reply. The thought of Carlos being in Dallas sickened him.

"I take it from your silence that you are not fond of the idea."

"I'm not sure my opinion matters."

"True, but I would like an answer."

"If the authorities suspect I'm linked to you, it could be disastrous, Carlos."

"As it turns out, I agree. I was testing you, Roberto. Keep up the good work."

CHAPTER SIXTEEN

As he worked late one evening, Rob's private line rang. He glanced at his watch, assuming it must be Carlos calling.

"Chambers," he said. There was no response. "Hello?" Still no response. He was about to hang up when he heard her voice.

"Rob, it's me."

He let out a sigh. "I was beginning to think I would never hear from you."

"I've tried to throw that napkin away at least a hundred times, but I couldn't."

"I'm glad you didn't. There is so much we need to talk about."

"I couldn't stop thinking about what you said. Surely there's no harm in talking?"

"There's not."

"Then why do I feel so guilty?"

"You shouldn't . . . unless you're married." His heart started to pound.

"Not yet. The wedding is next month. I just need to get things settled in my head before . . . Before it happens."

"Your head or your heart?"

"You left me, remember?"

"And I was a fool. I love you, Wanda."

"You have to stop saying that. It only makes this worse."

"It gets worse every day we're apart."

"Peter loves me."

"But do you love him?"

"Maybe. I think I do."

"Wanda, you wouldn't have to think about it if you did."

"If I were to back out, my parents would be devastated. I was such a mess after losing you. I guess I let myself get talked into this." She paused. "And I only have to say that out loud to realize how stupid it sounds. Had I known you came to Tyler, I might never have agreed to marry Peter."

"You can get out of this, Wanda."

"We missed our chance, Rob."

"Don't say that." There was a long pause in their conversation.

"It's late, Rob. You need to go home."

"No . . . I mean, yes. Where are you? I can call you when I get to my apartment."

"I'm in my old apartment, but don't call. Shelly just got in from a long flight."

"Then you call me."

"I don't know. Let me think about it."

"Wanda!" The line hummed in his ear.

He hung up the phone, slid everything he was working on into a drawer, locked it, grabbed his briefcase, and went to the elevator. The roads were clear, but the drive home seemed endless.

When Rob got home, he tossed his briefcase and coat on the sofa, and got into his pajamas.

An hour passed, then two, and Rob figured Wanda was not going to call and was about to turn in. When the phone rang, he bolted into his living room and grabbed it.

"Is it you?"

She laughed. "It's me."

He dropped into a chair. "I was afraid you wouldn't call."

"I almost didn't."

He wanted to say a million things but didn't want to overwhelm her. "What should we talk about?"

"Anything but my engagement to Peter. Why don't we talk about work?"

"Gary gave me the Bridwell account."

"Oh my gosh. How did Horton take that?"

He told her about Hubert Oil, the presentation, and how the cases were given to Horton and someone else. Everything but what he was doing for Carlos. They talked for hours.

"Oh my gosh, it's almost five in the morning!" Wanda said, yawning. "You need to get some rest before you go to work."

"I'm afraid to hang up."

There was a long pause. "Our talking doesn't change anything, Rob. I'm still getting married."

"I know." She didn't respond. "Stop chewing your lip, Wanda," Rob said, and smiled when she laughed.

"How did you know?"

"I have everything about you memorized."

Another long silence, then Wanda said, "I will call again if you agree to something."

He sat up in his chair. "Anything."

"Let me control when and what we talk about."

"I promise."

"Thank you. Okay, good night."

"Not good night. Good morning." Wanda's laughter as they hung up relieved some of the pain of ending the call.

Rob glanced at the clock and decided to forget about sleep. He had to stay busy to avoid going crazy thinking about Wanda with Peter.

Jack called later that morning with a counteroffer on the two properties. They were still a great deal, and he accepted the counteroffer. "We make a good team," Jack said. "I'm sure we'll do business again."

Rob left a message for Carlos that the two properties were his and spent the rest of the day preparing for a deposition in Van Zandt County on a Bridwell case.

By five o'clock, he was exhausted. He went swimming at the Y and then returned to his apartment to shower. He had just gotten out when he heard his phone ring and ran to answer it.

"Hi," Wanda said.

"It's so good to hear your voice."

"I've spent all day thinking about our conversation."

"So have I."

"I know you must be exhausted, but could we talk? I promise not to keep you up all night."

"I'm wide awake."

"Good. Tell me about your day."

As they talked, the tension between them vanished. When Rob heard Wanda giggle, he smiled and said, "You have no idea how much I missed that laugh."

"It feels like a lifetime since I laughed."

"Doesn't Peter make you laugh?"

There was a pause. "Not really. He's usually too busy telling me about some new medical procedure he's done."

"Maybe things will improve after you return to work."

Another pause. "Peter doesn't want me to work."

"But you loved your job! You should go back to work."

"Rob."

"I'm sorry." Rob paused a moment. "Can I ask you a question?"

"Only if I can refuse to answer."

"Does Peter spend all his time at the hospital?"

"Why are you asking me that?"

"I was just curious because you seem to have all this time to talk."

There was a long pause. "He's away at a medical conference. He'll be back at the end of the week."

"I see. That means when he returns, our talks are over."

"Yes."

"I have a crazy idea. I have to be in Canton tomorrow morning for a Bridwell case deposition. Would you like to drive over with me for the day? The deposition will only take an hour or two."

"I can't. I have to be here when Peter calls."

"When does that usually happen?"

"Before he goes to dinner, or after."

"What happens if you and Shelly are out?"

"Oh, I don't go out. Peter gets terribly upset if I don't answer."

Rob rolled his eyes, even though Wanda couldn't see him. "I'll have you home by four."

"Are you sure?"

"I promise." She didn't respond. "If you prefer, I could pick you up around the block from your apartment."

"Okay."

"Great. I'll meet you at Moore's Market around 7:30 tomorrow morning." He wanted to hang up before she changed her mind. "I'd better let you get some rest," he said.

"All right. Good night."

*　　*　　*

Rob left his apartment before 7:00 a.m. and parked near Moore's Market. He sat in the car, stumming his fingers against the steering wheel, willing himself not to check his watch. Finally he did, and discovered it was 7:40. He'd give it ten more minutes, and then he would have to go if he wanted to make his meeting on time.

Twenty minutes later, he gave up and started the car. He glanced in his rearview window before pulling away from the curb and saw Wanda approaching.

"Leave now before I change my mind," she said, sliding into the passenger seat.

"Yes, ma'am." Rob pulled away, and neither said a word for several minutes. "I thought you had decided not to come."

"I did at least a dozen times. Then Shelly saw me dressing and asked where I was going so early in the morning. I made up a story about going antique shopping in Weatherford with an old friend from college." She looked at him. "I lied to her."

"Not really. Almost everything you said was true. We are old friends, and you can do some antique shopping while I'm taking the deposition. So, you see, your premise of a lie could be disputed." He looked over at her and saw her smile.

"That sounds just like a lawyer. A twist here and there, and suddenly a lie becomes the truth."

"Gosh. You sure have a low opinion of my profession."

"You forget how many lawyers I've worked with."

He looked at her and saw that she was smiling. "Then I promise to only be a lawyer when I'm in the courthouse. After that, we're just old friends catching up on the old days." He glanced at her again and saw her eyes sparkle. "See. You weren't lying."

She twisted in her seat playfully and crossed her arms. "I think you're right."

Rob groaned inwardly when they reached the Canton town square, where he parked in front of the old stone courthouse. A group of men stood in a circle on the lawn, playing fiddles and guitars as people stood nearby to listen.

"I'm a bit overdressed for a country fair," Wanda said.

"You're perfect," he said as he got out. He opened the back door and got his hat and briefcase from the back seat. "I'll meet you back here at noon. Then we'll look for a place to eat."

"I'll ask some of these people for suggestions." She waved him away. "Go be a lawyer. I can handle this."

He got to the courthouse steps, looked back at her, tipped his hat, and entered through the large oak doors.

CHAPTER SEVENTEEN

When Rob met her after the deposition, Wanda was listening to music and holding two small bags. "I see you've been shopping," he said.

"Just a few things I thought needed to come home with me. Oh, I found us a place to eat. It's just a few streets over, near their fairgrounds."

"Great. I'm starving." Rob held the car door as Wanda got in, then he got behind the wheel. Per her instructions, he carefully circled the courthouse and crossed several streets before stopping at a four-way stop. To his right was the fairgrounds, filled with people going from one vendor to another.

He waited until it was his turn, then continued into the intersection. *Wham!* The impact threw them sideways in their seats and Wanda screamed as several objects pummeled the hood, smashing the windshield.

Rob shifted the car into park and reached for her. "Are you all right?" he asked as she raised her hand to her face where blood was trickling from above her eyebrow. "Don't. Let me look at it." He reached over and lifted her chin. "It's small. It won't leave a mark." He took a handkerchief from his pocket, took her hand, and made her press it against her forehead. "Keep it there until it stops bleeding. I need to check the damage."

He tried to open the door, but it was stuck. He gave it a firm shove and heard metal crushing, but the door opened enough to let him squeeze out. The road around them was covered with broken crates, dead chickens, and feathers, and an old, weather-faced man was running to and fro, trying to catch the chickens that were still alive. Rob watched the man grab two chickens and toss them into the cab of his old truck. "Hey," Rob called. "Are you all right?"

The old guy turned, holding two more chickens by their feet. Their wings flapped furiously, sending feathers into his face. "Damn birds. They don't even know I'm trying to help 'em." He opened the door to his truck, pitched the birds in with the others, and shut it. "Hey, mister, could you grab them two in front of your car while I snag the ones across the street?"

Rob sprang into action. When he'd caught the chickens, he held them up triumphantly, and saw Wanda laughing. He looked down. His suit was covered in feathers.

With the last live birds captured, Rob surveyed the damage to his car. The headlight was broken, the chrome bumper and fender detached, the windshield shattered, and the front tire slashed beyond repair.

The old pickup was so rusted and dented that it was impossible to tell if any of the damage was new. Rob went to the back of the pickup, took out his pen, and jotted down the truck's license number on one of his cards, then went over to the old man, who was now thoroughly covered in chicken manure and feathers.

"What's your name, sir?"

"I'm Henry. Henry Lemmon," the old man said, showing the one remaining tooth in his lower gums. He held out his weathered hand with dirty fingernails. "Glad to make your acquaintance." He looked past Rob to Wanda. "Is your missus all right?"

"I think she's fine."

"Sorry about your fancy car. I was takin' a load of chickens to the fair and didn't see ya comin.'"

"The police should handle this, I believe."

Henry raised a hand and pointed. "There's a phone over there. Just tell Luke that Crazy Henry hit ya. He'll know what to do."

"It sounds like this has happened before."

"Yeah, afraid so." He looked over at Wanda. "Don't worry. I'll wait here with your wife 'till you get back. Least I can do after ya helped me catch my birds."

When Rob returned, a crowd had gathered. In the distance, he heard a police siren, and a short time later, a black and white police car pulled up next to them, lights flashing. The siren went silent. A stocky police officer got out, hiked up his gun belt, and began surveying the damage. "Hell, Henry, this is your third accident this year. I thought I took your license after the last one?"

"You did, but I still gotta eat." Henry gave the officer a toothless grin.

Rob handed the officer his driver's license and business card.

"Looks like old Henry did a number on your car," the officer said, looking at Rob's license.

"I think you're right. I hope it gets us home once I get the bumper tied up and change the tire."

"Maybe, if the frame's not bent. You'll be lucky to get anything out of Henry if it is. He doesn't believe in insurance."

Rob shook his head. "I was afraid of that."

"Tell you what. See if you can pull your car into Sofie's parking lot. I'll call someone to help change your tire and tie up that bumper."

The distance to the lot was only about thirty yards, so Rob got behind the wheel and slowly turned the car to the right as debris crackled under the remaining tires. Suddenly, there was a loud pop, and the car tilted.

"What was that?" Wanda said.

"I'm afraid to look." Rob got out and saw his back-left tire was just as flat as the front one. He got back into the car. "We just lost another tire."

"What are we going to do?"

"Try to get this car off the street."

When they reached the lot, Wanda stepped out and came to his side. "Can they be patched?"

"I'm afraid not."

"Rob, I have to get home."

"Don't worry. I have a spare, and I'll buy a new tire."

The officer pulled in with a teenage boy in the passenger seat. "This is Lester," he said. "He'll take care of you."

The officer and the boy walked around the car, surveying the damage. "Dang, you got two flats," the boy said.

"Where can I buy a tire?"

"That'll be Floyd's Garage, but he's not there." The officer pointed to the fairgrounds. "He's over at First Monday Trade Days."

"Does the whole town shut down for this fair?"

"Pretty much," the officer said, then turned to the boy. "Lester, go to Floyd's booth and tell him to come runnin'."

The boy took off across the road and disappeared into the crowd.

"Look, why don't you take your pretty wife and have lunch at Sofie's? She makes the best chicken-fried steak in four counties. I still have to deal with Henry. When Floyd comes, I'll send him in to see you."

"Thank you." Rob removed his feather-covered jacket, pitched it on the back seat, and took off his tie before taking Wanda into the restaurant.

Almost an hour later, a man walked up to the table. "Looks like you met old Henry."

Rob stood and shook the man's hand. "It seems I did. How long will it take to tie everything together and replace the tires? We have to get to Dallas as soon as possible."

A frown crossed Floyd's face. "Well, if you drove a Ford, Chevy, or a John Deere, I would say a couple of hours, but I don't carry tires for a fancy Oldsmobile Fiesta."

"Then who does?"

Floyd chuckled. "Nobody. The best I can do is tow your car to my garage and order a tire while I tie everything up. I'll put a rush on it, but it will cost ya. With any luck, I should have you patched up by noon tomorrow."

Rob looked over at Wanda and saw the color drain from her face. He turned back to the garage owner. "Look, I don't care what it costs. I need that tire today."

"Mister, there ain't no way. If I don't order it now, getting one could take two or three days. How do I get ahold of you?"

"You tell me. I don't know anything about your town."

Floyd looked toward the restaurant counter. "Hey, Sofie, these people need a room for tonight. You got any ideas?"

The woman grabbed a towel and walked around the counter. "Are you crazy? You know it's the First Monday," she said, wiping her hands.

"You think Troy has something?"

"He might, but don't count on it."

Sofie looked at Rob. "My brother manages the Highway 19 Inn just outside of town. Wait here. I'll give him a call."

Within a few minutes, she returned, carrying three saucers of apple cobbler. "You're in luck. He just had something open up. I told him to hold it for you. Now have some cobbler."

Floyd picked up his plate. "I'll bring your saucer back, Sofie. Got to go order these people a tire."

Sofie chuckled as he left the table. "Troy said his renter checked out because the old goat he bought chickens from had a wreck and killed most of his birds. Any idea who that might be?"

"Small world," Rob said.

"When you're finished eating, I'll have one of my waitresses get you to the motel."

Wanda looked up at the woman. "Your cobbler is delicious."

"Glad you like it. It's on the house. You've been through enough today."

Rob went to the counter and took a moment to call the office. He knew Gary's secretary would send a search party looking for him if he wasn't at work the next morning.

It took hours to get his car towed to the garage. By the time they reached the motel, it was almost dark. Rob went into the office to book rooms for him and Wanda. When he left the office, he found Wanda twisting her hands together and chewing her lips.

"Wanda, it's going to be all right."

"No, it's not. I won't be home when Peter calls."

"Then call Shelly and tell her you and your friend were in a minor accident and to tell Peter you will talk to him tomorrow. I'm sure he will understand."

"She won't be home. She has a date."

"Then you call him before he calls you."

She opened her purse and started looking through it. "I must have left Peter's information on my nightstand," she said, looking up at him. "Rob, what am I going to do?"

He had never seen her like this, and it troubled him. "Wanda, there's a pay phone behind you. Give Shelly a call before she leaves and get the information." Rob took coins from his pocket and placed them in her hand. She went to the phone and dropped the coins into the slots. As she was dialing, Rob took a business card and pen from his pocket, handed them to her, and stepped away to give her some privacy. He saw Wanda writing, and then she hung up, glanced at him, lifted the receiver again and dropped more coins into the phone, and turned away.

After several minutes, Rob saw her cringe and hold the phone away from her ear. He resisted the urge to snatch the receiver and give the guy a good talking-to, but finally she hung up. When Rob got to her, Wanda had tears in her eyes.

"I—I don't think he believed me," she said.

"Wanda, can I ask, what does Shelly think of Peter?"

"What do you mean?"

"Does she like him?"

"They don't exactly get along."

"Why is that?"

"Peter thinks Shelly is disrespectful and too opinionated."

"But how does she feel about him?"

"Why?"

"Shelly sees all kinds of people working as an airline stewardess. I value her opinion."

Wanda took her time responding. "She thinks he's . . .It doesn't matter, Rob."

"Is it possible she sees a side of Peter you don't?"

"Stop. I can't do this."

"I'm sorry, Wanda. I hate seeing you upset. I should never have asked you to come."

She looked up at him with tears streaming down her cheeks. "It's not your fault."

He looked around. "It's getting late. Let's get you to the room."

"Room? There's only one?"

"It's all they had."

"Then we have to go to another hotel."

"I've already asked the clerk to check. Every hotel and motel around here is booked." When Wanda's bottom lip quivered, Rob said, "You take the room. I'll find somewhere else to sleep."

"Where? You just said everything is booked."

"Let me worry about that. Let's get you to the room."

They went down a walkway lined with dense, overgrown shrubs. When Rob unlocked the door to the room, the first thing to greet them was a large crack in the linoleum that left a sizable gap under the door. The furniture was decades old, scratched, and chipped. Even the paper-thin bedspread was worn out and faded.

Wanda ventured into the room and stopped short of the bathroom. "I'm afraid to look."

Rob gently moved her to the side and went in.

"How bad is it?" she asked.

"Let's just say it's somewhere between a gas station toilet and my high school locker room."

She peered inside. "I see what you mean, but the towels look clean. If this is it, it will have to do."

Rob handed her the key. "You get some rest. I'll check on you first thing tomorrow morning."

He was about to leave when she called out to him. "Don't go." She pointed to the bathroom door. You can sleep in the tub."

Rob closed the door and looked at her. "Are you sure? It would be better than sleeping outside your door."

Wanda nodded slowly. "I just need a minute to wash up."

"Take your time," Rob said as she went in the bathroom.

Rob sat at the foot of the bed until the bathroom door opened, and Wanda appeared with a towel draped around her slip. "You don't have to do that," he said. "I've seen you in your slip before."

"That was before. I'm engaged to Peter now."

"You're right." He went to the closet and took the spare blanket from the shelf and started toward the bathroom.

"Wait," she said and tossed him a pillow.

"Thanks." He went into the bathroom and closed the door.

CHAPTER EIGHTEEN

Rob sat on the tub's edge, untying his shoes, before undressing and spreading the blanket over the cold tub. His legs were too long to fit inside, so he hung them over the edge and tucked the pillow under his head, twisting his body in an effort to get comfortable.

"I'm sorry," Wanda called from the next room.

"Don't be. This was my doing, not yours."

The strip of light under the door went out, and everything went silent. Then Rob heard Wanda laughing. "What's so funny?"

"I can't get the sight of you chasing chickens, covered in feathers and bird poop, out of my head."

"That old guy needed help." He paused for a moment. "Wanda, I'm getting you home tomorrow even if I have to carry you on my back."

"I hope it doesn't come to that. Good night."

After a few more minutes of contortions, Rob had just settled in when he heard Wanda scream. He leaped from the tub, rushed into the room, and found her standing at the head of the bed.

"What happened?"

"Something slithered under the door."

Rob switched on the bedside lamp and looked around. Seeing nothing, he threw back the bedspread and looked under the bed. "Found it," he said. He stood up and held the creature out as it wrapped around his hand. "A harmless little grass snake."

"Get it out of here!"

Rob opened the door and tossed the snake into the scrub. He closed the door and started back to the bathroom, but Wanda screamed again. "Two more came in!"

Rob caught the second intruders, tossed them out, then grabbed a towel and stuffed it as tightly as possible under the door before going over to Wanda, who was standing in the middle of the bed.

"Sorry, sweetie. There must be a nest of them in the shrubs."

She squealed and launched herself into his arms. "I hate snakes!"

He could feel her shaking. "They're harmless."

"I don't care. A snake is a snake."

"Don't worry," he said softly. "I'm not going to let them near you."

"You promise?"

He kissed her cheek and whispered, "Cross my heart." He kissed the soft spot below her earlobe and felt her melt into his arms. She took his face in her hands and kissed him. He slipped an arm under her legs, laid her on the bed, and kissed her again.

She pulled back and locked her eyes on his. "Rob, what are we doing?"

He brushed a strand of hair from her eyes. "What people do when they're in love."

She shook her head, then said, "I know this is where I'm supposed to say no, but I can't."

*   *   *

Hours later, Rob stirred and reached for Wanda. He turned on the lamp and saw her sitting in a chair by the window. "How long have you been up?"

She shrugged. "I don't know. A couple of hours."

"Are you having regrets?"

"Regret is too mild a word. I'm disgusted and angry with myself for allowing this to happen again."

"Don't say that. I take the blame for last night."

"I'm not talking about us, Rob. I'm talking about Peter."

Rob sat on the bed across from her and took her hand. "Talk to me, Wanda."

"I started dating Peter in high school. We had been together so long I didn't realize how controlling and angry he was until I left for college. But it wasn't until I moved to Dallas and went to work at the firm that I was strong enough to end it with him. It wasn't until I met you that I realized what love really was."

"Then why did you go back to him?"

"I don't know. After you left, I didn't have the strength to fight Peter or my parents, and I let it happen." She took her hand from him. "But soon after we became engaged, Peter's bullying got worse."

Rob got down in front of her. "You have to get away from him, Wanda."

"Shelly's been telling me that since I returned. She's afraid he's going to hurt me."

"If he lays one finger on you, I'll—"

She touched his lips with her hand. "It's okay, Rob. I'm ending this as soon as we get back." She grabbed her handbag, slid the engagement ring from her finger, and dropped it into her coin purse. She placed her bag on the nightstand and held up her ringless hand. "I'm done with him for good."

Rob stood and took her in his arms. "I'm so sorry you've been going through this, sweetheart. Please let me make it up to you."

She leaned back and looked into his eyes. "Hmm. That depends. I need to be sure you're worth it?"

A smile crossed his lips. "I'll give it my all to prove I am."

"Then start now."

He scooped her in his arms and laid her down on the bed.

*   *   *

Rob had just gone to sleep when he heard knocking on the door. He got up and opened the door a crack, concealing himself behind it.

"Sorry to bother you, Mr. Chambers. Floyd's Garage called. Someone is coming to pick you up."

"How much time do we have?"

"Maybe fifteen minutes or so."

"Thanks for letting me know."

Rob closed the door and glanced back at Wanda. She was sleeping so peacefully that he regretted having to wake her. He touched her shoulder, and she opened her eyes.

"Sorry, sweetheart. The garage is sending someone to pick us up. You need to get dressed."

"Now?"

"I'm afraid so."

She nodded and hurried to the bathroom.

Rob had just finished dressing when he heard a horn sound outside their room.

"Wanda, he's here."

"I'm not ready."

Rob grabbed his coat and briefcase. "I'll have him wait." He went out to speak to the driver and minutes later, Wanda rushed out of the room, running her fingers through her hair, her handbag looped over her arm.

As they drove away, she leaned over to Rob and whispered, "Sorry for taking so long. I dropped my purse between the nightstand and the bed, and everything fell out."

"Do you have your coin purse?" he whispered.

"I do. I gathered all I could, but I knew you were waiting and rushed out."

"You always look beautiful, sweetie."

Less than ten minutes later, they were at the garage. "I'll let Floyd know you're here," their driver said. "You can wait for him inside."

They went in, and a few minutes later, the garage owner walked in, dressed in shop coveralls, wiping his greasy hands on an oil-stained rag. "It should get you to Dallas, but that's about it."

"That's great news. I thought you said it wouldn't be ready until this afternoon."

"I made some calls and found a tire and rim in Longview. I called in a favor, and the shop stayed open long enough for one of my guys to pick it up last night."

"I appreciate that."

"Don't thank me until you see my bill."

"I don't care. It's worth it. Would you mind if I make a call to my office?"

"Sure, just reverse the charges. I'll go check on your car."

Rob dialed the operator and placed his collect call to Mr. Tolland's secretary.

"Thank goodness," she said. "I've been frantic trying to figure out how to reach you. Mr. Tolland needs to speak to you. Let me get him on the line."

Rob glanced back at Wanda as she sat quietly in the corner of the office.

"Rob. I heard about your accident. Were you hurt?"

"I'm fine, sir. My car wasn't so lucky."

"How soon can you get back?"

"I'm picking up the car now."

"Great. Get here as soon as you can. Hubert Oil referred you to a company in Kilgore. You have an appointment with them this afternoon. The owner of East Texas Crude Oil is a close friend of Wendell Stern's."

"That's great, but the front end of my Oldsmobile is held together by wire, and it's a mangled mess."

"Don't worry. I'll have a car for you when you arrive. Be safe."

Rob wrote a check for the bill and thanked Floyd for taking care of them. The drive back was much slower than he expected because every bump in the road had the potential to shake his car apart. But truthfully, he welcomed the delay. It gave him more time with Wanda, who was chatty and laughing all the way back.

As they entered the city, Rob realized that he would need to keep Wanda out of his apartment until he could figure out what to do with the boxes of files and documents related to his work for Carlos.

"I can take you to your apartment if you like," he asked as they approached Wanda's neighborhood.

"No need. Drop me off at the market. I need a few things, and it will save me a return trip. You have to get to the office."

"I would rather spend the day with you," he said as he stopped at the curb.

"So would I, but I need to handle this with Peter. Call me before you go to Kilgore." She kissed him, got out, and went into the market.

The Oldsmobile creaked and rumbled all the way to the office. When Rob exited the car, he shook a few lingering feathers from his coat and grabbed his briefcase. When he walked in, he found Horton near the door.

"You've finally done it this time, Chambers."

"Done what?"

"Not only have you disgraced the firm, but you may have cost us the Hubert Oil account."

"What are you talking about?"

"Gary was discussing a new case with the operations director of Hubert Oil when a certain Doctor Peter Lawrence came in, yelling at the top of his lungs. He said you lured Wanda, his fiancée, to Canton and spent the night with her." Horton wagged his finger in Rob's face. "I should have known this would happen after I found you sneaking around with her. He is demanding we fire you, or he will spread the word all over Dallas about the low moral character of people we employ."

"Where is Peter Lawrence?"

"He left yelling something about getting Wanda straightened out."

Rob spun around and headed for the elevator, with Horton hot on his heels.

"Excellent," Horton said as Rob punched the call button for the elevator. "You're disobeying orders. Now I'm certain Gary will fire you."

"I'll save him the trouble. I quit." Rob opened his briefcase, took the files from the Canton deposition, and shoved them into Horton's arms. The doors to the elevator opened, and he stepped in. "Tell Gary I'm sorry, but I have to get to Wanda," he said as the doors closed.

The drive to Wanda's apartment seemed endless. When Rob arrived, he left his car running. He could hear a man's angry voice cursing and yelling as he approached the apartment, and heard Wanda scream as he opened the door. Peter was standing over her with his fist raised.

Rob grabbed him and threw him across the room. "You lay another hand on her, and I'll crush every bone in your body."

"Get away from me, or I will have you arrested."

"Wanda," Rob said, not taking his eyes off Peter, "Go down and get in my car. We're going to the police station to file battery charges against Doctor Lawrence."

"Good luck with that. We're engaged," Peter snarled. "She belongs to me."

Wanda grabbed her handbag, took the ring from her coin purse, and shoved it in his hand.

"I'm done with you, Peter. You don't get to hit me anymore. I never want to see your pathetic face again."

"You heard the lady," Rob said, pointing to the door. "You come near her again, and I'll make sure you regret it for the rest of your life."

Peter stumbled to the door. "That's fine, Wanda. But when he tosses you out again, don't come begging me to take you back. The last thing I want is discarded trash."

Rob lunged for Peter, but Wanda took hold of Rob's arm and held him back as Peter ran out the door. "He's not worth it, Rob. Let him go."

Rob looked down at the red mark across Wanda's face. "No man should ever do this to a woman."

Wanda touched her face. "He was so angry I was afraid he would kill me." She looked up at him and paused. "But how did you know Peter was here?"

"He went to the firm before he came here."

"Oh, no. What did he do?"

"A lot of yelling. Demanding I be fired. Saying if I wasn't, he would damage the firm's reputation all over the city."

"That's horrible."

"Horton said Hubert Oil executives heard the whole thing."

"Oh, Rob, I'm so sorry. Please tell me they didn't lose the account."

"I don't know. I was told to wait and speak to Gary, but I knew Peter was coming here, so I told Horton I quit."

"Rob, no. You have to go back and explain to Mr. Tolland why you left."

"I don't think it will do any good."

"I'm so sorry."

"It's not your fault. What bothers me is how Peter knew we were in Canton."

Wanda started looking around her living room and found a crumpled piece of paper beside the sofa. She picked it up, unfolded it, and gave it to him.

"Shelly gave this to Peter when he came here early this morning looking for me."

Rob read the note. "This is the name and phone number of the motel."

"Remember when I told you I dropped my handbag on my way out of our room?"

"Of course."

"Well, my checkbook fell between the mattress and the bed frame, and the housekeeper found it and gave it to the motel manager. My name and phone number are printed on my checks, so he called here and asked Shelly to have me call him. She wrote down the information of the motel, and then Peter came here looking for me."

"He must have called the motel and they gave him my name," Rob said. "Well, no matter. I'm staying with you in case Peter comes back."

"I don't think he will. You scared him half to death. Go sit down and I'll make us some coffee."

Rob stayed with Wanda until she insisted he go home and change out of his filthy suit. As he drove to his apartment, all he could think about was losing his job and how much he hated ruining his relationship with Gary Tolland. As soon as he was home, he picked up the phone and called Gary's office.

"Well, well, Rob. I have to say, you've been quite the topic of conversation around here today," the secretary said.

"Did we lose the Hubert Oil account?"

"Mr. Tolland handled it, but unfortunately, he had to give them a guarantee it wouldn't happen again. I'm afraid there's no way he can take you back."

"I understand. That account is too valuable to lose."

"Let me see if Mr. Tolland can speak to you."

Rob took a deep breath and waited.

"You disappointed me today, Rob."

"Yes, sir, I know. I'm so sorry. I want you to know how much I appreciate all you've done for me, sir. I feel I've lost more than a job. I've lost my family."

Gary's voice broke as he spoke. "I wish there were a way to fix this, Rob, but at this moment, I don't see how that's possible."

"I understand, sir. I just wanted to apologize for leaving without talking to you first."

"Why did you leave?"

"I had to get to Wanda. I was afraid Peter Lawrence would hurt her."

"Is she all right?"

"He hit her, and would have done it again if I hadn't showed up."

"Did you punch his lights out?"

"I wanted to, but Wanda held me back. I think he understands what will happen to him if he comes near her again."

"Good. And if you need a lawyer, call me."

Rob chuckled. "I will." He paused for a moment. "Gary, I will pay you back every dime you gave me for my mother's bills and to finish school."

"Forget it, Rob. You saved this firm from a costly mistake and brought us Hubert Oil."

"Well, I appreciate that, but I promised I would stay at the firm for three years, and I didn't." Rob heard Gary's intercom buzz. "I need to let you go."

"Take care of yourself, Rob."

"Yes, sir. Same to you."

Rob hung up and laid his head against the back of his chair. Minutes later, he took a deep breath and left a message for Carlos to call him at the apartment.

It was almost an hour before his phone rang.

"Roberto, why are you calling from your home?"

"I lost my job at the Tolland Firm."

There was an unsettling pause before Carlos spoke. "I would ask why, but it is too late for that. How quickly can you find another firm? We still have much to do."

"That may not be easy."

"Is it because of James Horton?"

"Not exactly. But I'm sure he's been warning the Dallas legal community about hiring me."

"Where are my documents?"

"In my apartment. The only documents at the firm are for the shopping center we purchased."

"Good. Do not leave your apartment until you hear from me."

Rob hung up and started to pace, trying to think of where he could take Wanda and hide out. He was still trying to figure out a workaround to his wrecked car and empty bank account when his phone rang again. Rob's chest tightened as he answered.

"Perhaps this new development will be beneficial for both of us."

"How?"

"Your work for me has been hindered because of your obligations to the firm."

"True. But our arrangement will be difficult wherever I go."

"I agree."

"I understand where this leaves us, Carlos. I will give you everything I have and forget everything that has transpired between us. We never have to see each other again."

He heard laughter on the other end of the line. "You misunderstand, Roberto. I am not letting you go. You will open your own law practice."

"That's impossible. I don't have the money or the client base to open a law office."

"Money isn't a problem. And there is no need for clients because you are only working for us."

Rob shook his head. "That's not going to work. A law firm without clients will draw attention."

There was a long pause on the other end of the line. "Then I will allow a few, but I must insist my work comes first. Now that we have that settled, we must address another problem. It's time to move my files into a more secure place. As I recall, I now own an office building."

"Yes. The top floor offices are vacant."

"Perfect. Now, do you see how working with me has its rewards? You should be thanking me, Roberto."

"That will never happen, Carlos," Rob whispered as the dial tone sounded. He got to his feet and felt something prick his legs. It was a chicken feather, sticking out of the fabric of his pant leg.

Rob showered, dressed, and drove to Wanda's apartment. When he got out of his car, he saw her coming down the staircase with a suitcase.

"Where are you going?" he asked.

"I tried to call your apartment."

"Why are you leaving?"

"Peter told my parents he caught me sleeping with you and ended our engagement. They are devastated. Mom was crying so hard she couldn't speak. I have to go and handle this in person."

"I'm going with you."

She shook her head. "It's best I do this alone. You're the last person my father needs to see right now."

"At least wait and go in the morning."

"I need to go now. It's time to tell my parents the truth about Peter."

"Call me as soon as you arrive."

"I will."

Rob carried her suitcase to her car, kissed her, and watched her drive away.

CHAPTER NINETEEN

It was late when Wanda finally called. "Sorry to call so late. This was my first chance to call," she said.

"How are your parents?"

"They saw the bruise on my face and were appalled. It made it easier to tell them how he has treated me all these years."

"I'm sure it did."

"They are furious with him. And with me for not telling them sooner."

"Did you talk about us?"

"We did. I told them you protected me from Peter."

"They're good people."

"I know." She yawned. "Sorry. It's been an exhausting day."

"Get some rest, sweetheart."

"I'll try. It's been a difficult day for both of us."

Rob went to bed and tried to sleep, but thoughts of everything that had transpired kept him tossing and turning. The sun was just beginning to come up when his phone rang.

"Hello?"

"A courier will deliver a package to you. It is cash to cover your expenses until you open your office. I will add more to your account as needed. In the meantime, I need you to purchase transportation companies for me. I don't want to pay someone else to transport our goods when we can do it ourselves."

"What kind of transportation?"

"I need trucks but, more importantly, access to shipping docks."

"Trucking companies shouldn't be a problem, but I know nothing about shipping docks."

"Then I suggest you learn. To help you understand how important this is, I am also sending you a gift in addition to the cash."

"What kind of gift?"

"You will see." Carlos hung up.

Early the following morning, his phone rang.

"There are two packages at your doorstep," Carlos said. "Get them. I will stay on the line."

Rob went to his door and found the packages wrapped in brown paper on his doorstep.

"I have them," he said, returning to the phone.

"Open the larger box first and then the other. I will wait."

Rob unwrapped the box the size of a man's shoebox and found it filled with bundles of hundred-dollar bills.

"Carlos, I don't have a job. I can't start flashing this kind of money around."

"Then find another way for me to give you money. Now, open the second package."

Rob set the phone aside and opened the package. It was a photo of Wanda dressed in a cap and gown, standing between her parents. He grabbed the phone.

"Carlos, this picture was in Wanda's parents' home. How did you get it?"

"I had my men pay them a visit last night. I was surprised to hear that she was there."

Panic surged through his body. "Carlos, if your men touched her, I'll—"

"Careful, Roberto. She was not harmed. In fact, they never knew my people were there. I did this as an example of how easy it is for me to get to anyone. Do you understand?"

"I understand," Rob said through clenched teeth.

"Good."

Rob hung up and dialed Wanda's parents. He had to make sure they were all right. Wanda's mother answered.

"Mrs. Snow. This is Rob."

It took a moment for her to respond. "I don't know if I should thank you for saving my daughter or hang up on you."

"I understand. Could I please speak to Wanda?"

"Just a moment."

As Rob waited for Wanda, he wondered if Carlos had actually sent men to place bugs in Wanda's phone.

"Rob, you shouldn't have called," Wanda whispered. "My parents need time to get over this."

"I'm sorry. I'm just anxious to reconcile things with them."

"I appreciate that, but this isn't the time. I will call you tonight."

"Tell her to hang up," he heard Wanda's father shout.

"Rob, I need to go," she said, and then the line went dead.

Rob dropped into the chair and ran his hands through his hair. Obviously the FBI wasn't going to help him. His eyes went to the clutter of boxes. Carlos was right about one thing. He had to get these boxes out of his apartment. But he needed a decent car before that could happen.

Rob got his keys and drove the Oldsmobile to a used car dealer. He made a deal on a dark blue 1957 Scotsman Studebaker sedan, paid for it with his savings, and sold his old car for scrap. He wasn't about to touch Carlos's money.

The Studebaker was a comfortable ride, and Rob's first stop was the building he had purchased for Carlos. He went up to the top floor and looked around. It had a direct view of the elevator and staircase. There was a small secretary's office connected to a larger office he could use, with an adjoining room that would make a good library. Rob had another thought. If he put up a wall in just the right place with a hidden entrance, it would be a perfect place to conceal file cabinets and a safe, leaving the rest of the office to look like any other law office in town.

The next two days, Rob searched for trucking companies and found several, but they were spread across many states, which would mean traveling.

Wanda finally returned from her parents' home in Tyler, and they went to dinner. After several minutes of conversation about her time in Tyler, Wanda asked how his job search was going. "Have you decided what you're going to do?"

"Not yet. I'm sure Horton has done a great job of making it impossible for me to find a position in Dallas."

"You worked too hard to give up on a legal career."

"I'm not giving up. I've been making calls out of state and have a couple of interviews."

"You want to leave Dallas?"

"I don't, but no firm here will hire me."

"When are your interviews?"

"I leave tomorrow morning."

"Why didn't you tell me? I would have come back sooner."

"You needed to be with your parents."

She sighed. "I just can't stand the thought of us being separated again."

"Neither can I, but I need to interview with these firms before they hire someone else. I'll be back before you know it."

It was late when he returned to his apartment. Instead of going to bed, he packed his suitcase and a box containing corporation and business documents and set them by the door. The following day, he loaded everything into the trunk of the Studebaker and drove out of Dallas.

Rob traveled from state to state, meeting with trucking companies and opening accounts. A couple of days into his trip, he called Wanda from his hotel in Nevada. "How are you?"

"Exhausted, but in a good way. I found a job. It's only temporary, covering as research assistant for someone who just had a baby, so if you find something, I can relocate."

"That's wonderful! With whom?"

"Mackenzie Law Firm. I start tomorrow. It's much smaller than the Tolland Firm, but I'll enjoy working there."

"Will you like researching family and corporate law instead of oil and gas?"

"I'm looking forward to it. I'm ready for a change. What about you? Does anything look promising?"

"Too soon to tell."

"When are you coming back?"

"Tomorrow night. My last appointment is in the morning." He glanced at the time. "You need to get some rest. You shouldn't be late on your first day at work."

"My alarm is already set. Good night, Rob. I love you."

"I love you too," he said and hung up the phone.

The next day, in a hurry to get back to Wanda as soon as possible, he did a quick tour of the trucking company with the owner, spoke to the mechanics, and inspected the trucks. He asked for the last two years' financial statements and other company records, shook hands with the owner, and left.

*   *   *

When he reached Wanda's apartment late that night, she jumped into his arms as soon as he opened the door. "It feels like you've been gone a month. Did you see the car?"

He put her down. "Which car? I saw dozens out in the parking lot."

"The car with the man watching my apartment. He's been there every night since you left."

"What kind of car?" he said, going to the window.

"I think it's a Chevy. It may be black or dark blue. It was dark, so I'm not sure."

"I can't see anything from here. I'm going down to look. Keep the door locked." Rob went down to the parking lot and looked around, but every car he saw was empty. He went back upstairs.

"Did you see him?" Wanda asked, locking the door behind him.

"I didn't see anyone. Are you sure the man was watching your apartment?"

"He always parks at the end of the row just beneath here. And there has also been a car parked outside my office."

He went to the window and looked again. "Has Shelly seen him?"

"She's been on an international flight for the last four days."

Wanda was chewing on her bottom lip.

"I'm staying with you tonight," Rob said.

She closed her eyes, sighed, then whispered, "Thank you. I haven't slept since you left."

"Why didn't you tell me about this?"

"I didn't want to worry you."

"If someone is bothering you, I need to know." He tapped the end of her nose. "Even if it's me." He held her close and rocked her in his arms, his mind spinning.

The next morning, Rob followed Wanda to work before going to his apartment. He sat at his little kitchen table and started making meticulous notations from memory of every routing and account number for each business and corporation bank account he had opened. Once that was done, he reviewed the documents for the trucking companies he had visited.

When he finished, he called each company owner and made an offer. One owner changed his mind about selling. Two others wanted time to talk to their partners, and one agreed to sell. He dreaded telling Carlos they only had one deal.

Rob spent the rest of the day researching other trucking companies to purchase. That night, as they lay wrapped in each other's arms, he could feel Wanda's heart beating against his chest. He took a deep breath and closed his eyes before he spoke. "I heard back from two of my interviews."

She rose up on her elbow. "That's great news. Did you get an offer?"

"Both firms went with someone else. I spent the day calling around to make more appointments."

"When do you have to go?"

"Tomorrow."

She sat up. "But you just got home."

"I know, but I don't have a choice. No one will hire me here."

"How long will you be away this time?"

"At least a week, possibly longer."

"Oh," she said and lay back, pulling the sheet to her chin.

He sat up and looked into her eyes. "When will Shelly be back?"

"I don't know."

"I want you to stay with Joey and Sybil until she returns. I don't want you here alone."

"I can't do that. They have a baby, and Lewisville is over an hour's drive from my new office."

He lifted her chin. "Then promise me you will call the police if that car returns."

"Oh, Rob, it's probably nothing."

"Wanda, I'm serious."

"All right. I promise to call the police if I see the car again."

CHAPTER TWENTY

It took several days more than Rob had planned to convince three trucking companies to sell. When those deals were finally wrapped up, he spent a few days in Galveston, trying to get someone to talk to him about access to shipping and dock locations along the Gulf Coast. Each time he asked someone about the docks, they would tell him to leave or walk away. He was about to give up when a man finally responded. "Mister, everyone here is afraid to talk to you."

"Why?"

"Have you heard of Marcel Pascal?"

"Pascal. I've heard he's connected to the New Orleans mafia?"

"He's not just connected. He runs it. Anything about shipping or docks has to go through him."

"How could one man own everything on the Gulf Coast?"

"He doesn't, but he controls it. If you want access to anything, you gotta go through him."

The last thing Rob wanted was to get involved with the mafia, but he knew Carlos wouldn't give up. "How do I find Pascal?"

The man shook his head. "You didn't hear it from me, but his office is above Savoy's Restaurant in the New Orleans Garden District." The man's eyes bore into Rob's. "Be careful. Pascal doesn't appreciate uninvited guests. Watch yourself."

"I will. Thank you for your help."

Rob's anxiety increased with every mile he drew closer to New Orleans. He crossed the river into New Orleans and found Savoy's. When he climbed the stairs to the upstairs offices, he was surprised to see the door open. Sitting behind a fancy desk was an Andy Warhol figure of a man, impeccably dressed. Rob walked up to the desk, but the man seemed oblivious to his presence and continued writing with an expensive-looking pen.

"Excuse me, sir," Rob said. The man leisurely raised his gaze and looked Rob up and down.

"You aren't from here, are you, handsome?"

"Uh, no, sir. I was hoping to make an appointment with Mr. Pascal."

"An appointment." The man chuckled behind his hand. "Who are you?"

"Robert Chambers, Mr. . . ."

"DuMont. Jean-Claude DuMont."

Rob gave him his card. "I have clients who wish to contract with Mr. Pascal for use of his docks."

DuMont looked at his card. "Lucky for you, I'm amused by your naïveté, Mr. Attorney. No one comes to this office unless invited. Since you were not, I can assure you that Mr. Pascal is not interested. Now, good-bye, and don't come back."

"Mr. DuMont, please. My client's offer is substantial. Shouldn't you at least allow your employer to hear the terms of our offer?"

DuMont placed a finger on a button near his phone. "Listen closely, handsome. Leave now, or I will make sure your lifeless body is floating in the river tomorrow morning."

Rob took the assistant at his word. "Sorry to bother you, Mr. DuMont. Good day."

Rob got out of New Orleans as quickly as possible, trying to think how he'd make Carlos content with trucking companies instead of docks.

Outside the city, he pulled off the road and called the number of Wanda's new office. "Sorry to bother you at work, sweetheart. I'm just finishing up and about to drive home."

"Any offers?"

"Not yet. I'm going to stay at my apartment tonight. I don't want to wake you and Shelly."

"Shelly's still in London. I don't care how late it is."

He could tell by the sound of her voice that something was wrong. "Wanda, has that car returned?"

"It's been there every night."

"You should have told me."

"You were interviewing. I didn't want you to worry."

"Did you call the police?"

"Yes, many times. And every time they arrived, the car drove off. The officer drove around the complex a few times and then left. As soon as he was gone, the car returned. The same thing happened every time I called. One of the officers finally came to the door and said he would come by every hour, but each time he did, the driver was gone. It's like the driver knew he was coming."

"I'm calling Joey."

"Absolutely not."

"When you get home, lock yourself in."

"I do. I even prop a chair under the doorknob. I'll be fine. Don't speed and get into a wreck getting back."

"Keep everything locked until I get there. I love you."

"And I love you."

He hung up and called Joey.

It was after 2:00 a.m. when Rob pulled into Wanda's parking lot. He drove slowly and checked every car on his way to her apartment. When he saw the vehicle and the man behind the wheel, he turned the Studebaker so the headlights gave him a full view of the car as he approached. A puff of cigarette smoke escaped the driver's open window, then suddenly, the car started and pulled up beside Rob. The two men locked eyes briefly before the man drove away. Rob waited until the taillights disappeared before parking his car. He was so angry he flew up the staircase without looking and almost trampled the man sitting on the top step.

"What are you doing out here?"

"Waiting for you," Joey said, tapping a tire iron in the palm of his hand. "I've been playing cat and mouse with that dude all night. Every time I tried to confront him, he drove away. So I decided to sit out here, and we've just been watching each other ever since."

Rob put a hand on his friend's shoulder. "Sorry for putting you through this, but I didn't know who else to call."

"You would do the same for Sybil." He yawned. "Now that you're here, I'll head home."

"Thanks, Joey."

"Don't mention it. See ya."

Rob stood near the staircase until Joey drove away before unlocking the door to Wanda's apartment. She was sound asleep on the sofa. Rob went to her bedroom, brought back a blanket, and covered her, then stood watch for the rest of the night at her window.

"When did you get in?" Wanda asked when her alarm went off the next morning.

"About 2:00 a.m.," Rob said, sitting next to her on the sofa. "I'm taking you to work this morning and bringing you home after work."

Rob stepped outside and scanned the parking lot. The car was nowhere in sight. He went in, made coffee, and waited for her to dress. He whistled when she walked out of the bedroom.

"Glad you like it," she said, stroking her new suit. "It's a copy of one Jackie Kennedy wore."

"I didn't realize you were a fan of politics."

"I'm not, but I find the Kennedys fascinating." She glanced at the clock. "We need to go."

He drove her to work, then went to his apartment to await Carlos's call. Rob was so angry that he was actually looking forward to the call, but it was mid-afternoon before his phone finally rang.

"Have you secured my trucking companies?"

"Carlos, keep your people away from Wanda."

Carlos chuckled. "I was told you met my man last night."

"You'll have to replace him if he shows up again."

"My people are there for a reason, Roberto."

"What reason?"

"Wanda is your weakness. She is your Achilles' heel. As long as I have her, I have you. Now stop wasting time and tell me what you found."

Rob realized this was going nowhere. "I found three trucking companies willing to sell."

"Excellent news. How soon can we make the purchases?"

"I'm finalizing in a couple of days."

"Good. Now, how soon can I use the docks?"

"You can't. The docks are controlled by the New Orleans mafia. They're not interested."

"Then make them interested. Find out what they want, and I will double it. I need those docks, Roberto. I am not giving up."

"Carlos, if I keep pushing, I won't come back alive."

"Who runs the docks?"

"Marcel Pascal."

"Offer Pascal more money."

"Pascal's assistant wouldn't even allow me to present your offer."

"Find a way, Roberto. I need those docks."

Rob could hear someone speaking Spanish in the background.

"We will discuss this later. It seems I have a more urgent situation needing my attention."

"Keep your people away from Wanda, Carlos."

"Her well-being is totally up to you, my friend. Now get me those docks."

Rob smashed the phone into the receiver.

He spent the next few days closing the trucking company sales, then left a message for Carlos. He was surprised when Carlos returned the call so quickly. "The deals are done on the trucking companies, Carlos."

"Where are they located?"

"Oklahoma City, Memphis, and Ames, Iowa."

"Those are good locations, but we need more. Now, tell me, when are you moving into my building?"

"There are modifications I want to make before I move in."

"What kind of modifications?"

"Reinforce the walls. Enclose an area to conceal documents."

"Conceal them from whom?"

"From everyone. The last thing we want is to have these corporations traced back to you."

"I agree. It pleases me to know you are looking out for me, Roberto."

"I'm not doing this for you, Carlos. I'm doing it for me. I don't want to spend the rest of my life in federal prison."

"Whatever the reason, I am pleased. Something has happened here we must discuss."

Rob's gut twisted.

"Our bank accounts in México were compromised," Carlos said. "It seems some of my most trusted employees betrayed me."

Rob shuddered to think what Carlos had done to them. "Sounds like you know who was involved."

"Not exactly. It is still too soon to know, but I have made an example of the ones I found. You and I have something in common, Roberto. When someone does harm to me, I never forget. Until I am certain I have eliminated all the rats, we must change how we transfer our money to you."

"What kind of changes?"

"The money will no longer be wired into accounts."

"Then how is it getting here?"

"It will be transported across the border to a certain location, and you will handle it from there. It is now your responsibility to devise a method of retrieving and depositing the funds into the appropriate accounts."

"Carlos, I have accounts set up all over the country. There is no way I can do this and handle everything else."

"Then I strongly suggest you find a trustworthy person to assist you. If I discover they have taken my money, you know who I will come for first."

Rob pulled the receiver from his ear and shook it violently. He closed his eyes and returned the phone to his ear. "How much time do I have before you start this process?"

"Two weeks at the most. Our revenue is growing, and with this last turn of events, we have no place to secure it. This new responsibility also comes with rewards, Roberto. Handle this well, and your compensation will be doubled."

"I'm not doing this for money, Carlos."

"You say that now, but you will change your mind. I suggest you get started, Roberto."

CHAPTER TWENTY-ONE

After days spent agonizing over how to move Carlos's money, it had become clear to Rob that the only possible way to do it and still keep up with Carlos's demands was to get someone else had to handle the money. But who? Rob tossed his pen onto the table, threw his hands in the air, pushed himself up and out of his chair, grabbed his keys, rushed out the door, and ran smack into Joey.

"Dang it, man," Joey said, stumbling backward. "You trying to kill me?"

"What the heck are you doing here?"

"I came to check on you. I haven't heard from you since the night at Wanda's."

"I know. I'm sorry, Joey. I promise we'll talk soon, but now isn't the time."

Joey crossed his arms. "Nope. I'm not moving. Something's going on with you, buddy. You haven't been yourself for months."

"It's nothing, Joey."

"Good, so let's go in and catch up."

Rob reached behind him and pulled his apartment door shut. "Let's talk out here. My place is a mess."

Joey slapped him on the shoulder. "Dang, man, I own a garage. Every day of my life is messy." He took a seat on the steps to the apartment. "I know losing your job is rough, but you got Wanda back, right? So what's going on with you? Does this have anything to do with that dude watching her?"

Rob ran his sweaty palms down his pant legs. "I don't want to discuss it."

Joey leaned over and punched Rob lightly in the shoulder. "Might as well, 'cause I'm not leaving until you do."

"Don't you have a business to run?"

"Garage is closed for repairs and Sybil and the baby are at her folks." Joey leaned back against the step. "I can sit right here for days."

"Yeah, well, some things are none of your business."

"Not where we're concerned. We swore never to keep secrets from each other."

"When we were eight years old!"

"An oath is an oath. Start talking."

Rob eyed his friend. "You're not leaving, are you?"

"Nope."

Rob sighed. "If you must know, I have a problem. A big problem, and I don't see an answer."

Joey propped himself on one elbow. "Are you and Wanda having trouble?"

Rob shook his head. "She's the only thing that's going right."

"Then maybe I can help."

"No. I just need to find someone to do a difficult job for me."

"I know a lot of people. What are you looking for?"

Rob took a deep breath and exhaled. "It has to be someone I trust. I mean, really trust." Rob dropped his eyes. "It's dangerous, Joey."

"Man, what the hell kind of job is this?"

"I can't tell you."

"How long do we have to find this person?"

"It's not *we*, Joey. Me. It's *my* problem. I only have a couple of days."

"And if you don't?"

"Let's just say the beating I took months ago was nothing compared to what will happen if I don't find this person."

There was a long silence.

"Goll-lee. It sounds like squeaky clean Rob Chambers has finally gotten his hands dirty." He reached over and slapped Rob on the knee. "Welcome to the rest of humanity, old buddy."

"This isn't funny, Joey."

"Didn't say it was. So, what are these bad guys asking you to do?"

Rob shook his head. "I can't tell you."

"I don't need details. Just give me the short version."

Rob paused as he calculated his response. "I'm looking for someone I can trust to move something of value for these people and take it to different locations."

"What's in it for the sucker who agrees to do it?"

"Oh, he's going to be paid well, but the risk isn't worth it."

"Man," Joey said with a shake of his head. "You do have a problem."

"Trust me, I know." Rob got to his feet. "Sorry, Joey, you have to go. There's a good chance I'm being watched, and the last thing I want is to put you in danger."

"Wish there was something I could do to help," Joey said as he got to his feet.

"I know, but it's my problem, not yours." Rob gave his old friend a gentle shove. "Until I get this handled, I don't think we should be seen together. I've got enough on my plate without worrying about you."

"Yeah, but two minds working on it doesn't hurt. We've been through tough times before. We'll get through this one," Joey said, then went down the staircase, got in his truck, and drove away.

Rob went inside and left a message for Carlos to call him. He didn't hear from him until later that day.

"We'll have to think of a different way to deposit your money, Carlos. I can't find anyone I trust to handle it." There was an unnerving silence. Rob's insides twisted in knots as he waited.

"Roberto, three and a half million in large bills are crossing the border in three days, and there will be another drop a week later. Either you handle it, or I will handle you and Wanda simultaneously."

Rob wiped his clammy palm on his shirt. "Give me the information, and I will do it myself."

As Carlos explained the procedure, Rob realized how great the danger was of something going terribly wrong.

He took a second to gather his composure. "I know you don't want to hear this again, but depositing this much cash will create more issues, Carlos."

"That is why I pay you so well. I expect the money to be in my accounts in less than four days. Don't disappoint me, Roberto."

Rob hung up, wondering just exactly how he was supposed to perform miracles.

Early the next morning, Rob's phone started to ring. One of the trucking companies that had previously rejected his offer had changed their mind. If he was still interested, they were willing to sell. Rob said he was and was told their attorney would contact him in the next few days to iron out the details. He had no sooner gotten off the phone than another trucking company called and said that if he came up on his offer, they would also be willing to sell.

Rob knew Carlos wanted the trucking companies, and he had to close them quickly or lose the sale, but if he stayed to do the closings, he couldn't be in Laredo to pick up the money, much less go from state to state to deposit it. That thought was still in his head when his phone rang again. Rob sighed as he picked up the phone.

"Hey, buddy. Remember Leroy Griffin, Sybil's cousin?"

"What are you talking about, Joey?"

"Your problem, stupid. Leroy wants the job."

"No. Absolutely not. I'm not dragging your family into this. Besides, Leroy's just a kid."

"You need to shut up and listen. Leroy's all grown up now and works as a bouncer for a roadhouse outside Channelview. He deals with drunken oilfield workers, cowboys, and biker dudes, always looking for a fight. He's used to handling bad guys. Besides, he needs the money. His old man isn't doing well, and Leroy's helping out. So just tell me when you want him to start."

Rob shook his head in frustration. "Joey, this could get him killed."

"He deals with that possibility every night."

There was a long silence.

"Hey. Say something," Joey said finally.

"Your wife will never forgive you or me if something happens to him."

"Nah. We're all surprised he's lived this long. You wouldn't believe all the stupid stunts he's pulled growing up."

"If he's that dumb, why should I trust him?"

"Because he's family and I'll tell his mama if he messes up. Now give me the details, and I'll get him on the road."

"I've got a bad feeling about this, Joey."

"One day, old buddy, you'll learn you can't protect the whole world. Leroy knows the risks and wants the job. Tell me when you want him, and I'll make sure he's there."

"I'll meet him," Rob said, after weighing the pros and cons in his head. "But I'm sending him home if I don't think he can handle it."

"Fair enough. I'll have him here tomorrow."

"No, I'll meet him in Channelview tomorrow morning. I'll put him on the road if I like what I see. What's his number?" Rob asked, then committed the number to memory.

"I know Leroy will do you proud, old buddy."

"We'll see. Thanks for your help."

"Go ahead, admit it. You need me. Talk later."

Rob wished he felt relieved. But even if, by some miracle, Leroy was the answer, he would need a complete description of bank locations, deposit slips filled out with amounts and account numbers, and maps for every stop he would make. It was going to be a very long night.

The next morning, Rob stood beside his Studebaker at a roadside park outside Cloverleaf and Channelview. A Chevy pickup pulled into the roadside park and stopped, and a broad-shouldered man exited the pickup and approached him.

Rob glanced at his watch. Leroy was only two minutes late.

"It's been a while," Leroy said in a deep husky voice.

"I'll say. You've grown up." Rob watched him kick a rock with one of his well-worn cowboy boots.

"Yep, my mama fed me well."

Rob took a step closer. "Did Joey tell you the risk involved with this job?"

Leroy grinned. "Yeah, he tried to scare me off, but it didn't work. Tell me what you need, and I'll handle it."

Rob hesitated before opening his car door and taking out his briefcase. "Leroy, this job involves handling a large sum of money."

"I do that now. After we lock up, I take the money from my boss's bar and several other businesses to the bank each night."

"Does Joey know that?"

"Nope. Some things you don't talk about."

Rob let out a sigh. "Good answer." He spent the next hour describing the location of the drop, the bank deposits, and the amount of money involved. The only reaction he got from Leroy was an occasional raised eyebrow.

"After you pick up the money, find a motel and lock yourself in. You need to bundle the money into the amount listed on each deposit slip I give you and deposit it into the bank on the account. I've done the calculations, and you should be back in three days. Call me at this motel in north Dallas if you think you'll be later than 6:00 p.m."

Rob saw a police car drive past them on the road. Then, to his horror, it made a U-turn and pulled up next to them.

"You boys all right?" the officer asked.

Rob could hear the blood pumping in his ears. "We're fine. I just hired this big guy to do some work for me. I was giving him directions."

"Well, all right then. Take care."

"Thanks for stopping."

Rob turned to Leroy after the policeman drove away. "Are you sure you want to do this? This could get you in major trouble."

Leroy laughed. "Joey said you were a worrywart."

"Maybe so, but for good reason. If you have any trouble, call the numbers I gave you. Be careful, Leroy."

The big man pushed away from the car hood. "Just because I have muscles don't mean I'm dumb. I know what you want me to do. Unless you got something else, I better get on the road." Leroy gathered the maps and information in his large hands and went to his truck.

As he drove away, Rob felt an uncomfortable tightness in his chest. He had just placed the lives of everyone he cared about in the hands of a roadhouse bouncer.

CHAPTER TWENTY-TWO

Rob had told Wanda he had to be out of town interviewing, but he was actually at his apartment. He needed to deal with the trucking companies, but more importantly, he had to be near his phone if Leroy called. When the day came for Leroy to return and Rob hadn't heard from him, he waited until almost 5:00 p.m. before driving to north Dallas and checking in to the motel. Hours passed, but there was no word from Leroy. Just before midnight, Rob grabbed the phone and dialed Joey's number just as someone knocked on the door to his room. He slammed the receiver down.

"Surprise," Joey said when Rob opened the door. He was grinning from ear to ear.

"What the hell! Where's Leroy?"

"Do you want to talk out here or let me in?"

Rob pulled Joey inside and glanced around outside before closing the door.

Joey tossed his bag onto the bed. "Why don't we start with 'Good to see you, old friend' before you bombard me with questions."

Rob grabbed Joey by the shoulders. "What happened to all the money, Joey?"

Joey pulled away from his grasp, opened his bag, and handed Rob a large envelope. "It's all where it's supposed to be. Those are the slips, receipts, and my expenses."

Rob took the envelope. "What do you mean, your expenses?"

"Just open the damn envelope." Joey sat on the bed as Rob spread everything out across the bedspread and inspected every deposit slip, calculating the totals. When he was done, Rob pushed it all aside and slumped onto the bed, exhaling loudly.

"You satisfied?" Joey asked.

"Every dime is accounted for."

"You feel better?"

"I will after you tell me what happened to Leroy."

"Man, I just spent three days and nights saving your ass. A thank-you would be nice."

"Stop stalling and tell me what happened."

"Leroy called me from Oklahoma City. He said he called home, and his mama told him an ambulance was there, loading up his dad to take him to the hospital. Leroy panicked and called me and said he was going home. I knew his running out on you would put you in big trouble, so I told him to stay put until I got there."

"He was supposed to call me, not you."

"He wasn't thinking straight. When I got to him, he told me what to do, and I did it." Joey twisted his neck from side to side. "I pushed you into hiring him, so it was my place to make sure the job was done." He glanced at Rob. "Now I know why you were so close-lipped about all this. Dang, that was a lot of cash."

Rob shook his head. "I know, and it belongs to some very bad people. That's why I didn't want you involved."

Joey shoved him with his shoulder. "Relax, Mommy. I'm home safe and sound."

Rob put his arm around Joey's shoulders. "I would never forgive myself if something happened to you."

Joey pulled away. "You're not going to kiss me, are you?"

Rob smiled. "I was thinking about it but changed my mind." Joey laughed. "Did you have any trouble?" Rob asked

"Nope. I was a little concerned that the banks would question a guy in a work shirt and blue jeans depositing tens of thousands of dollars in cash, but they didn't seem to give it a second thought."

"That's because I set up the accounts for businesses that only take cash. Carnivals, laundromats, and vending machine companies."

"Well, it worked. No one questioned a thing." He yawned and rolled the kinks from his shoulders. "Truth is, this was easier than the stuff I do at the garage. By the time I got to the last bank, I knew what they would say before they did." He turned and pushed down on the mattress with his open palm. "Are you staying here tonight or going back?"

"Going."

"Good. I need some sleep."

Rob went to the dresser, opened his briefcase, and tossed Joey a package wrapped in brown paper.

"What's this?"

"Your pay."

Joey opened the package. "Daaaannnng, man. How much money is this?"

"Five thousand dollars."

Joey gathered the cash in his hands and looked up at Rob. "Are you telling me whoever does this job gets paid this much every trip?"

"Joey, this was a one-time deal."

"No, it ain't." He jumped to his feet. "When's the next job?"

Rob gathered the receipts and deposit slips and placed them into his briefcase. "We're not having this discussion. Take the money and consider yourself lucky you're safe."

Joey stepped closer. "No way, buddy. You're not leaving here until I get this job."

Rob took hold of his friend's shoulders and squeezed hard. "Stop. These are dangerous people. You have no idea what you'd be getting into."

"So why don't you tell me everything and let me decide?"

Rob backed away. "I can't. If you say anything to anyone, they will kill us."

"Stop being so dramatic and talk."

Rob ran his hands through his hair, paused for a moment, and then began to speak. He told Joey about purchasing the lab equipment and his ordeal in the Mexican jail. He explained why he had broken off his relationship with Wanda. Joey's jaw dropped when he heard that Carlos and his partners were expanding to the States.

"That's why I don't want you mixed up in this," Rob said. "Think of your wife and daughter."

"They're the reason I need this," Joey said. "Can you at least wait a couple of days before you give it to someone else?"

"Wait. What's going on, Joey? Why would you even consider this?"

"We're having another baby."

"That's good news, isn't it?"

"Yeah, but I'm still paying off the first one. And last week the car lift broke, almost crushing one of my men. It's so bad I had to send Sybil and the baby to her mama's. I can't pay my guys and feed them without that lift." He pointed to the money on the bed. "It's going to take all that to fix the lift, and I still have bills to pay."

"Why didn't you tell me you needed money?"

"You've got your own problems. Besides, caring for my family is my job, not yours." He reached out and grabbed Rob's arm. "All I ask is a few days before you give this to anyone else."

Rob could see the desperation in his eyes. "Four days, Joey, but that's it."

"Thanks, old buddy." Joey yawned, sat on the edge of the bed, and started unlacing his work boots. "Now, get out of here. I need some sleep."

"Lock the door behind me."

Joey got to his feet, gave Rob his two-finger salute, and pushed him out the door.

*   *   *

Rob drove back to his apartment and threw himself across the bed. A ringing phone woke him, and he stumbled to the next room to answer.

"Where is my money?"

Rob was suddenly wide awake. "In your accounts."

"Good. I got the contracts for two trucking companies, but they are small. We need companies with more trucks."

Rob closed his eyes and shook his head. "I'll see what I can do, Carlos."

"Good. Now, we need to discuss the next money drop. It will be in Laredo the first of next week, and this shipment is larger than the last."

Rob's heart pounded in his chest. "Carlos, we need more accounts before the next drop arrives."

"Then do it, and find me more trucks."

Despite thinking of nothing but possible solutions, two days passed, and Rob still hadn't come up with an answer. As he was pacing his apartment, someone knocked at his door. He went to the window to see who it was. "Damn it," he said, opening the door. "Don't even start, Joey."

"Not leaving, old buddy, so might as well let me in."

Rob paused, then stepped aside to let him in.

"What's in all these boxes?" Joey asked, looking around the room.

"That's none of your business. And you're not making another drop."

Joey perched on the arm of the sofa. "What if I told you I figured out a way to get your trips handled faster without you or me being the ones doing it?"

"I'm not sending, Leroy."

"I'm not talking about Leroy. We get the guys from my shop to handle it, and I'll manage the whole operation. It's perfect."

"No, it isn't. We're talking about more money than your crew has ever seen. We can't risk a dollar of it going missing."

"I promise you, my guys won't take a penny. I've known them almost as long as I've known you."

"Joey, I learned the hard way that people you think you trust can turn on you."

"Not my guys. I'd trust them with my life."

"Are you in such desperate need of money you're willing to go to prison?"

"I'll do whatever it takes to feed my family and keep a roof over their heads. And look on the bright side. If we get caught, there's a chance we might get locked up in the same cell."

"That isn't funny. How will you care for your family if you're in prison?"

"Let me worry about that. Besides, I've already told my crew about the job, and they want in."

"You what?"

His friend shrugged. "Had to. How else was I to know if they were willing? I'll manage the guys while you handle the other stuff."

"Why are you so dead set on doing this?"

"I'm way behind on my garage payments. I'll lose everything, including our house if I don't get some money soon."

"You've put me in an impossible position, Joey."

"Look, all I ask is you come to the garage and talk to the guys. What have you got to lose?"

Rob started to pace again. After a couple of minutes, he stopped and looked at Joey. "I'll go, but if it doesn't feel right, the answer is no."

Joey grabbed Rob's hand and started shaking it. "You won't be sorry, I promise." Joey all but skipped to the door. "Got to go. Can't wait to give my guys the news."

Rob followed him to the door and watched as he ran down the stairs, jumped into his pickup, and pulled away. Rob closed the door and shook his head. This hole he had dug had just gotten deeper.

*　*　*

It was after dark when Rob walked into Joey's garage. The car bay was empty except for Joey and his men. All five men were scrubbed clean, wearing pressed jeans and work shirts, and watching every move Rob made.

"Brandon, Gus, Martin, Doyle, Trey. Are you sure you want to do this?"

Brandon stuffed his hands into his pockets. "We understand the risk, but the garage is in trouble, and we're about to lose our jobs. Things are tough out there, and nobody's hiring. We can't care for our families without a paycheck, so if you give us a chance, we'll do you right."

Rob looked each man in the eye. "Are you sure? Once I give you the details, there's no backing out."

The five men huddled a moment, and then Brandon stepped forward. "We're in. What do you want us to do?"

Rob spent the next few hours describing the job's details and the consequences if anyone messed up. By the time he finished, the men in the room were still eager to get started, but Rob was still conflicted about bringing them in.

*   *   *

Carlos called early the following day to give him the drop information, and when he hung up, Rob called the garage. "Joey, I need you here this afternoon."

"I'll be there in a couple of hours. I'll call my guys and have them come to the garage tonight."

"Joey."

"Don't say it. I've already drilled it into their heads. They know not to tell anyone, not even their wives."

"The same goes for you."

A few hours later, Joey arrived and saw everything was packed in boxes. "You moving?"

"As a matter of fact, I am."

Rob cleared the kitchen table of boxes, and the two men sat. He took a card from his pocket, slid it across the table, and tapped on the card with his finger. "This is the address and the phone number for my new office. The number on the back is a separate line. It's the only number I want you to use."

Joey picked up the card. "The Chambers Law Firm. Sounds impressive." He flipped the card over and looked at the number. "What happens if I need you late at night? Do I call you here or at Wanda's?"

"If you ever call her apartment, don't say anything about our deal."

Joey gestured to the boxes. "So she doesn't know about this."

Rob shook his head. "Absolutely not, and neither should your wife. We have to keep them out of this."

Joey studied Rob's face for a minute. "You afraid she'll dump you if she finds out?"

"I lost her once. I can't do it again."

"Then marry the girl. You can tell her after. I mean, if she's with you, she's already involved."

Rob nodded slowly. "You may be right."

"She loves you. It's time to tell her the truth." He stretched his arm and started rolling up his sleeves. "All right, tell me what to do so I can get my guys on the road."

Rob handed him a large envelope and spelled out the information in detail.

Joey flipped through the deposit slips. "Got it."

"I've put all the information on accessing the money in the envelope on top of the deposit slips. As soon as your guys finish, have them return to Dallas and give everything to you. If they must make a call, have them use a pay phone, but only when no one's around."

Rob handed Joey two large envelopes of cash. "This is expense money. Do you have all that?"

"Yeah, yeah. Remember, I did this already." He tucked the envelopes under his shirt. "I better get going."

Rob grabbed him by the shoulders. "Tell them to deposit every penny, Joey, and be careful."

"I will." He glanced at Rob's hands and smiled. "Can I go now?"

Rob released him. "Call me if there's a problem."

"You said that already."

Rob followed Joey all the way to his truck. He pushed the door closed but didn't let go. Joey started the engine and looked down at Rob's white-knuckled grip on his door.

"Let go, buddy. I need to get my guys on the road."

Rob released the door and stepped back. Joey gave him his two-finger salute, then back out onto the street.

Rob was thinking about Joey's advice as he climbed the stairs to his apartment. He went to his bedroom, opened the drawer of his nightstand, and took out the photo Carlos had taken from Wanda's parent's home. Rob laid it on the bed, then pulled the box holding Wanda's engagement ring out of the drawer and stared at it. There was no way he could ask her to marry him without telling her the truth.

CHAPTER TWENTY-THREE

When Rob and Wanda arrived at The Club that night, Jack ushered them in with gusto and sat them at his best table. They danced for a while, then returned to their table.

"Hey, mister," Wanda said. "Are you all right?"

"Yeah, sure. Why do you ask?"

"Your body's here, but your mind is somewhere else."

His brow furrowed. "Wanda, we need to talk."

Her eyes widened, and she pressed her hand to her chest. "Are you leaving me again?"

"No. I love you, sweetheart. But there are things about me you should know."

She reached for her clutch bag. "Then pay the bill so we can get out of here."

Neither said a word as they drove back to her apartment. Rob took his briefcase from the car's back seat and walked her to her apartment. He could see the concern on her face as he sat beside her on the sofa. He reached for her hand and held it between his.

"You're scaring me, Rob. What's this about?"

"I want to marry you, Wanda."

She blinked. "What did you say?"

"I want to marry you. But before I ask, there are things you should know."

She took her hand from his and pressed it against his face. "Rob, I love you. Nothing you say will keep me from saying *yes*."

He took her hand from his face. "It might. I've been lying to you about my traveling to interview."

Her eyes widened as she searched his face. "What were you doing?"

"I've been working for Carlos Rojas and his partners."

"Why lie about that? That's great news."

Rob closed his eyes and shook his head. "Wanda, what I'm doing for them is illegal."

She gasped and drew back. "Illegal? What are you talking about?"

He took a deep breath before answering. "I've been setting up fake corporations, opening bank accounts, and purchasing trucking companies and buildings to hide Carlos's drug money."

She cupped her hands over her mouth. "You're laundering drug money? Rob, you could go to prison." She grabbed his arm. "You have to stop."

"I can't." Rob picked up his briefcase and took out the photo.

Her eyes went from him to the photo and back again. "This was in my parents' home. How did you get it?"

"Carlos had his people take it the first night you were there. I called you the next morning to make sure you and your parents were safe."

"Why didn't you tell me?"

"I couldn't. I'm almost certain Carlos had his men bug your parents' phone lines."

"Why? My folks have nothing to do with him."

"He did it to keep track of me . . . and you."

"Me? What does he want with me?"

"He's using you to keep me in line."

"But why bring my parents into this?"

"He did it to prove he could get to you and your parents."

Wanda jumped to her feet and started wringing her hands. "Oh, my God. Oh my God." She pointed to the door. "Was the man in that car one of Carlos's men?"

"He was." Rob stood, took her into his arms, and felt her trembling. "This is why I ended our relationship. I thought you would be safe if Carlos knew we weren't together. It almost killed me to do that to you. But it didn't work, and when I saw you at that restaurant, I knew

I couldn't live without you." Rob closed his eyes for a moment, then looked at her. "And now Joey's involved."

She pushed back from him. "How did he get into this?"

"Joey helped me deposit some of Carlos's money. He's doing more of it now and being paid lots of money. I'm telling you this because if we're married, there is a good chance the authorities will think you're part of this if I'm caught."

"Well, now that you've told me, I am involved. If I don't report you, I'm aiding and abetting."

"I'm sorry, sweetheart. I've gotten you into a real mess." He watched as she began chewing her bottom lip.

"Have you gone to the authorities?"

"I tried to tell the FBI without implicating myself, but so far, all of Carlos's drug dealings are in Mexico, and the FBI has no jurisdiction."

"You said so far. Does that mean Carlos is bringing his drugs here?"

"He is."

She covered her face with her hands. "Dear God." She looked at him. "Rob, you have to get out of this."

"I can't. If I try, Carlos will hurt you." He took hold of her shoulders and looked into her eyes. "Wanda, If you want nothing to do with me. I'll understand."

Tears filled her eyes. "I can't let you go. I would rather fight this with you than be without you again." She smiled despite her tears. "I love you, so stop stalling and just ask me to marry you."

Rob took the ring box from his briefcase, opened it, and got on one knee. "I've waited far too long to do this. Will you marry me?"

"Yes, you *have* waited far too long. Of course, I will marry you."

Rob slipped the ring on her finger. "I love you, Wanda, and I promise I will get us out of this mess as quickly as possible."

She pulled him to his feet. "Stop talking and kiss me."

He took her into his arms and kissed her.

*   *   *

A few days later, Rob met with Joey at the apartment. "Any problems with the drop?"

"Not a one," Joey said, taking a large envelope from a canvas bag. "Look for yourself." Joey handed him the bag, then went to the sofa to stretch out. "I was up all night waiting on my guys. Wake me when you're done."

Rob opened the bag and began sorting through the slips. It didn't take long, but he let his friend sleep. A couple of hours later, he nudged Joey awake.

"Is it all there?" Joey asked with a yawn.

"Every penny accounted for."

"See, I told you."

Rob pointed to the three bundles wrapped in brown paper on his coffee table.

Joey jumped to his feet and picked them up. "Once the guys see this, I'll never get them to work on a car again."

"Tell them not to get used to it. I hope Carlos will return to wire transfers as soon as things are settled in Mexico."

"Don't change anything on our account. We still have mouths to feed." He went to the door. "Let me know when you get another call."

*   *   *

It wasn't long before Joey got his wish. Once again, his men were dispatched and returned without problems.

Rob moved into his new offices, and Joey's men handled the drops. While this was happening, Rob and Wanda visited her parents so Rob could ask permission to marry her. Her parents, especially her father, were hesitant initially, but when he saw how happy Wanda was, he agreed.

A few weeks later, they had a small ceremony at the courthouse. Joey, his family, Wanda's parents, and her roommate Shelly were the only guests. Just as the ceremony ended, a courier arrived with a box.

"I have a package for a Robert Chambers."

Rob stepped forward. "I'm Chambers."

He signed, and the courier left.

Wanda came to Rob's side. "That was strange. Who is it from?"

"I don't know." Rob set the box in a chair and opened it as the others joined them.

Inside the box was a beautiful Waterford crystal bowl with an envelope inside. Rob handed the bowl to Wanda and opened the envelope.

"It's from Carlos."

Joey leaned in to look as Rob showed the note to Wanda. "Did you tell him you were getting married?" he asked.

"I never said a word."

Joey took the note from his hand and started reading out loud. "Congratulations to you both. I would have attended had I gotten an invitation."

Wanda put the bowl back into the box and set it on the floor. "This is staying here."

"Why?" Wanda's mother asked. "It's beautiful and expensive."

Rob glanced at Wanda before answering. "It's from a former client of the firm we would prefer not to be associated with."

"I see," her mother said.

Rob smiled at Wanda and took her hand. "This is our day, and you're all celebrating with us. That's the only gift we need."

*   *   *

They took one day to honeymoon in San Antonio before returning to Dallas to set up Rob's new office. He was arranging law books on bookshelves when Wanda came over and draped her arms around his neck.

"I gave my official notice last week," she said.

"Why? I thought you liked your job."

"I do, but how will you keep your association with Carlos a secret with anyone other than me in this office?"

"Absolutely not. If you're here, you can't be the innocent wife."

"Too late. Like it or not, I'm showing up next week." She placed her hands on both sides of his face. "All I ask is you take on some clients so we don't have to live on drug money."

"I've already told Carlos a firm without clients would only draw attention."

"Good. The thought of living on Carlos's dirty money makes me sick."

"I feel exactly the same."

*　　*　　*

It took a week to get settled. Rob was sitting behind his desk when the private line rang. "How are you enjoying your new office?" Carlos asked.

Rob looked up to see Wanda standing at his door and shook his head. "I'm getting settled in."

She nodded and closed the door.

"Good, because our next shipment will arrive in four days."

"And it's larger than the last?"

"I see you finally understand my business. I have selected Corpus Christi as the best location for Luis's headquarters. We are in the process of having the complex remodeled to accommodate our needs. Before that is finished, I must know I have access to the docks."

"Carlos, we've had this discussion. The only way in is by Pascal's invitation."

"Then we must make the man an offer he cannot refuse."

"What kind of offer?"

"I will tell you when I have every detail completed. In the meantime, you have a drop coming in four days. Be ready, Roberto," he said and hung up.

Rob took a moment before picking up the phone and dialing.

"Joey, tell your guys to get rested. The next drop will happen in four days. I'll call you when I get the final details."

"We'll be ready."

Rob got up, went to the window, and looked down at the Dallas traffic and the people milling about on the sidewalks. Those people have no idea how fortunate they were.

*　*　*

Rob was forced to open more corporations and businesses to support the growing amount of money he had to funnel for Carlos. Carlos had not mentioned a word about New Orleans in weeks, and Rob prayed he had given up on the idea.

Joey's guys made runs every four to seven days, and Rob spent endless hours posting every deposit into ledgers for Carlos's accountants in Mexico. Rob took on a few clients to keep him sane and Wanda happy.

He was at his desk when Wanda came in and wrapped her arms around his neck.

"Guess what?" she said. "We're moving."

"Moving where?"

"A larger apartment near White Rock Lake. It has an enormous swimming pool just steps from our door." She released him and sat on the corner of his desk. "The stress you're under and working for hours without resting has taken a toll on you. You've been so busy you haven't had time to drive across town to swim. Now you won't have to. You can swim anytime you like."

"It sounds great."

"I can't wait for you to see it." The phone in her office rang, and she rushed to answer it. Minutes later, she returned.

"That was strange. That call was the owner of Miller's Oil in Midland, Texas, asking for an appointment."

"How did a company in Midland hear about us?"

"The owner said the Tolland Firm referred him."

"Are you sure he said *Tolland?*"

"Positive. Miller said Gary Tolland referred us."

"Why would Gary be sending us business?"

"Maybe this is his way of reconnecting with you."

"I hope you're right." Rob picked up the phone and started dialing as Wanda went to her office.

"It's so good to hear your voice," Tolland's secretary said when Rob greeted her. "How are you and Wanda? I heard you were married?"

"We're doing great, thanks. We had a call this morning from Miller's Oil in Midland. The owner said Gary referred us."

"He did, and there will be more."

"I don't understand. Why didn't Gary give the lead to one of his associates?"

"The firm has become so busy we have to limit the number of new clients we take."

"Does Horton know about this?"

"Oh, you haven't heard. Mr. Horton is no longer with the firm. Shortly after you left, he went to Mr. Tolland and insisted he be named a partner, but after the Mexicana codicil, there was no way Mr. Tolland would allow that to happen."

"That's surprising news."

"It was for everyone here, but it's been for the best. The associates and the staff are much more productive without him constantly hovering and criticizing them. It's amazing how one person could create such an atmosphere of stress and friction in an office."

"I understand that, but with all the firms in Dallas, why is Gary referring me?"

"The Tolland Firm is having its best year in history. I've heard Mr. Tolland say he attributes much of it to you."

"That's not possible. I wasn't there long enough to do anything."

"Rob, you saved the firm's reputation. We would have lost Black Pond and possibly many other accounts, and you brought us Hubert Oil. But I think Mr. Tolland's main reason for referring business to you is because he misses you."

"I miss being there. Is Gary in? I would like to thank him."

"He's in court today on a Black Pond case."

"Well, please let him know I called to thank him."

"He will be pleased you called. Take good care of that sweet wife of yours. We still miss her around here."

"She misses all of you. So nice speaking with you."

He hung up and saw Carlos's ledgers spread across his desk. "Damn you," he yelled, raking them off his desk. He got to his feet and started to pace.

Wanda came running into his office. "What happened?"

"I'm so sick of this dirty business. I've done this for so long, I'm beginning to feel like I'm turning into them."

Wanda took hold of him. "You're a good man, Robert Chambers. Don't let Carlos take that from you."

"You're right. He's taken enough. Why don't we get out of here?"

"Great idea! I can show you our new apartment. We'll go right after you lock up that mess."

"Yes, ma'am." Rob picked up the ledgers and was about to open the door to his hidden file room when his private line rang.

"I have great news, Roberto," Carlos said. "Luis is now in Corpus Christi and will soon be selling our products directly to customers. Why should we take less for our product when we can do it ourselves?"

"The distributor in that area won't like that, Carlos. Those men are dangerous. Are you sure Luis can handle this?"

"That problem was resolved weeks ago. They were given the choice of working for us or being eliminated. Diego is a master at this sort of thing."

Rob felt a knot forming in his gut. "So, when are you moving here?"

"Our business is so large, I can never be tied to one location. Because of that, except for certain matters, Luis will be communicating with you instead of me. You are to do everything he tells you as if it came directly from me. Is that clear?"

Rob shook his head. "I understand."

"Good. We are expanding very fast, Roberto, which means we will have large amounts of our product coming into your country."

"Are you asking me to find more trucking companies?"

"No. I am telling you it is time for you to return to New Orleans and secure the docks. I will call you shortly with the new details you will present to Pascal. When you return, I expect to have access to all the docks I need."

CHAPTER TWENTY-FOUR

"I know you said no new clients," Wanda said, entering Rob's office. "But Jack called and asked to see you this morning."

"Jack from The Club? Did he say what it was about?"

"I asked, but he said he'd rather talk to you."

Rob glanced at his watch. "Okay, I'll finish this and put everything in the safe room before he arrives."

His personal line rang and Wanda rolled her eyes. "That's my cue to leave."

Rob waited for his door to close before answering. "Yes, Carlos."

"The details of our offer to Pascal have been completed."

"What am I presenting?"

"Favors, Roberto."

"What do you mean by favors?"

"The type he would prefer not to handle himself."

"Are you offering to do his dirty work?"

"I am, and I will also pay whatever he asks for use of his docks. If Pascal is as smart as I think he is, he will accept my offer."

"You realize if he doesn't like this offer, I may not return?"

"Then I suggest you make sure he does not refuse."

"How soon do you need an answer?"

"As quickly as possible. Once Pascal agrees, I must rework our entire transportation system. Also, Luis will contact you shortly with the details of our next drop. You have much to do, Roberto. Get me those docks."

The thought of going back to New Orleans made Rob feel sick. He dropped his head in his hands.

"Are you okay?" Wanda asked, coming back into his office.

"I just need a minute."

"I will ask Jack to wait."

"He's here?"

"He just came in."

"Just give me time to clear my desk."

She nodded and left his office.

Rob took a deep breath, gathered all the ledgers, put them in the safe room, and went to get Jack.

"It's good to see you, Jack. Come in."

The round-faced man dipped his head to Wanda and hurried into Rob's office.

"Take a seat. What can I do for you?"

"I'm here to set up a trust for my niece and nephew's college education."

Rob took out a legal pad. "Who are you naming as executor of the trust?"

"I was hoping you could handle it."

Rob leaned back in his chair. "Are you sure? Why not their parents?"

"I would prefer it if someone outside the family handles this. I want to cover all their expenses while they are in school. Is that possible?"

"Yes, but it depends on how large a trust you are making." Rob put down his pen. "I'm happy to help you, but why not handle this yourself? You could open a savings account or even put them in your will?"

"No. It has to be done in a trust."

"Okay, then let's get started."

Jack reached into his coat pocket and placed a check on Rob's desk. "Here is two hundred dollars to open the escrow account. I prefer you do it in your name instead of mine." Jack cleared his throat. "The rest of the money will come in two installments of two hundred thousand dollars each. The first will come in three weeks, and the second will follow in a few months. Do you think that will be enough to cover their college?"

"It should be more than enough," Rob said. "Are you selling your businesses?"

"No. The money is coming from something else," Jack said, tugging at his shirt collar. "How soon can we get this done?"

"I'll have Wanda make an appointment for you on Friday. In the meantime, you will need to get your niece's and nephew's birthdays, full names, and social security numbers, and your specifications for how you want them to receive the funds. Unfortunately, I won't be able to open the escrow account until next Monday or Tuesday."

"I was hoping we could do it sooner."

"Normally I would, but I have to finish up here before I go out of town tomorrow morning."

"Then I guess that will have to do," he said as he nervously turned the brim of his hat. "Rob, there's something else we need to discuss." Jack glanced at the next room, where Wanda sat typing. "May I close the door?" He jumped up before Rob answered, closed the door, and returned to his seat. "I got a call from some, shall we say, acquaintances of mine in New Orleans asking about you after you paid them a visit."

"Really?" Rob squirmed in his chair. "I didn't know you had friends in New Orleans?"

Jack shook his head. "These people aren't friends. They asked me if I knew you."

"And what did you tell them?"

"That you were a lawyer and visited The Club." He paused for a moment and looked directly into Rob's eyes. "Take my advice and stay as far from these people as possible. It's not healthy to be anywhere near them."

Rob swallowed hard. "Thank you, Jack. I appreciate the warning. But some things are beyond our control."

He was conscious of Jack's searching gaze. Something—some kind of calculation—was going on behind that expressionless face. Then

Jack said, "I thought it might be something like that. It's easy to fall in with people and then realize getting to know them was a mistake." He smiled, but the smile didn't reach his eyes. "Believe me. I know all about that, but if you insist on trying to meet with Pascal, I'll make a few calls to certain people. That way, if you return to his office, you have a better chance of leaving it alive."

Rob felt a tightness in his chest. He wasn't about to ask Jack how he knew Pascal. "I'll be grateful if you can do that."

"Give it a day before you go. I think you'll find the door that was closed has opened."

Rob stood. "I'll be in your debt. Now, if there isn't anything else, let's get Wanda to set your appointment." He walked Jack out to Wanda's desk. "We need to make a two-hour appointment for Jack on Friday. It's important."

Wanda opened her calendar. "If it's that important, I can work him in on Thursday instead of Friday."

"I may not be back by then."

She glanced up at Rob, then looked back at her calendar. "How does 9:30 Friday morning work for you?"

"That's perfect."

"Good. I'll start your file and get the rest of your information on Friday."

"Thank you."

Rob walked Jack to the door and returned to Wanda.

"When did you decide to go out of town?" she asked.

"Carlos wants me to handle something."

"Should I be worried?"

"I do enough of that for both of us."

*　*　*

Instead of driving, Rob flew to New Orleans without luggage. He didn't want to be there any longer than he had to be. During his taxi ride to the Garden District, he rehearsed Carlos's proposal for the twentieth time. Just thinking about it made his heart pound.

When they arrived, the driver turned and looked at him. "Mister, Savoy's Restaurant isn't open yet."

Rob handed him the fare. "Thanks, but I'm not here to eat," he said, sliding out of the taxi. He closed the car door and the taxi pulled away from the curb and sped down the street.

Rob took the stairs to the second floor and approached the assistant at the desk.

"You have friends in the right places, handsome. You should have said so the first time you came. Mr. Pascal has agreed to your meeting."

"But he hasn't heard our proposal."

DuMont giggled. "Mr. Pascal doesn't waste his time with the messenger. He prefers to look into the eyes of the person requesting a business deal like this. Now, do you want this meeting or not?"

"Yes, sir, I do."

DuMont uncapped his pen, scribbled something on a monogrammed card, and handed it to Rob. "Have your clients call that number."

Rob took the card and left for the airport. He wanted out of this town as fast as possible.

*   *   *

Friday morning, he was on his second cup of coffee when Wanda ushered Jack into his office.

"How are you, Jack?"

"Anxious to get this done." He took out a folded piece of paper and handed it to Rob. "This is the information you requested for my niece and nephew."

Rob opened the paper and reviewed the information. "Looks like everything's here. Do you have any special requirements before we start?"

"I think we covered everything at my last visit."

The process took a couple of hours to complete. When they were finished, Rob stood up behind his desk. "I'll have Wanda type this up and open your escrow account Monday morning."

Jack shook Rob's hand. "I want this kept between us."

"I'm your lawyer, Jack. Everything we do is confidential."

"Thank you. That takes a lot off my mind."

"My pleasure," Rob said and walked him out the door. He had barely gotten past Wanda's desk when his private line rang. He hurried in and closed the door before answering.

"I see you are still alive?"

"I am."

"Does this mean I have my meeting?"

"It does. You just have to call and set it up."

"What is the number?"

After Rob gave him the information, Carlos said, "I must admit, I was concerned something might have happened to you, but I am pleased it didn't. Once I have access to these docks, there are no limits to what we will accomplish. I would prefer to have you at my side as my friend and partner, Roberto, instead of our current arrangement."

"You are threatening the people I love, Carlos. You and I will never be friends again."

There was a long pause. "That is unfortunate for both of us," Carlos said, and then the line went dead.

Wanda came in after he hung up the phone. She took his coat from the back of his chair and handed him his hat and briefcase.

"What's this?"

"You're going home and getting into the pool."

"I have work to do, Wanda. And I'm not leaving here without you."

"I have my car. I'll finish Jack's paperwork and be home before you leave the pool." She crossed her arms and glared at him. "That's an order, Chambers."

"I guess I'm going home."

CHAPTER TWENTY-FIVE

Luis called two days later with the information on the next drop. "Roberto," he said as soon as Rob answered, "I am in charge of distributing our product."

"I know. Carlos mentioned that on his last call."

"The only way I can meet Carlos's distribution deadline is to use people who have done this before. The problem is they are in México. The authorities know these men, so getting them across the border will be risky. I need your help finding a way to get them here as quickly as possible."

"Isn't this something you and Carlos should discuss?"

"I cannot. I told Carlos I could handle it. What should I do?"

"How have you done it before?"

"The old way of crossing takes too long. Carlos will be furious if I don't have a plan by our next meeting."

Rob closed his eyes and shook his head. "Let me see what I can do." He hung up the phone and fell back in his chair. Smuggling drug dealers across the border was not supposed to be his responsibility. Next thing he knew, they'd be asking him to sell drugs.

*   *   *

Days later, Rob pulled into the Gulf Breeze Hotel Corporation parking garage and was approached by two armed guards. "State your business," said one as the other watched with a hand on his holster.

"I'm Robert Chambers. I have a meeting with Luis Rojas."

"Give me your briefcase and put your hands on the car's hood."

Rob did as he was told. One guard patted him down while the other searched his briefcase. When they finished, the guard shoved his briefcase into his arms, and Rob was escorted to the elevator.

It felt like a scene in a spy movie, except the men and guns were real.

The doors opened on the top floor. Rob stepped out and was frisked by another pair of guards before he was allowed to enter the office, where he found Carlos seated behind a desk and Luis standing at his side.

"You look surprised," Carlos said.

"I am."

"Sit. We have much to discuss." Rob complied, and Carlos leaned back in his chair. "I am pleased with the hotel chain. It was a good choice for our needs. Luis tells me you have the details of his plan to move our people."

Rob looked at Luis, who averted his eyes. "I do. The plan is to purchase a fishing charter service."

"Luis, how will owning a charter service work?" Carlos asked.

Luis's eyes shifted from Carlos to Rob, then back to his brother. "I do not wish to brag, Carlos. Let Roberto explain."

Both men looked at Rob.

"You will load a few of your people with proper documents onto a charter boat and head out into the Gulf on a fishing trip. If the Coast Guard stops the boat, the charter captain will verify the people and documents as hotel guests. Once out in open water, the charter will meet another boat carrying the men Luis needs from Mexico, and they will exchange places. If the Coast Guard has checked the boat once, it is unlikely they will do it again the same day."

Carlos glanced at Luis, then back to Rob. "This is a good plan," he said. "Have you purchased the charter service?"

"I'm waiting for a return call from the owner."

"Luis has done his part, Roberto, now, do yours. Get it purchased. Every day you waste costs me millions."

Rob had to do something to keep himself from saying what he wanted to, so he opened his briefcase and handed Carlos several packets and folders.

"What is this?"

"The packets contain the deposits and spreadsheets from the last two weeks. The folders are the documents for the new trucking companies that stretch from Houston to Chicago. These and the last companies purchase will link you coast to coast."

Luis leaned forward. "This will require more drivers, Carlos."

"I know what it means, brother. I have already planned for this. With these new companies, we can expand to the northwest sooner than I anticipated."

"The northwest? Who will handle those drops?"

"That is your job, Roberto."

There was a long pause as Rob calculated what it would take to handle this massive influx of money.

Luis broke the silence. "We have great news, Roberto. Carlos has just set the meeting date with Pascal concerning the docks."

"Luis! That was not to be shared."

"Why not? Roberto was the one who made this possible."

Carlos glanced at Rob, then looked away. "We are done with you, Roberto. Leave us."

Rob grabbed his briefcase and walked out. He was happy to not be part of anything dealing with Pascal and Carlos.

As he drove away, he felt a strange sensation. He could almost swear someone was watching him. He brushed it off as nerves brought on by the news that, with the northwest expansion, he would now need to deal with even more money coming in.

As he drove out of Corpus, he kept checking his rearview mirror. The feeling of being watched continued all the way to Dallas.

*   *   *

It took a week to close the deal with the charter service. Rob barely slept. Thoughts of the massive amounts of new money coming in kept him awake. After one very long night, the answer came to him: *offshore accounts.* He could transfer most of the money, and keep doing that as often as needed. That would put an end to opening corporations and businesses to conceal the source of the money, and he would not have to add more people to move it either.

*   *   *

The summer heat slowly gave way to cooler temperatures. Wanda was sitting at her desk when two men dressed in khakis came in.

"Where do you want your new television set up?"

"On that wall across from my desk," she said.

"What the heck?" Rob said, coming out of his office as the men positioned an RCA television console cabinet against the wall. "I don't recall discussing a TV for the office," he said, moving a chair out of the way of the delivery men.

"We didn't. I bought it to watch the president's visit while I work."

He shook his head. "Is it the president you're so fascinated by, or Jackie?"

She shooed him away with her hands. "Go back to your office, and we'll discuss this when they're done."

Rob closed the door and went back to work. Less than an hour later, Wanda came in.

"Did they get it set up?" he asked.

"They did." She sat on the corner of his desk. "You know, it's not every day the president comes to Dallas. I don't want to miss it. I'll still get the reports done before you leave for Corpus."

Rob put down his pen and reached for her hand. "Of course, sweetheart. Sometimes I forget there's another world outside of this office. I haven't given you much of a life, have I?"

"It's unsettling to hide things like we do, but that's not your fault. We were thrown into this."

"Sorry for being a grouch."

"You're forgiven." She gave him a smile. "Now go back to whatever you were doing. I have a television to watch."

He reached for her, but she slipped from his grasp and laughed as she closed his door.

*   *   *

Over the next several days, Wanda listened to the chatter on the television as she typed. On the day of the president's visit, she dressed for the occasion and tried to work, but her attention kept going to the television. Large crowds lined the streets and had gathered at the airport well in advance of the Kennedys' arrival, and when the newscaster announced that Air Force One had landed, Wanda forgot about work and pulled a chair in front of the console to watch.

"Rob, you need to see this."

"Enjoy yourself. I've got some things I need to do."

A few hours later, she ran into his office and rushed to the window behind his desk, standing on tiptoes to reach the latch.

"Help me, Rob! The president's motorcade just turned onto Houston Street. Can't you hear the cheering?"

Rob got up, opened the latch, and raised the window. Wanda grabbed his chair and climbed up, leaning out the window for a better view. Rob grabbed hold of her skirt. "What are you doing?"

"There they are!" She waved her arms. "Mr. President! Jackie! Oh my gosh, did you see that? I think they waved back." She scooted backward. "They're heading to Dealey Plaza. I have to watch it on the television."

When her feet hit the floor, Wanda rushed to her office, and Rob followed. They watched as the motorcade turned onto Dealey Plaza, every movement narrated by the newscaster. Suddenly, there were popping sounds, and Mrs. Kennedy scrambled over the back of the convertible. Wanda jumped to her feet and went closer to the television screen. "Something's happening."

Rob ran to his office window to look out. People were screaming and running down the street, and as he stood there watching, Rob was reminded of the Godzilla movie he'd seen. He went back in to Wanda. She was standing in front of the television with tears streaming down her face. "Someone shot him! The president's been shot."

Time stood still as they listened to Walter Cronkite try to make sense of the events unfolding below them. Then Cronkite paused, removed his dark-rimmed glasses, stared into the camera, and told all of America that President Kennedy was dead.

Wanda gasped, then started to cry.

Rob took her hand. "We should go home."

They closed up the office and waited a long time for the elevator, but it never came.

"Everyone must be leaving the building," Rob said. "I think we should take the stairs."

When they got to their car, the parking garage was almost empty. Neither of them spoke all the way to their apartment. As soon as they were inside, Wanda turned on the television. They watched until Wanda couldn't take it anymore and went to bed. Rob watched until he fell asleep on the sofa. They stayed home the next day and continued to watch the reports of the shooting as events unfolded, including the swearing-in of Lyndon Baines Johnson and the capture of a suspect named Lee Harvey Oswald who had also killed J. D. Tippit, a Dallas police officer.

Early the following day, Rob slipped out of the apartment and went to the pool to clear his head with an hour of laps in the pool. He didn't want to go to the office, but he knew Carlos would be waiting to hear from him, so he dressed, left a note for Wanda, and drove to his office on eerily empty streets.

When he got to his building, Rob took the elevator up and got to work. He didn't raise his head until he heard his phone ring.

"Turn on the television."

"What?"

"Transfer the call to the phone on my desk and turn on the television. Hurry!"

He scrambled to turn on the television before picking up the phone. "Okay, what am I looking at?"

"Wait--they are replaying it now."

Rob watched the scene from the Dallas police station's basement, which was filled with police, Texas Rangers, and detectives and reporters. He saw Rangers on each side of Oswald pushing through the crowd.

Suddenly, a familiar short, round-faced man lunged at Oswald and fired a gun. Rob watched as Oswald crumpled to the floor.

"Oh, my God!" he gasped.

"Rob, is that Jack from the--"

"Don't say it, Wanda. We can't get involved in this."

"But--"

"No. If we talk to the authorities, Carlos will kill us without asking why."

"It feels like the whole world has gone crazy."

"I'm afraid you're right."

"Please come home."

"I will, sweetheart."

He hung up and watched Oswald's shooting replay again, then headed home.

CHAPTER TWENTY-SIX

For weeks afterwards, it felt as if the country blamed Dallas for the president's death. Conventions were moved from the city, tourists canceled their trips, and businesses suffered.

One day at the office, Wanda came in, closed the door, and rushed to Rob's side.

"Sweetheart, what's wrong?"

"An FBI agent is here," she said, wringing her hands. "What are we going to do?"

He jumped to his feet. "Keep him out there until I get Carlos's stuff put away." She didn't move. Rob lifted her chin and looked into her eyes. "We're going to be all right. Stay calm and keep him out there until I clear my desk."

She nodded and went back to her office.

Rob quickly gathered ledgers and deposit slips from his desk, put them in his safe room, and secured the hidden door. Then he opened the door, where a man who looked to be in his mid-fifties, dressed in a dark suit and holding a hat, was waiting.

"I'm Robert Chambers. I understand you are here to see me?"

"I'm here to ask you a few questions," the man said, then walked past Rob into his office without an invitation.

Rob glanced at Wanda before following the man in. "Of course. Please take a seat."

The agent placed his hat on Rob's desk, reached into his suit jacket, and handed him a card.

"How can I be of help, Agent Neal?" Rob said, scanning the card.

"

"You set up a trust fund recently. I have questions about your association with the donor."

"The donor is a client."

"How long have you known him?"

"About a year."

"What services did you perform for him?"

Rob paused a moment. "Agent Neal. That information is confidential."

Neal's expression never changed. "Was the matter criminal, civil, or family law?"

Rob stalled by looking at the card once more. "Again, my work with my clients is confidential. Why do you ask?"

"Do you recall any conversation with your client regarding the late president?"

"There were none."

Neal stood, fixed his eyes on Rob's, and held them for a long moment. It felt like they were burning through his brain.

"If you think of anything, give me a call. You can reach me at that number." Neal took his hat from the desk. "And I'd advise you to stay around, kid. We aren't done."

Rob's heart skipped a beat. "Done with what?"

Neal didn't answer. He just walked out, tipping his hat to Wanda as he passed.

She jumped from her chair and went to Rob. "What was that about?"

"He was asking about my connection with Jack."

"All we did was open a trust."

"I know." He left it at that.

"Oh, Rob. What are we going to do?"

Before he could say more, his private line rang. Rob shook his head. "That must be Luis."

"Is the FBI going to arrest us?"

He held Wanda by the shoulders. "We're fine as long as we say nothing to anyone about this. Understand?"

"Who am I going to tell? You and Joey are the only people I see." She nodded toward the ringing phone. "You had better answer that."

Rob went to his office and closed the door. After talking to Luis, he tried to work, but the FBI agent's visit had shaken him.

The following day, he asked Joey to meet him at a small café on lower Greenville Avenue.

"Why are we meeting here instead of in your office?" Joey asked, sliding into the booth.

"I had a visit from the FBI yesterday," Rob whispered.

"The Feds?" Joey looked from side to side, then spoke in a whisper. "What did they want?"

"The agent was asking questions about my association with a client."

"Which client?"

"You don't need to know. But what he said before he left is troubling me."

"What did he say?"

"He said to stay around because we aren't done."

"Done with what?"

"I don't know." Rob leaned forward and locked eyes with Joey. "But I think it's time to start making plans. Pack whatever essentials your family needs. And cash. Lots of cash. Keep your gas tank filled and your family close. If he hears about this visit, Carlos is more deadly than the FBI."

Joey took a deep breath and nodded. "Do you think this agent knows what we're doing, or was he just trying to rattle you?"

Rob gave Joey a grim shrug. "I don't know, but if he does, we have to disappear."

"Can't we just quit?"

"It's not that easy. We're in too deep."

"Okay," Joey said. "Okay. I'll start putting some money away."

"What have you done with all the money you were paid?" Rob whispered.

"Paid off my debts. But I'll put some aside after our next run. What about you?"

"I've been putting it away since this started."

Joey nodded, looking down at his hands. After a minute, he looked up at Rob. "Remember the blood pact we made? I think it's time we do a grown-up version."

"What are you talking about?"

"If anything happens to one of us, the other will take care of our families. Are you good with that?"

"You know I am, but you have to promise me you will get out of here when I tell you."

"You got my word."

Rob slid a large envelope across the table. "This is a big one. Tell your guys to keep their eyes open and be extra careful.'"

Joey slid the packet under his coat. "You're making me nervous, buddy."

"I am nervous. No more coming to the office either. I'll get word to you when we need to meet." Rob looked over his shoulder. "You better go. We shouldn't be seen together."

Joey slid to the end of the booth. "Maybe we're making too much of this?"

"I hope you're right, but we can't take that chance. Take care, Joey."

Rob sat for a while before paying the bill and leaving the café. His mind raced with questions as he drove back to his office. What could the FBI know? Had one of the accounts been reported to the authorities? Did he overlook a connection to one of the corporations?

He returned to the office and checked and rechecked every transaction he had made. It was clear that, despite Agent Neal's order to stay in town, he would have to open an offshore account to handle the money flooding in and relieve the overloaded accounts. Rob booked a flight to the Cayman Islands and spent days going from bank to bank, meeting with their officers until he narrowed down his selection. On his last day on the main island, he entered an impressive building and surveyed a large open area filled with desks and well-dressed people speaking on the phones in a variety of languages.

A striking young woman dressed in a stylish light gray suit approached him and smiled. "May I help you?" Her sparking white teeth gleamed in contrast to her dark skin.

"I would like to speak with your director."

"Certainly. Is Mr. McKay expecting you?"

Rob handed her his business card. "Tell him I have returned with my decision."

She disappeared into the front office. Moments later, she reappeared with a portly middle-aged man with tanned skin and black hair sprinkled with gray.

The banker flashed a toothy smile as he grabbed Rob's hand with the zeal of a car salesman. "Welcome back, Mr. Chambers," McKay said in accented English. "I understand you have chosen our bank?"

"I have just a few more questions."

"Please step into my office."

The banker sat at his desk, laced his fingers together, and leaned forward. "What are your questions?"

"You said your bank could handle deposits of any size without restrictions on the amounts." When the banker nodded, Rob said, "And every transaction, as well as my identity, is kept concealed and secured."

A broad smile spread across the banker's face. "Our clients come from all over the world. There has never been a confidentiality breach during the seventy years of our existence. Why don't we do a tour of our facility?"

"Perhaps another time." Rob leaned forward and took McKay's business card from the holder on his desk. "How much notice do you need before a deposit?"

"None. The funds may be wired, carried, or shipped. Once the money is deposited, it is available to you at a moment's notice."

Rob paused momentarily and recalled all the people at desks in the bank's central area. "McKay, I insist you handle my accounts, not one of your staff."

"I would be honored to be your personal banker, as well as a source for any other services you may require."

"What sort of other services?"

"Our clients sometimes need skilled services such as identities, bodyguards, discreet travel arrangements, and other requests."

"Have any of your clients ever needed to . . ." Rob paused, thinking about how he wanted to phrase this question. "Have they ever needed to 'refresh' the money before placing it into your accounts?"

"I have heard that diamonds never lose value and are always in style." McKay said. "Would you agree?"

Rob nodded. "I agree, but I'm in no need of diamonds."

"This diamond broker specializes in cleaning all types of commodities, not just diamonds." McKay smiled. "You must be referred to this gentleman by people he trusts. Fortunately, I am in a position to refer my clients." McKay reached into his desk, took out several forms, placed them in front of Rob, and offered him a pen. A smile crossed the banker's lips when Rob took the pen. "The broker is very selective in choosing his clients, of course. I will make the call, but he may not respond."

Rob lifted the pen from the paper. "If he refuses, are there others you can recommend?"

"There are, but he is the best."

"Please make the call," Rob said as he started filling out the documents.

After completing all the required paperwork, Rob left the bank, took a taxi to the airport, and boarded his Trans World Airlines flight to Dallas. He arrived midafternoon and went to the office.

Hours later, Wanda came in with her purse and coat over her arm. "Time to go home," she said.

"You go. I have to meet Joey before my trip to Corpus tomorrow."

"You just got home!"

"I know, but I need Carlos's approval to move the money."

"You're exhausted. You have to rest."

"I can't until I get this done."

Wanda shook her head. "What's Carlos going to do if you drop dead?"

He looked at her and smiled. "No such luck. Go home, sweetheart. I'll get there as soon as I can."

Late that night, Rob crept into the bedroom. The lamp on Wanda's side of the bed clicked on and she sat up.

"Sorry," Rob said. "I was trying not to wake you."

"I wasn't sleeping." She glanced at the alarm clock. "It's after midnight. You can't keep this up."

"I don't have a choice. We're sitting on a ticking bomb."

"Can't you take a day to rest?"

"Not until I get this money moved."

She threw back the sheets. "Then come to bed so I can at least hold you before you go?"

He gave her a tired smile. "I don't deserve you."

*   *   *

Rob parked the Studebaker in the Gulf Breeze Hotel garage just before noon. After the usual pat-downs, he rode the elevator to Luis's office, and the guard let him in.

"I am glad you are early, Roberto."

Rob looked around. "I'd hoped to see Carlos?"

"Not today." Luis pointed to the seating area. "Our time together is short, Roberto." A smile spread across his face. "Congratulate me. I am getting married."

Rob shook his hand. "Congratulations, Luis. When's the big day?"

"It is the first of the month, and then we leave for our honeymoon. But I must return to Mexico soon because of all the festivities our families have prepared."

"How long will you be away?"

"Six, possibly eight weeks."

"That's a long time. Who will be in charge while you're gone?"

"Not your concern, Roberto. I have it all under control." Luis took a seat. "Do you have the books for our accountants?"

Rob opened his briefcase and removed the binders. He flipped one of the books open and ran a finger down the columns. "As you can see, the amounts in each account have more than tripled since my last visit."

"But that is good."

"Not when it exceeds the level of normal business for each of these accounts. It's time we move as much money as possible into offshore accounts. I've selected a bank in the Caymans that will best suit our needs."

"I see," Luis said as he scanned the notations.

"Once I have Carlos's approval, I will start the process."

"I agree with your assessment of the situation, Roberto, but there is no need to wait for Carlos. Move it now."

"Luis, I'm hesitant to do that without Carlos's knowledge."

"He is in a meeting and cannot be reached."

Rob wondered if the meeting had anything to do with New Orleans but didn't ask. "When will he be available?"

"Not for several weeks."

"That won't work. There will be more drops by then. We have to do this now."

"Carlos has entrusted me to act on his behalf. I am telling you to move the money. When I return, you can give me the information, and I will advise Carlos and our accountants about what we have done."

"I'm not comfortable with this. The last thing I want is for Carlos to think I've taken his money and run."

"My brother will be pleased, I assure you." Luis smiled. "And do not forget, Roberto, we have ways of tracking you no matter where you go."

A cold sweat covered Rob's body. "I'm sure you do."

"I have many things to do before my flight. If we are done, my guard will see you out."

"We are. Congratulations on your marriage, Luis."

"Thank you, Roberto. We will talk when I return."

CHAPTER TWENTY-SEVEN

Over the next few days, Rob converted the money into banknotes and cashier's checks, all made out to him from banks in and around Dallas, leaving enough money in each account to keep them open for future drops. When he had finished, he called his island banker to see if his appointment with the diamond broker had been set.

"I shared your request," McKay said, "but no date will be set until you return to the island." Rob could almost feel the ocean air in the banker's voice.

"I'm flying out tomorrow morning. I'll call you as soon as I land."

"I look forward to your arrival. Have a safe trip, Mr. Chambers."

Rob flew to George Town and contacted the banker from a pay phone at the airport. McKay told Rob he would need to contact the diamond broker directly, and gave him the man's number.

"How will the money get from the broker to your bank?" Rob asked.

"It is wired from his account to the bank, and I will transfer it into your accounts."

Rob took a taxi to a local hotel and called the broker as soon as he was in his room. No one answered, so he tried again. And kept trying for two days, when a woman with a strong German accent finally answered.

"Who is this?" she asked

"Robert Chambers. I'm calling to set an appointment with the broker."

There was a pause, then the woman said, "Your meeting is tomorrow on the patio of the Ocean Spray Hotel on the edge of Rum Point. The meeting time is 2:34 p.m. Schulz will not waste his time with you if you are one minute late."

The next day, Rob arrived early and walked out onto the patio and stood looking at the turquoise Caribbean Sea.

"Are you here for the scenery or our appointment?" a man's voice said.

Rob turned and saw a man dressed in a seersucker suit sitting under a large umbrella. He had a walking stick in his hand, and his straw hat rested on the table in front of him.

Rob extended his hand. "Thank you for meeting me."

"Thank Clarence McKay," the broker grumbled. His German accent was even stronger than the woman's. "He is the only reason I am here." The broker pushed the chair next to him with his cane. "Sit. You are blocking my view."

Rob sat, and Schulz slid a pen and notepad to him. "Give me an estimate of this transaction and the approximate size of future ones."

Rob wrote the amounts and passed the notepad to Schulz. He expected a look of surprise or a raised eyebrow, but there was nothing.

Schulz jotted down something and returned the pad. "That is my fee for each transaction."

Rob looked at his quote. "This is twice the amount McKay said you charge for diamonds."

"That was before I knew you were American."

The broker took his cane and tapped the side of his leg. "One of your American bullets did this to me in Luxembourg. So, do you want my services or not?"

Rob glanced at the figure, then back to the man. "I'll take it."

Schulz wrote something on a page of the pad, then tore it off and handed it to Rob. "Be at that address tomorrow morning at 8:00 a.m."

Schulz positioned his hat on his head, pushed himself up from the chair, and limped away.

Rob arrived the next morning with his briefcase filled with banknotes and cashier checks. As he approached the entrance, an enormous, dark-skinned man blocked his way. The man held out his massive hand. "Passport."

"Why?"

"No passport, no meeting."

Rob's brow furrowed as he looked into the massive man's face. He took his passport from the inside pocket of his jacket and held it out to the man, who snatched it from his hand.

"The case," the man said. "Open it."

Rob clenched his teeth as he opened his briefcase. The man ran his large hand inside every pocket before stepping back. "You can pass."

Rob shook his head. "Not without my passport."

The man pocketed the document. "Not till you leave."

The interior walls of the building were painted sunshine yellow, with massive paintings on every wall, colorful rugs on the floors, and expensive fabrics draping the windows. The broker sat behind an enormous desk. Two men, each about the size of the man at the door, stood nearby, watching Rob's every move.

"What form is the money in?" the broker asked.

"Banknotes and cashier's checks."

The broker gestured to a chair and handed Rob a pen and a card with numbers written on it. "Sign them over to that account."

Rob's stomach twisted into knots as he signed millions over to a man he had just met.

As Rob finished signing, the broker verified the information and slid each document into a folder. Then he picked up his phone and spoke in German, hung up, and pointed to the door. "Leave."

"Has the money been transferred?"

"Go to your bank and find out."

"I'm not leaving here until I know it's done."

The broker set his phone in front of Rob. "Call McKay."

Rob dialed the number. The seconds it took for McKay to answer felt like an eternity.

"Have you received the transfer?" he asked the banker.

"I have. I am looking at the transaction now."

"What is the amount?" Rob exhaled when he heard the total. "Good. I'll be there soon."

The broker leaned forward and pointed his finger at him. "Doubt me again, American, and you will never see me again."

"I understand."

Rob took his empty briefcase and walked out, retrieving his passport as he did. He went to the bank and walked straight into McKay's office. "I need to see the transfer verification."

"Yes, of course. Please have a seat," McKay said, placing the document in front of him. "As you can see, all is in order."

Rob looked at the page and calculated the total. He sighed in relief after seeing it was all there. "I need to break down the deposit into numbered accounts."

"But of course. I will have my assistant set you up in a private office."

Rob divided the millions into different accounts and posted each number into a little black book for Carlos's accountants. When he finished, he went to his hotel and booked a flight back to Dallas, then left for the airport, trying to ignore the nauseous feeling he had about leaving the money behind without Carlos's knowledge.

Back in the US, Rob spent the next few weeks traveling from state to state, gathering the money and cashiers' checks before again flying to the islands and repeating the process.

When he had finally moved the bulk of the money, he flew home, eager to see Wanda. He parked the Studebaker in his garage, grabbed only his coat, and took the elevator to his office. He had barely cleared the door before Wanda was in his arms.

"It feels like you've been gone a year."

"Believe me, I know."

"How long do I get to keep you this time?"

"At least a week, maybe longer. You'll probably be tired of me by then."

"Never." She took him by the hand, led him to one of the high-backed chairs, and got in his lap. "I need to hold you for a moment."

"I need a lot more than holding," he said with a wink.

"We both do. Why don't we get out of here?"

"You're reading my mind." Rob kissed her. As he kissed her a second time, the door to their office burst open, and men in dark suits rushed in. Rob shoved Wanda off his lap and stood in front of her, shielding her.

"Who are you?" Rob shouted.

One of the men approached showed him a badge. "FBI. Stay where you are," he said as men began going through file cabinets and desks.

"Those files are confidential! Leave now, or I'm calling the police."

"Now that's a novel idea," said one of the men as he entered the office.

Rob recognized his voice from the call he had made months ago.

"I'm Senior Agent Randal Schneider," the man said, "and this is Senior Agent Tom Neal, but I understand the two of you have met."

"I don't care who you are," Rob said. "You have no right to storm into my office and take my files."

"Oh, I have every right, Chambers." Schneider looked Rob up and down. "It's time we talk."

"I have nothing to say to you without a warrant."

"Schneider snapped his fingers, and a much younger agent rushed to his side, took something from a briefcase, and handed it to Rob.

"That's your warrant," Schneider said.

Rob snatched the paper from the young agent's hand and scanned every line of the document before tossing it on Wanda's desk. "You're wasting your time, Agent Schneider. I've already spoken to Agent Neal." Rob tried to remain calm but could hear his heart pounding in his ears.

"I'm here on a different matter, Chambers. We should discuss this in private. Why don't we step into your office?"

Schneider went to the door of Rob's office and looked in. "Take what you have and give me the room," he said, and the men began filing out, their arms loaded with documents.

"Let's go, Chambers."

Rob nodded at Wanda. "It's okay. Just stay here."

Neal escorted Rob into his office. Rob's heart skipped a beat when he saw Agent Neal standing next to the hidden door, a feet away from where Carlos's ledgers were hidden.

"Sit," Schneider said, pointing to a chair near Rob's desk.

Rob lowered himself into the chair.

"Let's get down to business, Chambers."

"What business? You have no right to come here and frighten my wife."

Schneider chuckled. "Oh, your wife should be frightened, and so should you. I can put both of you away for a very long time." Schneider snapped his fingers and the young agent with the briefcase came to him and gave him a file. Schneider took a stack of photos from the file and laid them across Rob's desk.

Sweat rolled down Rob's back as he looked at the photos: Rob and Carlos in Mexico City. Alejandro and Diego coming out of a Mexican cantina. Joey entering a bank. Joey's crew at the Laredo bus station. Luis and Rob in the Corpus Christi office. Schneider was pulling out another photo when Rob held up his hand.

"Stop. The men in these photos are business clients." He looked up at Schneider. "When did that become a crime?"

"Are you sure that's how you want to play this?"

"I'm telling you the truth."

Agent Neal cleared his throat. Schneider glanced at Neal, then back at Rob. "You're lying, Chambers." He tapped the photo of Carlos with his finger. "*El Cerebro* and his companions are drug dealers, and you are laundering their drug money."

Rob leaned back and crossed his arms. "I'm not saying another word without an attorney." His mouth was so dry the words barely escaped his lips.

Schneider sat in the chair next to him. "Oh, Chambers," he said softly. "You have no idea how much I would enjoy taking you down. But all I would get for my efforts is a minnow." Schneider sat back and interlaced his fingers across his chest. "And I ask myself, what good is a minnow?" He released his hands and tapped his forehead. "A minnow is useful only as bait." Schneider straightened the lapels of his jacket and leaned towards Rob. "So, if you want to save yourself and your wife, I suggest you listen carefully. Help us, and I'll do my best to make it possible for you to spend your life with your lovely wife. Refuse, and you will not see each other again until you're old and gray."

Rob glanced at Agent Neal and saw the muscles in his jaw tighten. He turned back to Schneider. "You have no idea what you're asking. You think you know these people, but you don't. If I say anything to you, they will kill my wife."

"That's the beauty of this, Chambers. The organization won't know you've helped until you testify against them in court."

"You make it sound so easy."

"It is. All you have to do is tell me everything you know about this organization and help me put them away."

"Such as?"

"How I find them. How the money is moved. Who's involved. How deep the organization is in this country. All the information on companies, property, and bank accounts you've opened across the States."

Rob closed his eyes and shook his head. "I can't do that."

Schneider got up from the chair. "What do you think Carlos and his organization will do to your wife and your friend once they learn we have all of you in custody? He has ways of getting to them, Chambers. He's done it before. The only way to guarantee their safety is by helping me put them away for good." He looked at his watch. "You have one minute to accept my offer, or I'm arresting both of you. Is that clear?"

Rob's brain was ablaze with images of Wanda behind bars and what Carlos might do to her. "All right, I'll help you. But I have requirements."

"That depends on what they are," Schneider said.

"You will not prosecute Wanda, Joey, or me. And you protect all three of us, including Joey's family."

"That can be arranged if you do exactly as I say. Now, let's go over *my* requirements. When I call, you come. When I tell you I need something, you supply it. Under no circumstances are you to breathe a word of our agreement to anyone, not even your wife or your friend. Understand?"

Rob nodded his head.

"I didn't hear you."

"I agree."

"Good. Now that we understand one another, we can go."

"What about my files?" Rob asked.

"Oh, we are keeping those."

When Rob and the agents walked out of his office, Wanda jumped to her feet and ran to him.

"We're done here, men," Schneider said. "Take everything you have to the office." He looked at Wanda. "Sorry for upsetting you, Mrs. Chambers. Have a nice day."

Schneider waited as his men carried boxes to the elevator. When the agents had gone, Wanda closed the door behind them.

Rob went to her. "It's over, sweetheart."

"No, it's not. Once they see what's in those files, we'll be arrested and locked away forever!"

He lifted her chin. "All those files belong to our regular clients. None of it has any connection to Carlos."

"What about all the documents you brought back from the islands?"

"I left my briefcase and all the information under the spare tire in the trunk of my car."

CHAPTER TWENTY-EIGHT

They spent the next two days cleaning up the office and taking inventory of what had been seized. When they finished, Wanda dropped into a chair. "Thank God that's over."

"Not quite," Rob said as he closed a file drawer. "We still need to make new folders for the missing files."

"What good will that do? There won't be anything in them."

"I can rebuild the files from memory."

She pushed herself from the chair. "Let's get to it. I'm ready to put this behind us."

It was difficult to drop everything and lie to Wanda about where he was going once the meetings with Schneider started, but Rob had no choice but to do what the FBI ordered, even when it meant racing across town for a meeting with less than an hour's notice.

Each meeting's agenda was usually the same. When was the next batch of money being moved? Where were Carlos, Diego, and Alejandro? It didn't matter how many times Rob told Schneider he no longer had contact with Carlos; Schneider refused to believe him.

Rob needed to speak to Joey, but he was pretty sure his office phone was bugged after the raid. He called Joey from a pay phone outside a nearby pharmacy after checking to be sure no one was nearby.

"Hey," he said when Joey answered. "Don't say anything. Go to the business next door to your shop and use their phone to call me on this number. Make sure no one's around to hear anything." Rob gave him the number of the pay phone. "Hurry, Joey."

Rob paced back and forth until the pay phone rang.

"Have you been putting cash aside?"

"Yep, some," Joey said. "My uncle broke his leg and is out of work, so I had to pay his medical bills and lend him some money for his family, but I put some away."

"How much?"

"About twenty thousand. I'll have over thirty after my next run."

"Is your car packed and full of gas?"

"Yeah."

"Don't go anywhere but the garage or home. I have to be able to contact you."

"What about my guys?"

"You can't tell them anything." Rob paused for a moment. "It's time, Joey," he said finally. "After this drop, you and your family have to disappear."

"But—"

"No buts. Just do as I say. I'll call when I have the drop information. Be careful."

Rob hung up and drove home. He took a suitcase from the hall closet, packed clothing for Wanda and him, and returned the suitcase to the bottom of the closet. Then he grabbed his large gym bag, emptied the contents, and laid it over the suitcase before returning to his car. When he got back to the office, he tapped on the door, and Wanda let him in.

"Any calls?"

"None."

"Well, I need to make a few. When I finish, we'll close up and go home."

She pressed the palm of her hand to his forehead and crinkled her brow. "Are you all right?"

"I'm fine, just need to get out of here."

"I couldn't agree more."

Rob closed the door to his office and took his phone off the hook so his private line would look busy if Wanda checked, then opened the door to his secret room and moved boxes aside to reach his safe.

He wiped his sweating palms on his pant leg and turned the combination dial until it clicked. He transferred the bundles of cash inside into his briefcase, then locked the safe and secured the door to his safe room. Rob hung up the phone receiver and slid his briefcase under his desk.

"Chambers," he said when his private line rang a moment later.

"We need to meet," Schneider said.

"Where?"

"There's an abandoned movie house in Terrell on West Rockwall and East Nash Street. Park your car on West High Street and come in through the back door of the building. You have an hour and a half to get there."

Rob grabbed his briefcase and went out to Wanda's desk. "Sorry, sweetheart. There's something I have to do."

"Any idea when you'll be back?"

"Not sure. If I'm not back by five, go home and lock yourself in." He kissed her on the forehead. "Lock the office door after I leave."

"Don't worry. I will."

Rob locked the briefcase full of money in the trunk of his car before getting behind the wheel. It took him over an hour to reach the movie house in Terrell. He parked as instructed and went to the back of the abandoned building. The battered metal door was open.

As soon as he entered the building, Rob's nostrils tingled from the dust, mold, and pungent odor of decaying fabric. He walked past the dust-coated curtain into the small theater and looked around.

"Back here, Chambers," a voice in the darkness said.

Rob continued up the rows of torn and broken seats to find Schneider midway up an aisle.

"This place looks like it could fall down any second."

"That's the point." Schneider unfolded the seat beside him and patted the dry, cracked leather. Rob sat down.

"We're getting close to making our move. When the time comes, my people will take you and your wife to a safe location."

"Then what?"

"We'll keep you hidden until this goes to trial. Once these guys are convicted, you'll be relocated and given new identities."

"What about Joey and his family?"

"For now, your friend has to be kept out of it. I can't risk him doing anything to jeopardize my raid."

"But you agreed to get Joey and his family out before it happened."

Schneider pointed his finger at Rob's face. "I make the rules, Chambers. Mess this up, and I'll leave all of you to the drug lord."

"When is this raid happening?"

"You'll know when my men show up at your door." Schneider stood. "Stay put for the next twenty minutes, then leave."

As Schneider went down the aisle of the theater, several men dressed in black suits stepped from the shadows and followed him out the door.

Rob returned to his seat, thinking about the Corpus location being raided. Once it had been twenty minutes, he started to leave, but a voice behind him said, "Not yet, kid. We need to talk."

Rob spun around and saw Agent Neal coming toward him.

"You're a little late," Rob said. "Schneider's gone."

"He's not the reason I'm here. Take a seat."

Rob sat, and Neal took the seat next to him. "I told you this wasn't over in your office," Neal said.

"It could have been, if Schneider had listened to me months ago."

"What are you talking about?"

"I called the FBI main office. I told Schneider Carlos and his organization were moving to the States. But Schneider was more interested in finding out about my name than stopping them."

"So, that was you."

"You heard it?"

"I am notified about anything concerning Rojas, Martínez, or their organization. I've heard the recording several times." He leaned forward. "You mentioned people in danger when you called. I know about your wife, but who else?"

"Carlos said he would kill Wanda. Then he threatened Joey and the Tolland family. That's my former employer."

Neal placed his hand on Rob's shoulder. "Listen closely, son. Schneider is an arrogant glory hound. His word lasts only as long as he needs you. When he's done, Schneider will discard you like a soiled napkin. You're going to need my help to survive." Agent Neal reached into his breast pocket and pulled out a card. "Take this."

"You gave me one the first time you were in my office."

"That one didn't have my direct line on the back. Call that number anytime, day or night, and I'll get back to you as soon as possible." Neal paused. "And be careful when making calls from your office or home phones."

"So, they've been tapped?"

"It's highly possible."

Neal got to his feet, and Rob followed his lead. "Why are you being so open with me?" Rob asked.

Tom looked up at the peeling ceiling. "Let's just say you remind me of someone." He cleared his throat and pointed to the exit. "Now get out of here."

Rob took a couple of steps down the aisle and turned back. "Agent Neal, who do I—" he asked, but no one was there.

Rob got to his car and checked the time. It wasn't yet five, and he knew Wanda would still be at the office. Instead of going there, he went to their apartment and took his briefcase from the trunk and went in. Inside, he transferred all the money from his briefcase into the gym bag, zipped it closed, and put it under the suitcase before returning to the office.

When he got to the office, Wanda was putting on her coat.

"Are you all right?" she asked.

"I am. You go ahead home. I have a few things to finish before I go."

"Are you sure?"

"Positive." He kissed her. "I'll be there soon." When she'd gone, he went into his office and unlatched the lock on his hidden door and opened the safe. He took an empty file box from a shelf, filled it with the rest of the money, and put a large envelope containing their passports and other important documents into the box. Then he picked up the little black book of account information and flipped the pages. That book was his best insurance that Agent Schneider would keep his word.

Rob put the book into the envelope and relocked the safe. His private line was ringing as he secured the door to his secret room.

"Roberto, I was beginning to think you weren't there," Luis said.

"What can I do for you, Luis?"

"I have the information for tomorrow's drop."

"Go ahead, I'm ready." Rob grabbed a legal pad and wrote down the information. "I'll see it's handled."

"I am meeting with Carlos and our accountants at the end of the week. I must present the ledgers and all the documents on the offshore accounts."

"I have them ready."

"Perfect. Be here tomorrow. I must review everything with you to answer all questions."

"The earliest I can get there is afternoon."

"I will see you then."

Rob hung up, tore the sheet from the legal pad, pocketed it, and took the little black book and two large bundles of cash from the box. He put the book of accounts into his briefcase and stuffed the money into two separate envelopes, then carried the box, envelopes, and briefcase to his car and drove to a gas station with a pay phone across town.

"Joey, it's me. We need to meet."

"Where?"

"The place you hit your first home run. Hurry."

When Joey arrived at the lot they had used as a baseball field next to Love Field Airport, Rob was standing next to his Studebaker.

"I haven't been here in ages," Joey said. "What's up?"

Rob took a folded piece of paper from his pocket. "It's the information for your last drop." He opened the door, took the two large envelopes from the front seat, and handed one to Joey.

"This one is for you and your family, and this one is to pay your men. Remember what I said, Joey. As soon as it's done, take your family and get as far from here as possible."

"Sybil and the girls are already gone. I sent them to her parents' place days ago."

"That's great, but once this drop is completed, get your family and leave the state. And don't tell her parents, me, or anyone where you are."

"Wait a minute. How will we find each other?"

"We won't."

"Hold on. Are you telling me we can't even talk?"

"We can't. At least not until these guys are put away."

"But that could take years."

"I know."

Joey looked away. "I never thought it would come to this," he said when he turned back to Rob. "We've done everything together since we were kids."

Rob placed his hand on Joey's shoulder. "This is the only way to protect our families. When it's over, I'll find you."

"You swear?"

"I swear." Rob lightly punched his shoulder. "I don't like this any more than you do, old buddy, but we don't have a choice." His voice broke. "Take care of yourself, old friend."

Joey grabbed Rob and held on for a long moment. "You too."

Before Joey drove away, he gave Rob his signature two-finger salute, and then he was gone.

That night, Rob paced his living room. He wanted to tell Joey to forget the drop and just leave, but if Schneider had tapped his phones, he would know Rob had gone behind his back, and that would mean Wanda and Joey would spend the rest of their lives in jail.

Rob slipped back into the bedroom and put on his pants and shoes, careful not to wake Wanda, then went out to his car. He retrieved the box from the trunk and carried it into the apartment, got the money and the envelope of documents from the box, placed it all into the gym bag, and zipped it up. He set the suitcase on top of the gym bag and closed the door, then got into bed and stared at the ceiling for the rest of the night.

CHAPTER TWENTY-NINE

The next morning, Rob was making coffee when his telephone rang. As soon as he answered, Agent Neal started talking.

"Carlos is coming, kid. Schneider raided the Corpus compound early this morning, and Carlos discovered you're helping us. Take your wife and get out of there."

"How does Carlos know?"

"Doesn't matter! You have to go."

"What about Joey?"

"I'll take care of him."

"And Gary Tolland's family?"

"I'll handle it. Go."

"Who was that?" Wanda asked, coming in from the bedroom.

"Get your purse and my briefcase."

"Why?"

"I'll tell you in the car." He rushed to the closet, grabbed the suitcase and gym bag, and met Wanda at the door.

"I didn't lock the door," Wanda said when they got to the car.

"It doesn't matter. We're not coming back."

"What?"

"Get in the car."

Rob tossed the suitcase and gym bag onto the back seat and got behind the wheel. As he was about to start the vehicle, a car raced past them and stopped in front of their apartment.

"Get down," Rob ordered.

Wanda slumped in the seat. "What's happening?" she whispered.

Rob inched up just enough to see two armed men kick their front door open and run inside the apartment. He started the engine and sped out of the parking lot, catching sight in the rearview mirror as the men ran out of the apartment and jumped into their car.

"Get as far down as you can. Carlos's men are here with guns."

"Oh, my God!" she said, slipping on to the floor.

Rob raced down the street, his eyes on the car speeding toward them in his mirror. "Hold on!" he shouted, pressing the gas pedal to the floor.

Wanda screamed as he took the corner and raced through the Highland Park Shopping Village traffic light, barely missing several cars in the intersection. He glanced at his mirror and saw Carlos's men rip the bumper off one of the cars and keep coming.

"Brace yourself!" He turned into a multistory parking garage, went to the far side of the structure, and exited onto a different street.

When he finally slowed down, Wanda looked up at him. "Please tell me you lost them."

"For now."

"What are we going to do?"

"We're going to crisscross the city until we reach Interstate 35 and head north."

"And go where?"

He tore his eyes from the road and glanced at her. She was crying. "I'm not sure, sweetheart. All I know is we can't stay here."

"How did you know they were coming?"

"Agent Neal."

"Why did he warn us?"

"That's a long story."

Rob waited until they were out of town before allowing Wanda to get off the floorboard. They drove for almost an hour and a half to Gainesville, Texas, where Rob pulled behind a small gas station to hide their vehicle.

"Why are we stopping?" Wanda asked.

"I need to check on Joey." He went to the pay phone, dropped in a few coins, and dialed the number of the garage. The person who answered wasn't Joey or one of his men. Rob hung up and dialed Joey's home. Again, a stranger answered. Rob hung up and dropped his head. "Please be all right," he whispered.

"Did you reach him?" Wanda asked when he returned to the car.

"No. Someone else answered."

He backed away from the gas station, drove another hour and a half to Paris, Texas, and stopped at a used car dealership.

It took an extra five hundred dollars to ensure the dealer's silence. Rob packed everything into a pale gray '57 Plymouth Fury and drove off the lot.

Wanda turned to him as they joined the traffic headed out of town. "Tell me why Agent Neal called you."

Rob spent the next hour telling her everything. The agreement with Schneider, the arrangement to keep them and Joey out of jail, and his meeting with Agent Neal at the movie theater. "I wanted to tell you," he said, "but I was told I couldn't. The only thing I hated more than lying to you was leaving you to meet Schneider. Each time I did, I was afraid Carlos would come while I was away."

She crossed her arms and glared out the window. "There's a lot you've been keeping from me. I thought we promised to tell each other the truth."

"I'm sorry, sweetheart. I thought I was keeping you safe."

She turned and looked at him. "I'm a grown woman, Rob. I handle things better when I know the truth. Next time, remember that."

*   *   *

They drove on back roads for hours before stopping at a small motel just south of Jefferson City in Rolla, Missouri. Rob checked them into a room, then said, "I need to find a pay phone."

"There's a phone in the room."

"I need to call Agent Neal, and I don't want the FBI tracing my call."

Rob found a pay phone a few blocks away and dialed the long-distance operator. "I need to place a call to Virginia." He gave her Agent Neal's direct number.

"That will be a dollar and twenty-five cents," the operator said.

Rob inserted the coins. A few seconds passed, before the agent answered.

"Neal."

"Where are you, kid?"

"Somewhere in Missouri. Where's Joey?"

There was a long pause. "Sorry, kid. Carlos's people got to him before I arrived."

Rob's gut clenched. "How bad is he hurt?"

"He's dead."

"Was he--Oh, God. Did they torture him?"

"It's best you don't know."

Rob dropped his head against the side of the phone booth.

"The Tollands are safe," Neal said. "I have people watching them around the clock."

"Where was Schneider when Joey was murdered?"

"In Corpus, digging through his botched raid."

"How did you know Carlos was coming for us?"

"Our people intercepted a call from Carlos to Luis telling him to get the records and get out."

"How did Carlos know about the raid?"

"I believe someone from the Corpus Police Department is on Carlos's payroll. Schneider contacted Corpus PD just before the raid, and we think Carlos was tipped off."

"Why would he kill Joey before coming for me?"

"Who knows?" There was a brief pause. "Kid, Schneider thinks you warned Carlos about the raid. He has warrants for you and your wife."

"But you just said it was someone from the Corpus police? Neal, I'm not the leak."

"What I believe doesn't matter. It's what Schneider told the director that matters."

"Damn it! Get Luis to talk. He knows who's on their payroll."

"Luis was killed in the raid."

Rob closed his eyes and dropped his head. "Carlos will blame me for the death of Luis."

"That's why I have to bring you in."

"Why, so you can arrest us?"

"Let's worry about that once you're safe. I'll meet with the director once you are in custody. There's a good chance I can get him to honor the agreement."

"No, thank you. My wife's not spending one night in jail because of me."

"You have to trust me."

"I trusted Schneider, and now Joey's dead. You're crazy if you think I'll let Schneider take my wife. We're better off on our own."

Neal sighed. "You're not thinking this through. Rojas will find you. I saw what they did to your friend. You don't want that happening to your wife."

"Good-bye, Neal." Rob returned the receiver and stood motionless for a moment as rage swept over him. He began pounding the side of the phone booth with his fist.

Finally, he drove back to the motel. Wanda was sleeping and Rob stood by the bed, looking at her, for a few minutes before lying down beside her, letting her hair soak up the tears he cried for his best friend.

The next morning, they got in the car again and Rob drove through the night. By noon the following day, they desperately needed sleep and rented a room in a motel on a back road. Rob got the suitcase and gym bag from the trunk and followed Wanda into the room, but after showering, neither could sleep.

"Rob, talk to me. You've hardly said ten words to me in the last two days."

He turned to her with tears in his eyes. "Joey's dead. Carlos's men killed him."

"What happened to Sybil and the babies?"

Rob pushed himself up against the metal headboard. "They weren't there. Joey told me he sent them to her folks days before this happened."

"Thank God." She leaned against him. "Poor Joey. I can't believe he's gone."

"There's something else. The Feds raided the Corpus compound, and Luis was killed. I'm certain Carlos is blaming me for his death."

Wanda pulled the sheet under her chin. "But if you had a deal with Schneider to protect all of us, why didn't he protect Joey?"

"Neal said Schneider thinks I warned Carlos about the raid. He's issued warrants for our arrest."

"Are you saying we're running from Carlos *and* the FBI?"

"I'm afraid we are."

She went silent for a long minute. "How are we going to keep them from finding us?"

"By staying away from cities and constantly moving. At least until I can figure a way out of this."

Wanda leaned against the headboard, and neither of them said a word. Finally, Rob turned to her. "I'm not letting either of them get to you."

"Us," she said and looked at him. "It's *us*."

"You're right. I'm not letting anything happen to us."

"How will we survive without any money?"

Rob got out of bed, picked up the duffel bag, and placed it on her lap. "Open it."

She pulled the large zipper tab across the top and took out a bundle of bills. "Where did this come from?"

"It's some of the money Carlos paid me."

"How much is here?"

"Around two hundred and fifty thousand. The rest of it is in a Swiss bank account." He zipped the bag and set it on the floor. "I've kept some of the money Carlos paid us hidden in the secret room."

She was silent for a moment. "What's in the Swiss account?"

"A little over four and a half million."

"Did you say *million?*"

"I did. We won't live long enough to spend it all."

She pulled the sheet up to her chin again. "You didn't have to put it like that. Carlos won't stop until he finds us."

"I'm not letting anything happen to you, sweetheart." He kissed her. "Now, lie down and try to rest."

Rob lay beside her, but visions of Joey's tortured body filled his dreams and he woke, covered in sweat and shaking. He glanced at Wanda, slipped from the bed, and crept into the bathroom, where he slid to the cold tile floor and smothered his sobs with a towel as visions of Joey, smiling and giving him his two-finger salute, ran through his memory.

"Don't worry about your family, buddy," he whispered. "I'm going to take good care of them. I promise."

They left early the next day and drove for several hours before Rob pulled off the road by a small market near Grand Island, Nebraska. "I need to call someone."

"You can't tell anyone where we are."

"This person has no connection with Carlos or the FBI and no way of tracing us." He opened the door. "Why don't you get us something to eat while I make the call?"

They went into the market, and Rob exchanged a few bills for coins, then left Wanda to shop as he went to the pay phone outside the building. When he found her again, they got back in the car and Wanda made a bologna sandwich.

"Who did you call?"

"My banker in the Cayman Islands."

"Are you sure you can trust him?"

"I've entrusted him with over ninety million dollars, so I'm pretty sure he wants to keep me happy. He knows people with some, um, unique skills, and we're going to need new identifications to disappear."

"But if he's your banker, Carlos knows about him?"

"He doesn't. I never got the chance to give Luis the information."

"I can't believe you moved almost a hundred million dollars of drug money without Carlos knowing. Did Luis know?"

"He's the one who told me to move it. Carlos may know it was moved but doesn't know where. Luis died before I could give him the ledger and the banks' locations."

"That's another reason for Carlos to be hunting us."

Wanda was biting her bottom lip. "You have to trust me, sweetheart. This is the best chance we have of staying alive," Rob said.

The next day, Rob made another call near Grand Junction, Colorado.

"Was the banker able to help?" Wanda asked when he returned to the car.

"He was. The person I need to see is in Chicago. We need new passport photos."

"How do we do that?"

Rob took some paper from his pocket and handed it to her. "I took a couple of pages from the phone book. Places that do passport photos. But we need to change our appearance. Have you ever dyed your hair?"

"I've never colored my hair. I don't know how."

"Okay, so those pages have names and addresses of hair salons. I'm getting mine colored too," he said.

She rolled her eyes and groaned. "When are you meeting this person in Chicago?"

"As soon as we can get there. He moves around a lot, apparently."

"I'm sure he does."

"Wanda, the best way to keep Carlos and the Feds from finding us is to leave the country."

"For how long?"

"For as long as it takes Carlos and the Feds to forget about us."

CHAPTER THIRTY

Wanda opened her compact, looked at herself in the mirror, and groaned. "I'll never get used to looking like this. I barely recognize myself."

"The less we look like ourselves, the better. Now we need to take those photos."

After having their photos taken, they drove out of town. Getting to Chicago on back roads took three full days. When they arrived, Rob bought a city map, and Wanda called out directions as he wove through the city to an area called Englewood. The sidewalks were littered, the alleyways were cluttered, and there were metal bars across every door and windows. Wanda looked at the men smoking and talking on the streets. "Are we in the right place?" she asked.

Rob pointed to an old apartment building. "That's where I'm supposed to meet him."

"Then why aren't you stopping?"

"I'll come back after I find you a safe place to wait."

"No. I'm going with you."

"Sweetheart, I have a better chance of getting out of there alone than with you."

Rob found a small hotel several miles away and got them a room. Once the door was locked, he put the gym bag on the bed and removed eight one-thousand-dollar bills.

"It's going to cost that much?"

"It's worth every cent if it works. I need your driver's license, social security card, and our new photos."

She took them from her wallet. "Are you sure about this?"

"No, but it has to be done." Rob undid his belt and unzipped his pants.

Wanda's eyes widened. "What on earth are you doing?"

"Concealing the money." He put the bills into his briefs, zipped his pants, and secured his belt. "It's safer there than my wallet."

"If you feel something is wrong with these guys, get out of there."

"I will." He took her hand. "Chicago isn't Dallas, Wanda. Don't leave this room until daylight."

She looked at him for a long moment before nodding. "Please be safe," she whispered.

"I'll do my best. Keep this door locked until I return." He kissed her and walked out.

Wanda locked the door, then collapsed on the edge of the bed.

*   *   *

When Rob finally returned to the motel room with several small paper sacks in his hand, Wanda threw herself into his arms.

"Did you get any sleep?" he asked when she finally let go of him.

"Sleep?" She punched him in the arm. "All I could think about was you bleeding to death in some filthy gutter." She threw her arms around him again. "Next time you do something like that, I'm going with you."

"We'll see about that." He picked up the sack he'd dropped. "I got us some food."

Wanda stood at the end of the bed as he opened the bags on the small end table, then unbuttoned his shirt, took out a packet, and gave it to her.

Wanda dumped the passports, birth certificates, driver's licenses, and several business documents onto the bed. She held up the passports and read the names and addresses.

"So, now I'm Rhonda Campbell from Ontario, Canada?"

"I picked a country that spoke English. I chose that name because Wanda is close to Rhonda, and I'm Richard. Campbell is a common name in Canada. It makes it easier for us to hide."

Wanda chewed her lip as she looked at her passport. After a long moment, her questioning eyes went to his. "Can I say good-bye to my parents before we leave?"

He went to her and lifted her chin. "I'm sorry, but you can't. I'm certain Schneider has ordered your folks to contact him if they hear from you. And remember, Carlos probably has their phones bugged."

"I can only imagine what my dad and mom are thinking right now."

"They love you, Wanda. That will never change. Now, eat something before it gets cold. Tomorrow is a busy day. We have shopping to do before we walk into banks."

"Why are we going to a bank?"

"Not one bank. Several. We can't take this much cash through customs, so we need to deposit it under our new names. When we get to Canada, we'll have the money transferred."

"How long is that going to take?"

"I'm not sure. Each country has its own rules. We have to be patient, Wanda. I mean Rhonda."

She squeezed her eyes shut. "Please don't call me that when we're alone. I don't want to forget who I am."

He wrapped his arms around her and held her close. "I know this isn't easy, sweetheart, but we must do it if we're going to survive."

*   *   *

They visited several stores the following day to purchase luggage and clothing, and then drove to a fine hotel.

"Are we staying here?" Wanda asked as they pulled up to the Chicago Hilton.

"You've had to spend too many nights in dirty motel rooms, sweetheart. It's time I treated you better."

Before she could respond, the bellman opened her door. "Are you checking in?"

"We are."

"I'll get your luggage."

"I'll take the gym bag," Rob said, climbing out of the car.

After changing into new clothing, they visited several banks and opened accounts. Rob kept back enough cash to tide them over until they could transfer the money.

By the end of the day, they were both exhausted. Rob ordered room service, and then they went to bed.

* * *

The next morning, Rob booked a flight to Toronto. Then he left Wanda at the hotel and drove the Plymouth to a used car lot in the same part of the city where he had gotten the documents. He took what the dealer offered in cash and flagged a cab back to the hotel. As glad as he was to be moving forward with their plan, Rob couldn't shake the horrible guilt he felt over forcing Wanda to leave behind her parents, Shelly, her history, and everyone and every place she'd ever known. He couldn't even think about Joey.

* * *

Their flight landed in Toronto, and they went to customs with the other passengers. As they stood in line, Wanda put her arm through his. "The only reason we have survived this is because of you. You're the smartest, strongest man I have ever known."

Rob kissed the top of her head, overcome with love for his wife, and they approached the counter. The customs agent scrutinized their documents carefully, and Rob wondered if the man could hear his heart pounding. Finally, the agent stamped their passports and waved them through. They gathered their luggage and hailed a cab and Rob asked the driver to take them to the nearest hotel.

Wanda stood at their hotel room window, looking at the city. "I had no idea Toronto was so beautiful. How long are we staying?"

"Just long enough to move our accounts to Canada. Once that's done, we move on."

"Move where?"

"Wherever you want. Just make it as far from Dallas as possible."

"I've always wanted to visit Sicily."

"Sounds perfect."

By the time the money was transferred, Rob was in a state of nervous exhaustion. As soon as the verification came in, he booked their flight to Rome, dismissing the echo of Luis's warning that Carlos could find them wherever they went that played in his head.

As they went through the lobby behind the porter pushing the cart with their luggage, Rob noticed a man at the hotel desk with dark hair and tanned skin, wearing a black leather jacket with a red stripe down the sleeve. The man gave the clerk a photo and asked if she had seen the people in it. His accent was definitely Mexican.

Rob grabbed Wanda's arm. "Stay calm and walk to the door as fast as possible."

When they were outside, Rob was relieved to find the taxi and luggage waiting. "Get in," he said to Wanda and went to help the driver with the luggage.

"Airport and hurry," he said to the driver as soon as he got in. As they pulled away, Rob glanced back and saw the man run out of the hotel. He stopped at the curb and watched their cab merge into traffic.

Wanda turned to Rob and whispered, "Was someone here for us?"

"I think it's possible."

"Thank God we're leaving."

*   *   *

They spent the night in Rome, then flew to Palermo, Sicily. Rob got them a room at the Grand Hotel et des Palmes, and they went for a walk, Wanda marveling at the ancient, flower-laden streets. Rob stayed alert for anyone trailing them, but never saw anyone, and they enjoyed their time there so much that a few days turned into a few weeks. Finally, Rob broached the topic of leaving.

"No," Wanda said, shaking her head. "I like it here. The people are friendly, and it's so beautiful."

"I know, but I'm concerned about being in one place too long."

"Have you seen that man from Toronto?"

"No, but I'm certain he isn't the only one Carlos has sent to look for us."

"We've been on the run so long already. We need time to recoup. Maybe it would be harder to find us if we were someplace other than a hotel?"

He pondered this for a day. "I'll agree to stay on one condition. If I see or hear anything suspicious, we're leaving."

She embraced him. "Yes. Of course. Thank you. When can we start looking for a place to live?"

He rolled his eyes and shook his head. "We'll start tomorrow."

They found a small bungalow to rent away from the busy part of the city and settled in. A few days later, they ventured out for dinner at a nearby cozy little restaurant called La Rosa, which quickly became their home away from home.

They introduced themselves to the owners as Rhonda and Richard Campbell, but the owners called him Ricky. Papà Emilio cooked, and Mamma Alessia managed him and their six children. The older siblings waited tables and washed dishes, and everyone cleaned.

One night, after finishing his last order, Emilio tossed his stained apron onto the counter and dropped his hefty frame into a chair at the family table across from where Rob was seated. He poured himself a glass of wine, drank it, then filled it again. "Life is good," he said, leaning back in the rustic wooden chair.

Rob pushed his empty plate aside and lifted his glass. "The *Pasta alla Norma* was outstanding, Emilio."

"Only the best for my friends." Emilio opened his arms and surveyed his surroundings. "I am a most fortunate man, Ricky. I do what I love, with those I love, for people I love. Why could any man want more?" His wife walked up to the table. "Alessia, why do you look so troubled?"

"Rosa called. Aunt Antonina is very ill. Rosa was helping her, but now her husband has injured himself, and Rosa must go home to Gela to help on their fishing boat. I will have to care for Aunt Antonina."

"You want to go to Catania? Alessia, I need you here."

"I know. I told Rosa this was our busy season. I will send Teresa to help."

"But we need all our children!"

"Let me help," Wanda said, reaching for Alessia's hand. "I can wash dishes, wait tables, whatever you need."

"Are you sure?" Alessia asked.

Wanda smiled and nodded. "I would love to help."

Alessia grabbed Wanda and embraced her. "*Grazie, grazie*, Rhonda. We are so grateful."

"When do I start?" She smiled as Alessia released her.

"I will let you know as soon as I hear from my cousin."

While Alessia and Wanda spoke, a man at a table with his wife and two young daughters caught Rob's attention. The way the father played with his daughters reminded him of Joey, which sent a sharp pain to his heart. "Ricky, why do you look so glum?" Emilio said.

Rob forced a smile. "It's nothing. I think it's time we go so you can close up for the night."

Emilio suppressed a yawn. "You are right. It has been a busy night."

Rob and Wanda bade them good night and walked to their bungalow.

"Why are you so quiet?" she asked.

"Just thinking."

"Well, stop it. It's a moonlit night, we're surrounded by beautiful flowers, we had a delightful meal with the first new friends we've made since we got married. You should be enjoying it."

Rob looped his arm around her waist and pulled her close. "You're right," he said, trying to relax.

Wanda wrapped her arms around his neck and kissed him as soon as they entered the bungalow. She led him into the bedroom. Rob unbuttoned her dress, slipped it off her shoulders, scooped her up, and carried her to bed. They made love, and she fell asleep in the crook of his arm.

As he lay holding her, thoughts of the man in the black leather jacket at the hotel in Canada flashed into his mind. Rob glanced down at Wanda, then slid from the bed, dressed, got his briefcase, and stole softly into the kitchen. He removed the packet containing their documents from the briefcase and placed it on the table. He took everything out and started going through them.

If Carlos knew of their new identities, they needed new ones as soon as possible. Rob took a sheet of paper and wrote down double the costs of the ones they'd purchased in Chicago, then tabulated the money they had on hand and estimated the cost of multiple airfares, not counting food and hotels. They had more than enough in their Canadian accounts to cover all of it, but if they had to run before transferring the money to Palermo, then how far they could go would be limited.

Rob looked at the documents from the packet, regretting that all their stocks and securities were in their real names, making them impossible to liquidate. He slipped the documents back into the large envelope. The small black notebook containing Carlos's offshore accounts was the only thing left in the envelope. He was about to return it to the packet when a thought crossed his mind. This could be a bargaining tool.

The bedroom door opened, and Rob slid the book under the paper. "Why are you up so early?" Wanda asked.

"I've been trying to figure something out."

She pulled out a chair and sat down. "Maybe I can help."

He looked her in the eyes. "I've been thinking about the man we saw in Toronto. There's a good chance the hotel clerk gave him our new names. If he did, it's only a matter of time before he tracks us here."

"Then get new documents so we can stay."

"First, I would have to find someone who does it, and the cost of new ones could take a large portion of the money we have on hand."

She looked down at the numbers on his pad. "You said we had two hundred and fifty thousand when we left Dallas."

"We did, but most of it is in the Canadian accounts. The fastest way to handle this is for me to return to Canada, close those accounts, and bring the money here."

"Absolutely not. If Carlos sent that man, I'm sure there are more men looking for us."

"The only other option is to go to Zurich and take money from our Swiss account."

He saw her chewing on her bottom lip. "If that's the only way we can stay in Palermo, then we have to do it."

"After we visit the bank in Zurich, you can stay there while I check on the Cayman accounts."

"If we get money from the Swiss account, why risk your life going to the islands?"

"I have more reason than that for going." He took the small leather-bound book from under the pad and gave it to her. "This book contains all the account information on Carlos's money. Without this, it's impossible to access those accounts."

"Then it can stay where it is until it rots. We don't need it."

Rob caught her hand as she rose from her chair. "Wanda, I have to know it's all there."

She shook her head. "What difference does it make? We have no need of it."

Rob picked up the book and put it in his briefcase. "But there could come a time when we do."

"Until it does, that money needs to stay where it is."

CHAPTER THIRTY-ONE

Rob approached Wanda the following morning as she was dressing. "We need to get you a heavy coat for Zurich. It's freezing there this time of year."

"Rob, I can't leave. I promised Alessia I would help at the restaurant. Can't we wait until her daughter returns?"

"No, we can't. We need new identities, and I'm not leaving here without you."

"I won't be alone. I will spend all my time with Emilio and Alessia at the restaurant."

He crossed his arms. "Not at night, you won't."

"They are counting on me. I can't desert them."

"Then you'll have to stay with them."

"I can't. They have a houseful as it is."

"Either you go with me or you stay with them. Those are the only two choices."

Wanda started to protest, but seeing the look on Rob's face, she relented. "All right. I'm sure Alessia won't mind."

*　*　*

Rob flew to Zurich two days later. The roads from the airport were covered with ice patches, and snow was packed six feet high on the roadside. He checked into a hotel and called Wanda to tell her he was there, then, less than an hour later, met his banker at the Union Bank of Switzerland.

Rob settled into one of the expensive leather chairs beside the banker's massive desk, noting the precise placement of every object on its surface.

"How may I help you?"

"I'm withdrawing a million from my account and want twenty thousand in cash. The rest will be placed into a new account under my wife's maiden name."

The banker opened his desk drawer, removed several forms and slips, and placed them on his desk. "Where would you like to have the million wired?"

"Put it in banknotes. I'm taking it with me."

"I would not recommend that, Mr. Chambers."

"I understand, but that's how I want it done."

"As you wish." He slid documents across the desk, and Rob filled out the new account information, withdrawal, and deposit slip.

The banker gathered the forms and stood. "I'll return shortly."

Minutes later, a young woman appeared with a cup of coffee. Before Rob had even finished, the banker returned with a new leather briefcase and a folder. Rob set aside his cup and watched as the banker counted his banknotes.

"Seven hundred, eight hundred, nine hundred, one million dollars in notes. Here is the confirmation and account number of the three million, five hundred and seventy-eight thousand you requested transferred into the new account." He placed the documents into the new briefcase and gave it to Rob.

"Thank you."

Rob paused for a moment as he contemplated his next question. "Has anyone asked you questions about me or my accounts?"

"No one. Even if there had, no information is given without the client's approval."

Rob exhaled. "Thank you. That's important."

"Is there more I can do for you?"

Rob got to his feet. "Thank you, but no."

"Be mindful of that briefcase, Mr. Chambers, and have a safe trip."

Rob wished him farewell and left his office. He asked the doorman for a taxi, and within minutes, one arrived.

"Where to, sir?" the driver said with a German accent.

Rob hesitated for a moment. "Is there a jeweler nearby?"

"*Ja.* I'll have you there shortly."

Rob looked down at the briefcase. The banker was right. Carrying this much money was risky, but they could stay hidden for the rest of their lives with a million at their disposal.

The driver stopped before a sizable jewelry store and turned to Rob. "Good store."

After some time, Rob returned to the cab holding a small blue bag with a white bow. The driver looked over the seat. "A special gift?"

"Yes. For a special lady. Hotel Ostzeile, please."

The ride back to the hotel was tedious. Between the weather and crowded streets, they were barely moving. Moments later, the taxi came to a complete stop. The driver threw up his hands, followed by a loud protest in German.

Rob sat for a time, drumming his fingers on the new briefcase, and looked idly out the window. He watched people navigating the icy sidewalks while others huddled behind the windows of cafés and shops. Suddenly, one of them caught his eye.

He rubbed the frost from the window to make sure what he saw was real. A man bundled in a heavy coat looked exactly like Joey. Rob watched as a woman with one little girl on her hip and another holding her hand joined the man. The little girl in the woman's arms reached for the man, and he took her and held her close.

Rob closed his eyes and shook his head. Joey was dead. He opened his eyes and realized the man was staring directly at him with a huge grin on his face. The man gave him a two-finger salute and Rob gasped and fell back against the seat.

The taxi driver pressed the horn, yelled out the window in German, and started inching the taxi forward as Rob turned back to get another look at the man, but he and his family had disappeared. His body started to shake, but not from the cold, and his mind was racing. He didn't want to take money from Wanda's Swiss account because he wanted her to have it in case something happened to him, so he would need to provide for Joey's family from the Cayman accounts.

He picked up the phone to call Wanda as soon as he entered his room and sat on the corner of the bed, waiting for the operator to place the call. It rang several times before it was answered. "La Rosa," said the youngest of Emilio's daughters.

"Sofia. It's Ricky Campbell. May I speak to my wife?"

"Sorry, Signore Ricky. We are overrun with customers. I will ask Mamma to have her call you. Good-bye."

"Wait!" The line hummed.

A moment later, he dialed again and was connected to Pan American Airlines. The next flight to George Town left at six that evening, and if he didn't make it, he would have to wait another day. Rob grabbed his belongings and raced to the airport. The plane was boarding when he arrived, and there was no time to call Wanda until he landed on Grand Cayman.

"Sorry, Signore Ricky, your wife is not here. But I told Mamma you called, and she told me Signora Rhonda left a message for you."

"What does it say?"

"Let me look. Mamma put it here someplace."

After a minute, Rob said, "Sofia, are you there?"

"I'm here, Signore, but I cannot find her note. Give me your number, and I will have her call you."

"I'm traveling, Sofia. Please tell your mamma I will try again later."

"I will. Ciao." The line hummed.

Rob went straight to the bank from the airport and was greeted by the same beautiful dark-skinned lady from his previous trip.

"Is Clarence McKay available?"

"Yes, Mr. Chambers. Please have a seat."

Hearing the woman say his name sent a chill up his spine. Rob took a chair by an open window, set his suitcase on the floor beside him, and held on to the briefcase. A rush of ocean air caressed his skin as the gauze-thin curtains danced in the breeze. It was refreshing after breathing recycled air on the seventeen-hour flight from Zurich.

McKay came out of his office and shook his hand. "I am glad you are here, Mr. Chambers. We have much to discuss."

Rob reached for his suitcase and briefcase.

"No, my assistant will take care of your suitcase." McKay snapped his fingers to get the young lady's attention and then pointed to his luggage.

Rob noted the man's demeanor when he entered the office with his briefcase and took a seat. "What's wrong, McKay? Has anything happened to my accounts?"

"No, they are just as you left them."

"Then what is it?"

"A group of men arrived on the island seeking information about you."

Rob fought to remain calm. "What did you tell them?"

"We told them we had no knowledge of you."

"Do you know who they were?"

"I do not. But they spoke to each other in Spanish."

"Were they Mexican?"

"Perhaps. These men went to every bank on the island asking about you."

"How do you know this?"

"We bankers share information when we have unwanted visitors."

Rob took a moment to absorb the news. Now, he knew Carlos was aware he had moved the money offshore.

"I need to make some changes," Rob said, and saw McKay go pale. "I'm not moving the money, McKay. I just want you to make my name disappear."

"If I do that, how will we identify the accounts?"

"With passwords that only I can change."

"This is a strange request."

"Can you do it?"

"Of course. I will make it work."

Rob took a piece of paper from his shirt pocket and slid it across the desk. "This is another thing I need you to do. Transfer five million from the Transmark account and put it into a new account in the name of Mrs. Sybil Evans. I insist you handle that personally, McKay."

The banker took the page. "Of course. I will address this immediately."

"Is there someplace I can make a long-distance call?"

"Of course." McKay took Rob to a private room down the hall and introduced him to a young woman.

"Evette will assist you with the accounts. Feel free to make as many calls as you wish."

"Thank you."

Rob placed the black briefcase on the floor by his feet, took the small leather book from the breast pocket of his jacket, and checked his watch. It was dinnertime in Palermo, and Wanda should be at the restaurant.

He picked up the phone and placed the call. Minutes passed before someone answered.

"La Rosa," said a voice he didn't recognize.

"I am Rick Campbell. My wife, Rhonda, should be there helping Alessia."

There was a pause on the line. "Signore, I am Mario, Emilio's nephew. All that are working are family. Perhaps your wife is at home?"

"Could I speak to Emilio?"

"That is impossible. My uncle cannot leave the kitchen."

"I was told a note was left for me. Can you look?"

"Signore, there is no note," the young man said after a brief pause. "Sorry, more customers have arrived. I must go."

Rob hung up and redialed the operator. He gave the operator the number of the bungalow and took several deep breaths as the phone rang and rang. Rob hung up and glanced at his watch. Cold fear washed over him.. He had to get back to Palermo.

There was a light knock on the door, then Evette entered, followed by a boy wearing a short-sleeved uniform and what resembled an organ grinder's monkey's cap perched on his head. He pushed a cart stacked with packets next to Rob, touched his cap, then left.

"Sir," Evette said, "these are your first documents and the forms required to change your accounts. Your next batch is being printed." Then she left, closing the door behind her.

Rob looked past the documents and reached for the phone to call Pan Am. "When is your next flight to Palermo, Sicily?"

""The next flight is 2:15 p.m. tomorrow."

"Tomorrow? There's nothing earlier?"

"No, sir. There is only one flight from the islands."

"Then book me on that flight."

When he finished making the reservation, he hung up the phone, took the first packet from the stack of documents, and got to work.

It was nearing the end of banking hours when Evette gave him the last account files. A couple of hours later, Rob turned to the final page of his book and placed a check next to the numbers. He was leaning back in the chair, flexing his tired shoulders, when McKay walked in. "I see nothing has been touched since my last deposit."

"As I said, sir, they are as you left them. Have you made your notations of the passwords on the accounts?"

"I have. Are you certain you can erase my name from every document in this bank?"

"I've had my people doing that since you made the request. The first stack of accounts has been completed and will be brought to you for review. You can finish the rest tomorrow."

"I have an urgent flight out tomorrow. I'm not leaving here tonight until it's all done."

Evette returned with another cart of documents. Rob made notations of each new account number and its password in the small black book. By the time he finished, it was after midnight. He left the bank and checked into a hotel. As soon as he entered the room, he glanced at his watch, calculated the time in Palermo, and realized it was 4:10 in the morning. Rob fell across the bed, fully clothed, intending to close his eyes for just a few minutes.

When he woke up, it was after 10:00 a.m. He grabbed the phone and dialed the operator, but once again, Wanda did not answer the phone at the bungalow.

Rob took an ashtray and matches and the black book of accounts out to the balcony table. He licked his finger to test the wind, then ripped the pages containing the old account information from the book, crumpled them into the ashtray, struck a match, and watched them go up in flames. He repeated the process until every page of the old accounts was ashes. The he carried the ashtray to the bathroom, dumped the ashes into the toilet, and flushed them. Then he flushed them again. Once all trace was gone, he took his things and went to the airport.

CHAPTER THIRTY-TWO

It was midday by the time Rob landed in Palermo, exhausted after fifteen hours of airports and planes and terrified by what he might find at the bungalow. He raced outside the airport after retrieving his bag and hailed a cab. "I'll double your fare if you get me to Palazzo Senatorio as quickly as possible."

"Double?" the driver responded.

"Double. Now go!"

The taxi pulled from the curb and zigzagged between cars as they left the airport, then swerved to miss a pair of pedestrians, sending them running to the edge of the cobbled street. When they arrived, Rob pushed the double fare into the driver's hands, grabbed his bags, and ran to his door. Panic rushed over him when he saw the window glass was broken above the lock on the door. He reached in, unlocked the door, and ran in, calling for Wanda. He dropped his suitcase, tossed his briefcase onto a chair, and went from room to room, but she was nowhere to be found.

Rob left the bungalow and ran down the cobblestone streets all the way to La Rosa's. He darted past tables of guests to reach the kitchen.

"Emilio," Rob shouted breathlessly. "Where is Wan--where is my wife?"

"Ricky, she is in the *ospedale.*"

Rob grabbed Emilio's arm. "She's where?"

"The *ospedale.* My Alessia is with her now."

"Are you saying the hospital?"

"*Sì.* Centro Médico."

Rob ran out the door and flagged the first taxi he saw. The drive was endless. Rob paid the driver and ran as soon as the vehicle stopped into the multistory building. He skidded on the tile floors as he reached the front desk.

"I need Rhonda Campbell's room number." The young lady looked at him. "Rhonda Campbell," he repeated. He glanced over the counter to a clipboard of names and pointed.

The girl called to her coworker, who walked over.

"*Buongiorno, Signore.* May I be of assistance?"

"Thank God you speak English. My wife, Rhonda Campbell, where is she?"

The man looked down at the chart. "When was she admitted?"

"I'm not sure. A day ago? Maybe three? I've been out of town."

"Ah, yes, room 344. That's down--Signore! You don't know where you are going!"

Rob ran up the stairs two at a time to the third floor. He burst into the hallway and approached several people dressed in white. "Room 344, 344!"

One of them pointed down a side hallway, and Rob took off in that direction. When he saw her room, he burst in.

Wanda was in bed looking as pale as the sheets that covered her. Rob rushed to her side and took her cold, pale hand. "Sweetheart, what happened to you?" he said, trying to conceal the terror he felt.

"Where have you been? Alessia called the hotel in Zurich, but they said you had checked out."

As if summoned, Alessia entered the room. "Ricky. I am so glad you are here. Rhonda was so worried."

He looked from Alessia to Wanda and back again. "Could one of you please tell me what happened?"

Wanda held out her hand, and Alessia came to her side. "Alessia and Emilio saved my life."

"Saved you?" he asked, his voice shaking as he scanned her face and arms for injuries. "Did someone hurt you?"

"No one," Alessia said. "Rhonda became ill. She was fearful it was the flu and refused to let me come to your home to check on her. I called later that day to say I was coming to bring her food, but she didn't answer."

Wanda looked from Alessia to Rob. "I couldn't. I was throwing up so much I couldn't get to the phone."

"The next day, I could not reach her," Alessia said. "I went to your home to check on her. The light was on, but she did not answer, so I went to get Emilio. He broke a window so we could unlock the door. Rhonda was unconscious on the bathroom floor. We brought her here." Alessia patted Wanda's arm, then looked up at Rob. "The doctors said she was severely dehydrated. It was good we found her when we did."

Rob grabbed Wanda's hand. "My God. Does the doctor know what caused this?"

"We haven't seen him," Wanda answered.

Rob glanced at the door, then turned back to Wanda. "That's ridiculous. We need answers."

"I understand your concern, Ricky," Alessia said. "But there are difficult cases and her doctor has been unavailable. Perhaps today."

"If we don't see him soon, I am getting her another doctor."

Alessia looked at Wanda, smiled, and shook her head. "He is just like Emilio. He has no patience where his family is concerned."

"My wife is all I have, Alessia," Rob said. "Thank you for taking care of her. I am forever in your debt."

"*Gli amici sono la famiglia che scegliamo noi stessi.*" She turned to Wanda and smiled. "Friends are the family we choose for ourselves."

"That is so sweet, Alessia," Wanda said. "We feel the same about you and Emilio."

Alessia leaned over and kissed Wanda's forehead. "Now that your Ricky is here, I will return to the restaurant. I am sure Emilio is overrun and driving everyone *pazzo*," she said, circling her fingers around her head.

"Does that mean crazy?" Wanda asked.

"Sì," Alessia said, and laughed.

Rob walked her to the door, returned to Wanda, and took her hand. "I'm so sorry I wasn't here when you needed me, sweetheart."

She looked into his eyes. "I was terrified something had happened to you. Where were you?"

"I went to Zurich like we discussed. Then . . ."

"Then what?"

"Then I flew to the Caymans."

Her mouth dropped open, and she pulled her hand from his. "We talked about this!"

"I had to go. I went for Joey and you."

"What are you talking about? Joey's dead, and the last thing I want is for you to risk your life going near that money."

Rob closed his eyes for a moment. "Wanda, stop. The last time I saw Joey, he asked me to take care of his family if something happened to him, and he would do the same for you." Rob's voice broke as he spoke. "Joey's dead because of me. I had to fulfill my promise to him."

"But we don't even know where they are."

"I know I can find them, but first, I had to set up a way to provide for them."

"You should have given them the money in the Zurich account. I would rather Joey's family have it than lose you."

"Joey's family deserved more."

"I agree, but four million is more than enough to take care of them for the rest of their lives."

"That's true, but you and I could be on the run for years. I took a million from the Swiss account to ensure we had enough in case that happened." He paused a moment. "And it was important I know the money in the Cayman accounts was still there."

She turned her head and gave him a questioning look. "Why? Who cares if Carlos finds it?"

"I do. I will trade those accounts for your freedom if Carlos finds us."

She closed her eyes and shook her head. "No. I don't want to live without you."

He took her in his arms and held her as she cried. "Please don't leave me like this again," she whispered.

Rob laid her back, kissed her hand, and looked into her eyes. "I won't, I promise."

He stayed by her side for the rest of the night. The next morning, he went to the nurse's desk, demanding to see Wanda's doctor or have another physician assigned to her. He was told no other doctors were available, but they promised Wanda's doctor would see her that afternoon. By late afternoon, Rob was out of patience and went back to the nurse's desk. "I don't care how busy he is. We need information."

"Signore Campbell, Signore Campbell, please. I am here." A man dressed in surgical scrubs hurried to the nurse's station. "I am Dottore Lozano. Let me get your wife's chart, and we will talk in her room."

Rob returned to Wanda and was standing by her bed when the doctor came in. "My wife has been here for days, doctor," he said. "You aren't leaving this room until you tell us what happened to her."

The physician closed the chart and stood at the end of her bed. "Signora Campbell is experiencing a condition called *hyperemesis gravidarum*."

Rob grabbed Wanda's hand. "Oh, God. Can it be cured?"

The doctor smiled. "The condition can be severe and, if not monitored, may again require medical care. However, it should dissipate long before the baby's birth."

Rob's legs folded under him. Wanda reached for him as he went down, nearly pulling the IV from her arm and yelping in pain.

The doctor grabbed Rob, sat him in a chair, and attended to Wanda.

"Baby?" Rob mumbled. He turned and looked at Wanda. "Did he say baby?"

"I thought you knew," the doctor said as he finished securing the IV. "The test and examination show that your wife is four months pregnant."

Rob composed himself enough to stand. "We . . .we didn't know."

The doctor extended his hand. "Then let me be the first to congratulate you."

Rob felt a surge of euphoria flooding him and shook the doctor's hand. "We're having a baby!" He let go of the doctor's hand and kissed Wanda. "When can I take her home?" Rob asked the doctor.

"Not for a few days. Once your wife is released, you must ensure she gets proper care. If she becomes this dehydrated again, it could be disastrous for her and the baby."

"I won't let her out of my sight."

The physician nodded. "*Va bene. Ciao, Signore e Signora,*" he said, closing the door behind him.

Rob turned to Wanda. "I can't believe this."

"It's a miracle," Wanda said, wiping the tears from her face.

"I just remembered I have something for you." Rob picked up his coat, removed the small box from his pocket, and watched as she opened the box.

She lifted the simple gold locket and chain from the box and held it in her hand. "Rob, it's beautiful."

"Open it."

She snapped it open. "These are our horrible passport photos."

"They are there to cover the engravings. Under one photo is the contact information of the Zurich banker. Under the other is your account number. I put it in your maiden name." Rob took the locket from her hand and secured it around her neck. "The account has over three million dollars for you and our baby. Promise me you'll never take this off. I'm not making the same mistake with you that I did with Joey. If there comes a time I tell you to go, you have to go. You have to protect our baby."

"I'm not going anywhere without you, Rob. I don't want to raise this child alone."

He shook his head. "Promise me, Wanda."

She squeezed her eyes shut as if to avoid seeing something terrible. "All right, I promise."

Rob wrapped his arms around her and felt the tension in her body evaporate. They talked for hours and were marveling at their good fortune when a nurse came into the room with her medication.

"The doctor wants her to rest," the nurse said, looking at Rob. "It is time for you to go."

"I want to stay with her."

"That is impossible. Visiting hours or over."

"It's okay," Wanda said. "Why don't you get some rest and go by the restaurant tomorrow to give Alessia and Emilio our news?"

"Are you sure?"

"I know you're dying to tell them. This is your chance."

"I am. I'll come straight to you after I'm done." He kissed her and went to their bungalow.

After he showered, he was too excited to sleep, so he dressed and was about to leave the bungalow when he noticed his briefcase. He'd been so worried about Wanda that he had left a million in banknotes and the book of accounts out in the open with their front door unlocked. He repacked the briefcase and took it with him.

The restaurant was humming with activity when he arrived. Alessia seated him at the family table and brought him food. He set the briefcase between his feet and ate. During a break, Emilio joined him at his table. "It is good you are back, Ricky."

"I'm glad to be back. I am so grateful to you for taking care of my wife."

"You would do the same for my Alessia. Oh, I told my nephew to repair your window today."

"No need. You've done enough." Rob paused a moment. "Emilio, I have something to tell you and Alessia," he said with a broad grin.

"Then, we must hear it." Emilio turned and bellowed, "Alessia!" and motioned for her to come.

She frowned at him when she reached the table. "*Amore*, stop your shouting."

"Sit, *cara*. Ricky has something to tell us." She quickly settled into a chair and leaned in.

"We finally spoke to the doctor. She is . . . We are having a baby."

Alessia clapped her hands, then jumped to her feet and kissed Rob on both cheeks. "*Un bambino!* What fantastic news!" She turned to her husband. "See, I *was* right."

Rob looked at her. "How did you know?"

Emilio gave his wife a swat on her backside. "She has given birth to six. Somehow women know these things." He raised a glass of wine. "You will have beautiful babies, Ricky," he said as Alessia hurried off to greet the first wave of customers that came in.

Emilio and Rob were still enjoying their wine when the family's middle son went to the table.

"What is it, Antonio?" Emilio asked.

"Papà, strange men just came to the door looking for Robert Chambers."

Rob muffled a gasp.

"Chambers? We don't know a Robert Chambers."

"That is what I told them," Antonio said, then turned and looked at Rob. "Then one of the men showed me pictures of you, Signore Ricky, and also Signora Rhonda. They said you also used the name Richard Campbell."

Rob grabbed the briefcase and got to his feet. "What did you tell them?"

"I said we knew no one by those names, and they left."

The blood in Rob's body pulsated in his ears. "Did they say where they were going?"

"They stopped speaking English and spoke Spanish. Of course, I could still understand what they were saying."

"Antonio!" his father shouted. "Tell us what they said."

"They went to check the shops and the neighborhood."

Emilio took his son's arm. "Say nothing of this and go back to work."

"Sì, Papà."

When they were alone, Emilio turned to Rob. "Ricky, who were those men?"

"They are evil people, Emilio. They forced me into their business. When I discovered how dangerous they were, I broke free, and now they want to hurt us."

"What can I do to help you?"

"You can't. I will get my wife and leave Palermo as quickly as possible." Rob reached into his pocket and gave Emilio the keys to the bungalow. "All of our personal things are yours." He put a hand on Emilio's shoulder. "Thank you for everything, Emilio. Take care of yourself and your family."

Emilio wrapped Rob in his massive arms, then whispered, "We care for you. Go out the back so no one will see you." Emilio released his grip, and Rob rushed to the kitchen.

He stepped out of the restaurant and hurried through the alleyways for several blocks before going to the street to hail a cab. He gave the driver the hospital's name, slid low in the seat, and prayed he would get to Wanda before Carlos did.

CHAPTER THIRTY-THREE

Rob pushed money into the driver's hand, draped his jacket over the briefcase to conceal it, and went into the hospital. He took the stairs instead of the elevator to Wanda's floor. With every step, Agent Neal's admonition that Rob would need him in order to stay alive played in his head.

Wanda was sleeping, so Rob slid the briefcase under her bed and left her room to find a pay phone. He dropped coins into the slots and dialed the operator.

"I need to call a number in the United States. Yes, I'll hold."

He dropped more coins into the slot at the operator's request and gave her the number. Several minutes passed, and finally a woman answered.

"Bureau Services."

"I need to speak with Agent Tom Neal."

"Sir, how did you get this number?"

"From Neal. It's urgent. Get him on the line."

"Your name?"

"Tell him it's someone who needs his help to stay alive." His mind was spinning as he waited for Neal to pick up. How was an FBI agent thousands of miles away supposed to help? Rob hung up and returned to Wanda. She opened her eyes as he approached her bed.

"Sweetheart, I have to get you out of here."

"Now?"

"Right now. Carlos's men came to the restaurant looking for us."

"How did they find us?"

"It doesn't matter. We have to go." Rob sat her up, and she almost toppled over. He reached out to steady her. "We need a wheelchair."

"No. I can do this."

"You aren't strong enough. I'll find a chair. Can you unhook your IV?"

"Yes. Go."

Rob went to the door and glanced around. There was a wheelchair pushed up against the wall just past the nurse's station, and he waited, hoping the nurse would walk away, but suddenly he heard shouting in the distance. The nurse hurried to the end of the hallway to see what the commotion was about. Rob followed her. Down the adjoining hallway, a nurse was being restrained by a man as several other men went from room to room. Rob ran back to the wheelchair and took it to Wanda's room.

"They're here!" he said, and pushed the wheelchair up to her bed. He flung open the small closet, grabbed her clothing and shoes, and brought them to her. "No time for you to dress." He lifted Wanda from the bed, sat her in the chair, laid the briefcase and clothing in her lap, then wrapped the bedsheet around her.

He pushed the chair to the door, put a finger to his lips, and looked out. There was no one in sight. "Hold on." He pushed the chair out the door and went in the opposite direction of the commotion. A woman came out of a room, and Rob swerved to miss her, almost toppling Wanda out of the chair. He grabbed her shoulder. "Are you okay?"

"Keep going!" Wanda said, and he picked up his pace. "There's an elevator."

Rob raced to it and pushed a button. "Come on! Come on!" he said through clenched teeth. The doors finally opened, and he pushed Wanda inside. She looked up at him with eyes as round as melons.

When the doors opened to the lobby, Rob saw that everyone's attention was directed toward the hospital's entrance, where several men were standing near the door. One wore a black leather jacket with a red stripe running down the sleeve, and when he lifted his jacket to tug on his pants, there was a gun holstered to his belt.

Rob stepped back into the elevator. "We'll have to get out another way," he said, pulling the sheet over her head. "Don't show your face." He pushed the chair out of the elevator and went to a hallway opposite the entrance.

After several minutes, they came to a set of exterior doors. Rob looked out and saw two parked ambulances. Beyond them was either a driveway or a parking lot, it was too dark to tell. He pushed her through the doors and stopped between the two ambulances. "We need to get you dressed." He stooped down, put her shoes on her feet, then slipped her dress over the hospital gown. "Can you hold on to the briefcase?"

"Give it to me."

"Get a tight grip. This could get rough." He pushed her down the drive to a parking lot and kept going until he came to the end of the block. He pushed her chair across the street and down a row of shops and stopped at the last one on the block. The lights were on, but the door was locked, and the man inside waved him away. He looked up and down the street, but all the businesses were closed. There was a door marked *Bagno*, but it was also locked. "We have to find a place for you to hide," Rob said, pushing the chair down a dark alleyway. "Stay here until I get back."

"Back from where?"

"I'm going back to see if we were followed."

He returned to the front of the alleyway and eased his way up the street toward the hospital. A few doors down, he saw a pay phone and hurried to it. He dropped the last of his change into the slots and dialed. As it rang, he checked the streets for any sign of the men.

"It's Ricky," he said, as soon as Emilio answered. "The men are at the hospital. I got my wife, but she is too weak to walk. We need a place to hide."

"I am coming. Where are you?"

"No, just tell me where to go."

"Ricky. Where are you?"

"On the hospital's north side, near a shop that sells rugs."

"I know the place. I will send my nephew, Mario. He will be there within the hour."

"Emilio, we don't have an hour. Once these men realize we've left the hospital, they will be out looking for us."

"Go to the end of the block to the street called Via Onorato. There is a bakery called Ciabatta on that street. I will send Mario to you there. He drives an old truck with two big, ugly dogs in the back."

"Thank you."

"Be safe, my friend."

Rob hung up and raced back to Wanda. "Emilio is sending help. He will meet us at a bakery not far from here."

Rob pushed the chair to the end of the block and turned down a narrow street lined with shops. Above the shops were apartments. The only light came from the lampposts dotting the sidewalks. Every few feet, Rob turned to look over his shoulder. When they reached the bakery, it was closed. He backed the wheelchair into the dark shadows next to the bakery.

"Stay here."

"Where are you going?"

"To see if we were followed."

Rob went back several blocks and stood in a doorway. Nothing was moving. The only sound came from a few cars on the main road and an occasional barking dog. He glanced at his watch and could just make out the illuminated hands. Twenty minutes had passed since his call to Emilio.

He ventured up to the main road, stood at the corner of a building, and again checked his watch. Thirty-five minutes had passed.

Just as he was about to relax, he saw a group of men run across the street and heard one of them shouting in Spanish. The men started turning in his direction, and Rob slipped backwards as fast as he could, hoping not to be seen, then darted through the alleyways back to Wanda.

"They're coming," he gasped. "We have to leave the chair. Wrap your arm around my neck and hang on to the briefcase." As Rob lifted her from the chair, he glanced over his shoulder and saw one of the men at the end of the block.

"*¡Aquí, aquí!*" the man shouted.

"We have to run," Rob said. "Hang on."

"Put me down!"

He lowered Wanda to the ground, and her legs buckled. Rob wrapped his arm around her waist and supported her as they ran down the street.

Rob glanced behind them. The men were closing in quickly. They were only yards away when a vehicle engine and the sound of barking dogs echoed in the narrow street. A horn blasted, and Rob looked back to see the men scrambling out of the way of a speeding truck. He pushed Wanda against the wall of one of the buildings as the Emilio's nephew skidded to a stop. "Get in!" Mario shouted.

Rob lifted Wanda, threw her into the seat next to Mario, and then jumped in. "Go, go, go!" The tires of the truck squealed, and they sped away.

He glanced out the back window. "Get down!" Rob shouted as gunfire echoed between the buildings.

Mario spun the steering wheel and turned a corner. "My dogs!" he shouted as yelps came from the rear of the truck.

Rob inched up to peer over the seat. "They're okay."

The truck made another sharp turn, and everyone swayed to the right. Rob checked the road behind them. "You lost them."

Mario took the weathered cap from his head and pitched it to Rob. "These men are looking for a man and a woman. Your wife must get down."

Wanda lay in Rob's lap as they sped through several more blocks before Mario eased off the accelerator.

Wanda was gripping Rob's leg. "Are you all right?"

She lifted her head. "Are they still chasing us?"

He glanced at the side mirror. "I think we lost them." Rob looked past Wanda to the driver. "You saved our lives, Mario. Thank you."

"I think we should crisscross the city to ensure we are not found."

"Good idea."

They drove for an hour before Wanda sat up, leaned against Rob's shoulder, and closed her eyes.

Mario glanced at her. "She does not look well."

"She isn't. I have to get her somewhere safe as soon as possible."

"My uncle told me to take you wherever you need to go."

"As far from Palermo as possible. But they're surely watching the airport, plus every train and bus station."

"Then I will take you to the airport in Naples. We will take the overnight ferry, and then I will drive you to the airport. Do you have documents?"

Rob glanced at the briefcase at his feet. "We have everything we need."

"Then, we go."

*   *   *

It was late the following afternoon when they arrived in Naples. Wanda was so tired and weak that Rob knew she needed time to rest before getting on a plane. He had Mario drive around until they found a small hotel, where he rented a room. Rob took Wanda inside and put her to bed and returned to Mario. "I wish you would let me get you a room."

"I prefer to stay out here with my dogs. But have no fear. If anyone comes, they will tell me, and I will warn you."

"Try to get some sleep." When Rob returned to Wanda, she was sleeping. He covered her with a blanket and sat beside her. The thought of Carlos's men getting so close to her made his skin turn cold. Rob lay down next to her and slept fitfully until dawn broke. He slipped from the bed and took his briefcase into the bathroom. When he came out, he went to check on Mario. As soon as he approached the truck, the dogs jumped to their feet, growling, and Mario popped up from the seat.

"*Tranquillo, tranquillo,*" he said to the dogs, and they dropped onto their bellies, keeping their eyes fixed on Rob.

"You weren't kidding," he said as Mario exited the truck. "Nothing gets past them."

Mario turned and scratched his dogs' heads. "They are my children."

Rob reached into his pocket and removed a roll of cash. "Take this. You'll need to buy a new truck and feed those two."

Mario looked up at him, then pushed his hand away. "This I did for my uncle," he said tenderly.

Rob took Mario's hand and folded his fingers around the bills. "You must, for your safety as well as your uncle's. Those men saw your truck, Mario. You must get a different one. Park this one on a side street in the city. Remove everything that could lead back to you or your family. Take the license plates and destroy them. Put the keys on the dashboard, and don't lock the doors. Then get back to Palermo."

Mario laughed. "You want to make it easy for my truck to be stolen."

"That's exactly right."

Mario glanced from him to the roll of bills in his hand. "Never have I seen so much money. When I return home, I will buy the finest truck in Palermo."

"You can't, Mario. If you do, you will attract attention." Rob took an envelope from his pocket and handed it to him. "Please give this to Emilio. Tell him thank you."

Mario took the envelope. "I will see he gets this as soon as I return." He grabbed Rob's hand and shook it. "Take care, Signore. If you return, remember, you have a family in Palermo." Mario got behind the wheel.

Rob waited until the truck was out of sight before returning to his sleeping wife. She opened her eyes when he came near the bed.

"Where were you?"

"I sent Mario back to Palermo," he whispered.

She bit her lip and looked at him. "Rob, I need to tell you something. I called my dad from the hospital to tell him about the baby."

"Wanda, why? Why would you do that? I told you Carlos may have bugged your parents' phones."

"I know. That's why I called Daddy's office. I knew it was safe."

"And who do you think your father called as soon as you hung up?"

Her face drained of color. "Oh, God, he called Mom. Rob, I'm so sorry. This is all my fault."

Rob started pacing.

"Please don't be angry."

He exhaled loudly. "Now we know he has our new identities. And how he found us."

"What are we going to do?"

"That's what we must figure out."

CHAPTER THIRTY-FOUR

Wanda spent most of the day vomiting. When the vomiting finally eased up, Rob carried her to the bed and pressed a damp cloth to her forehead. "Please tell me what I can do to make you feel better."

She laid the palm of her hand on the side of his face. "Take me home. I don't want to give birth to our baby in some dingy hotel room."

"Sweetheart, if we go back, we will have the FBI after us too."

"I know, but I think our baby has a better chance of surviving with them than it will if Carlos finds us." She put her hand to her belly and closed her eyes. "Will you please think about it?"

"I will. You need to rest."

Rob spread a blanket over her, then moved to a chair. When she fell asleep, he slipped from the room and went to the hotel lobby to make a few calls. Wanda was still sleeping when he returned.

He took a wire hanger from the closet and his briefcase into the bathroom. After closing the door, he removed everything from the case and set it on the edge of the sink. Then he twisted the hanger until it broke and used the sharp edge of the wire to tear the briefcase's lining where it met the side of the case. Rob slipped the banknotes and black book under the lining and smoothed it out as best he could, then used the small container of glue he had gotten from the hotel office clerk to dab the ragged edges of the lining, which he tucked back in place with the hanger edge. He set the briefcase on the bathroom floor to let the glue dry and returned to Wanda.

An hour later, her eyelids fluttered open, and Rob sat on the bed next to her. "Feeling better?"

"I think so."

"I've thought about what you said, and you're right."

"Right about what?"

"Going home. While you were sleeping, I went to the lobby and booked our flights to the States."

Her mouth dropped open. "Are you serious?"

"I had no choice." He placed a hand on her belly. "It's two against one."

"When do we leave?"

"Tonight."

She reached for him, and he hugged her. "Thank you, thank you, thank you." She pulled back and looked at him. "But we don't have our new identities."

"I know. But the longer we stay here, the greater our chance of being found."

"Where are we going?"

"Dallas. It's the last place the FBI or Carlos would think we would go," he said, trying to sound convincing. "With any luck, Carlos will be so immersed in hunting us here that he won't realize we are in the States."

*   *   *

After a long day's flight, they landed at Love Field in Dallas. Wanda squeezed Rob's arm when the plane touched the tarmac. "We're home."

"Yes, but far from safe," he whispered.

"I know. I'm just so glad we're here."

As soon as they entered the terminal, Wanda needed a restroom, so they hurried toward baggage claim where they knew there were several. Suddenly, they heard someone shout his name. "Rob . . . Rob Chambers, slow down."

"Keep moving, and don't look back," Rob said.

The faster they walked, the more the man called his name.

"That sounds like Gary Tolland."

"It is." Rob saw a women's restroom and handed Wanda the briefcase. He put his hand on the small of her back, propelling her towards the restroom. "Lock yourself in a stall and don't come out until you hear me call you."

Rob searched the corridor for a place to hide. He saw a shop with a large cutout of Madeleine L'Engle promoting her new book, *A Wrinkle in Time*. He positioned himself behind the display and waited. When Gary walked by, Rob called out to him. "Gary. In here."

"What are you doing?"

Rob motioned to Gary to be silent and follow him. He went to the back of the shop behind a tall rack of books.

"Helen and I have been worried sick about you," Gary said. "We didn't know what to think when the FBI told us we were in danger."

"You still are. Did the Feds tell you why?"

"Agent Schneider said you were involved with dangerous people. He insisted we call him if you contacted us."

"I see," Rob said, his pulse rate rising.

"Don't worry, son. You didn't contact me. I found you." Gary put his hand on Rob's shoulder. "Whatever this is, let me help you."

"You can't. It's too dangerous."

"That's why I hired people to watch Sissy at college and just put Helen on a plane to visit her sister. Everyone's safe."

"No, they're not. These people are killers. They murdered my friend Joey."

"The news said he was killed in a robbery."

Rob shook his head. "Not true."

"Let me help you."

Rob thought for a moment. "There is something." He reached into his jacket pocket, took out a pen and ticket stub, and started writing. Then he took a dollar bill from his billfold and handed both to Gary.

"What's this?" Gary asked.

"Your retainer. I'm officially hiring you to handle the estate of my friend Joey Evans. Sybil's father owns Moore's Market on Delaney Street in Bayton. Find her and tell her to call the phone number on that paper and ask for Clarence McKay." Rob pointed to a row of numbers on the stub. "That is the account number and access code. McKay will take it from there."

Gary glanced at the note, then at Rob. "Do I tell her I got this from you?"

Rob shook his head. "No. Tell her it's from her husband."

Gary tucked the note and dollar bill into his shirt pocket. "I'll handle this myself."

"I was hoping you would." Rob looked past Gary to the door. "I have to go." He extended his hand, but Gary pushed it aside and hugged him.

"Take care of yourself, son. You're important to me. To us."

The lump in Rob's throat made it almost impossible to speak. "It's safer for you if we aren't seen together." He glanced at his watch. "Give me twenty minutes to get to Wanda and get her out of here before you leave the store."

"How is Wanda?"

"Pregnant. I'd tell you more, but I don't have time. It's good seeing you, Gary. Please give Helen and Sissy my love."

"I will. I'm sorry things ended the way they did at the firm."

Rob felt the sting of tears in his eyes. "It was for the best."

"Take care of yourself, son."

"I'll do my best."

When Rob reached the restroom, he stopped a young lady about to enter. "Excuse me, miss. Could you please tell Little Mama that her husband said it's time to go?"

The woman giggled and walked into the restroom. "A tall, good-looking man is at the door waiting for Little Mama. He says it's time to go," she shouted.

Rob heard women laughing, and a moment later, Wanda came out with the briefcase.

He took the case and her arm, exited the airport, and flagged a taxi.

"Bus station, please," he said after getting her in.

"Yes, sir," the driver said. "Any luggage?"

"No."

Wanda leaned next to him and whispered, "Bus station?"

"I was wrong to come back to Dallas. Too many people know us here."

Wanda looked at him for a moment, then sighed. "Well, at least we're in Texas."

*   *   *

The Greyhound pulled into the station and came to a stop. "Houston," the driver said over the intercom.

With his briefcase firmly clamped in one hand and Wanda's hand in the other, Rob exited the bus. Wanda rushed inside the terminal to escape the diesel fumes and find a restroom while Rob called for a taxi. An hour later, they were in a hotel room, exhausted.

Rob went to Wanda's side as she stretched out on the bed and gently pushed hair strands from her face. When she fell asleep, he pressed a soft kiss on her forehead and slipped from the room. The desk clerk told him there was a phone he could use next to the window in the seating area. He went there, waited around until a man reading the newspaper left, and gave the operator Agent Neal's number.

"And your name?"

"It's Kid. I'm calling for Agent Neal. Agent Tom Neal."

"One moment, please."

It took a while before someone came on the line.

"Bureau."

"Will you accept a collect call from Mr. Kid for Agent Tom Neal?"

"One moment."

Rob was doubting his plan when she finally came back on the line. "We will accept the charges, operator. Mr. Kid, please hold."

Rob twisted the cord to the phone so tightly that the phone almost slid from the table.

"Glad you called back," Neal said.

"How did you know I called?"

"I don't give this number to many people."

"Carlos's people found us in Palermo, so we returned to the States."

"Schneider still has a warrant for your arrest."

"He's using me as his scapegoat. He already got Joey killed."

"And you'll be next unless you tell me where you are."

"Texas."

"Texas? That's the last place I thought you would go."

"That's why I chose it. The problem is Carlos knows our new identities."

"Then we have to assume he knows where you went."

"Wanda's pregnant. If I keep dragging her across the globe, I could lose both of them."

"A baby complicates things."

Rob glanced from side to side. "Neal, I have almost a hundred million dollars of drug money hidden, but I'm not telling you where until Wanda is safe and free of any charges. She's done nothing but love me. I'm the one to blame for this."

"If I don't get to you soon, it won't matter how much money you're hiding."

"Are we talking about Carlos or the FBI?"

"Look, you can trust me." Rob didn't respond. "But we're running out of time, kid. Let me help you."

Rob closed his eyes and paused before responding. "We're at the Bayou Vista Hotel on the east side of Houston."

"Room number?"

"107."

"Stay there and keep out of sight until you hear from me."

He hung up the phone. If this was a mistake, he'd just have to pay for it.

*   *   *

The following morning, Rob sat Wanda down and told her what he had done.

"If you're unsure of this, we still have time to go," she said.

"I nearly lost you once. I'm not taking that risk again."

She wrapped her arms around him and laid her head against his chest. "Please don't let them separate us."

"I hope that doesn't happen, sweetheart."

Rob and Wanda waited all day, but Neal didn't call. All she had eaten were crackers and cookies from a vending machine, so Rob took Wanda to a nearby café that evening. When they returned to the room, he switched on the light and found a man standing in the corner.

"I thought I told you to stay put," Agent Neal said.

Rob pushed Wanda behind him. "And you said you would call."

Wanda stepped to Rob's side. "You can't separate us, Agent Neal. Rob was forced to do what he did to protect me."

Neal's eyes smiled, but his face didn't. "I'm not here to separate you, Mrs. Chambers. I'm here to protect you. I'm moving you to a different location. You'll remain there until I can arrange to get you out of Texas."

"We're ready," Rob said. "We're wearing everything we own."

"We can take care of that later." Neal stepped to the window, pulled back the drape, then dropped it. Moments later, there was a light rap on the door. Neal looked through the peephole before opening it. Two men in dark suits entered.

"Time to go. My men will erase your names from the hotel registry. Don't say a word once we leave this room."

Neal peered down the hall before motioning them out. They found another dark suited man waiting for them by the door. Rob draped his coat jacket over the briefcase, took Wanda's hand, and walked out. They got into a car and were driven away, with another automobile following.

"Where are we going?" Wanda asked.

Tom looked over his shoulder from the front passenger's seat. "It's a small house in an area called Galena Park. It's on the end of a dead-end street and backs up to a creek, which I'm told they call a bayou here. It's not my pick of locations."

Rob glanced from Wanda to Tom. "What does that mean?"

"Let's have that discussion after you're in the house."

Wanda leaned against Rob in the dim light and took hold of his arm. They drove for about an hour before entering a neighborhood of middle-class homes built in the 1950s, all of them perched on cinder blocks several feet from the ground. At the end of a long and dimly lit street, the car turned into the carport of the last house on the left side of the road. Two men exited the second car. One stood near the door as the other went into the house. Moments later, the second man came out. "All clear."

Neal got out and opened the passenger door. "Get her into the house."

Rob helped Wanda from the back seat and took her and his briefcase into the darkened home. Neal switched on the lights, and Rob and Wanda saw they were standing in the kitchen. A drop-leaf table sat against one wall with a pair of chairs at each end. In the center of the table were two tarnished gold metal candlesticks holding green candles. A cheap copy of Norman Rockwell's Thanksgiving painting was pinned to the wall above the table. Across the room was a hallway that Rob assumed led to the bedrooms and a bath. To his left appeared to be the living room. Another door with windowpanes covered with a sheer curtain faced the back of the house, and behind him was a gas stove with white cabinets on either side. A yellow phone hung on the wall at the end of the counter, next to the windowpane door, and a creaky Frigidaire stood on the opposite wall.

"This is a safe house?" Rob asked. "I was expecting metal doors and bars on the windows."

Neal grunted. "That's what I would prefer."

"What happens now?" Rob asked.

Neal walked to the small table, lifted one leaf, and locked it. "Take a seat."

Rob and Wanda settled in. "How long will we be here?" she asked.

"Officially, I can't move you until I get the director's approval. You are still Schneider's case."

"Damn it, Neal. I don't trust Schneider with Wanda."

Tom held up his hand. "That's the reason I put you off the grid. I spent a day on the phone trying to get to the director, but he was in meetings at the White House. I'm flying to Virginia tonight to handle this in person."

"How long will you be gone?" Rob asked.

"As long as it takes. I'm not leaving until I get Hoover to turn your case over to me and reinstate your immunity agreement."

"Do you think he'll agree?"

"Yes, after I assure him you will assist the Bureau in capturing Rojas and the rest of his people. To make this work, I'm telling him you will give up the information on every company and account you set up across the United States."

Rob and Wanda exchanged glances. "Let me make sure I have this right," Rob said. "You're saying if I help you find Carlos and give you access to all the accounts I opened across this country, we'll be free of all charges?"

"That's what I'm offering. Of course, you'll still have to testify at trial."

"What will happen to us once the trial is over?" Wanda asked.

"We will set you up in a new location under different names and help you get a new start."

Wanda glanced from Rob to Agent Neal. "And you think your director will agree?"

"I do. You deserve another chance after what happened to you and your friend."

Rob glanced at Wanda, then back to Neal. "I've asked this before, but why are you doing this?"

"I have my reasons. Now, give me everything that has your names on it."

Rob reached for the briefcase and quickly produced their documents and stock certificates. He took out the cash he had gotten from their Swiss account, but Neal told him to keep it. Rob left the book of offshore accounts and banknotes hidden behind the case's lining.

Neal took the documents and got to his feet. "Stay inside with the curtains drawn until I return."

"Keep Schneider away from us, or I'll hurt him," Rob said. A smile played across Neal's face.

"Now that I would pay to see." Neal went to the door and let two agents in. "Keep this place locked up and them out of sight," Neal ordered.

"Any news on our second line of defense?" the sandy-haired agent asked.

"I'm working on it. But until then, your job is to keep them safe," Neal said, then went out and closed the door.

"I suggest the two of you get settled," said the agent.

"What are your names?" Wanda asked.

"I'm Agent William Frankston. My friends call me Bill. And this is Agent Andrew Hawkins."

Wanda looked at the second man. "And what do your friends call you?"

"Agent Hawkins, ma'am." He blinked but never smiled.

"Oh, I see. Thank you, Bill and Agent Hawkins, for protecting us."

Rob glanced at his watch and saw it was after 9:00 p.m. "How long is your shift?"

"We're here until 0700 hours or our replacements arrive."

"See you in the morning, gentlemen." Rob started toward the hallway, stopped, and took the two metal candlesticks from the table.

"What are you doing with those?" the agent asked.

"Just a little something to have on hand," he said, testing the weight of the metal candlesticks. "Good night."

Rob entered the bedroom and placed the candlesticks on his nightstand.

"Are you expecting the lights to go out?" Wanda asked.

"You never know," he replied.

"Rob, you said you would give them the accounts in the States. Shouldn't that also include the offshore accounts?"

"Not until I know we're free of prosecution."

"Do you believe Neal can make that happen?"

"He's the best chance we have." He kissed her on the forehead. "You need to get some rest."

"What about you?"

Rob picked up the candlesticks. "Until I know we're safe, I'm not taking any chances."

CHAPTER THIRTY-FIVE

Rob looked out the back door at the bayou from the exact spot he'd stood in at least a hundred times over the last few days. Wanda watched him as she sipped hot tea at the kitchen table. "What on earth are you looking at?"

"Nothing. This waiting is driving me crazy." Rob turned to the agent of the day sitting near the back door, reading the newspaper. "Have you heard anything from Agent Neal?"

The agent glanced at his partner leaning on the hallway doorframe. He shook his head. "Sorry, sir. Nothing yet."

"Why is this taking so long?"

"These things take the time they take." The telephone rang, and Rob moved to answer, but the agent laid the paper aside and stood up. "Sir, back away," said the agent. "Hello? Agents McMillon and Hathaway. Yes, sir. He's standing right here." McMillon handed Rob the phone.

"Kid, it's me."

Rob mouthed *Neal* to Wanda as she stood next to the table. "I was beginning to think you had forgotten us."

"Not likely. I've been fighting for you since I arrived. Did you receive the clothes I sent?"

"We did. Thank you."

"How are you holding up?"

"It's a good thing you can't die from boredom. At least Schneider hasn't shown up."

"That's because he's here. He flew up when he heard I was asking for your case."

"Is he fighting you on this?"

"Of course. But as it turns out, I'm glad he came. The director was very disturbed over the death of Luis and your friend, as well as the agency losing track of you."

"How disturbed?"

"Enough to give me your case and reinstate your deal."

Rob locked eyes with Wanda as he spoke. "So, we won't be charged if I cooperate with you?"

"That's right. I'm flying back after all the paperwork is handled. I should be able to move you to a more secure location tomorrow afternoon. I've also requested medical care for your wife once you're settled."

"That's great news."

"Kid, this isn't a gift. No one knows these people better than you. We need your help to find them and take them down. I'll see you first thing tomorrow morning."

Rob hung up the phone. "We have a deal."

"Are you serious?"

He wrapped his arms around her. "Neal said the director agreed to drop the charges against us if I assist them."

The stress on Wanda's face dissolved into a smile. "Oh, honey, that's wonderful."

"Neal's returning tomorrow afternoon to move us."

"I can't believe it's almost over."

"At least now we don't have to worry about Schneider," Rob said. "He's done enough damage."

That evening, when the shift ended for McMillon and Hathaway, Agent Bill returned.

"I'm told you're leaving tomorrow," he said.

"We are," Wanda said. "Who is your new partner?"

"Agent Donaldson, ma'am," the agent said with a dip of his head. "And since this is my first time here, I must check the house and yard to understand the layout."

"Help yourself. My husband is in the bedroom."

"Thank you."

The agent started down the hallway and put his hand on his revolver when Rob stepped out of the bedroom. They spoke for a moment, then Rob went into the kitchen. "What happened to Hawkins?" Rob asked.

"He was reassigned," Bill replied.

Agent Donaldson returned. "I'm going out to check out the property." He stepped outside, closing the door behind him.

"I'm sure you are ready to get out of here," Bill said.

"We are. Doing nothing all day is mind-numbing. I don't know how you stand it."

Bill chuckled. "Training. Lots of training."

Wanda tried to conceal a yawn, and Rob smiled. "It's getting late. Time to get you to bed." He nodded to Bill, and the couple went down the hallway to the bedroom.

Rob set his briefcase next to the bed as Wanda changed into a gown. He removed everything except his boxers, got under the sheets, and switched off the lamp.

He pulled Wanda close and began gently stroking the slight roundness of her belly. "Good night, Little Mama," he whispered. "Get some rest." He closed his eyes and went to sleep.

*　　*　　*

A sound woke Rob. He sat straight up in the bed.

Wanda grabbed his arm. "What was that?" she whispered.

"I don't know," he said, getting to his feet. "Get up and put on your shoes."

Rob opened the window, unhooked the screen, and let it fall to the ground.

"What are you doing?"

"I'm giving you a way out of here." He took the nightstand, positioned it under the window, and took her by the shoulders. "If I'm not back in two minutes, you climb out that window and find a place to hide. I mean that Wanda," he said with urgency.

"Not without you," she pleaded.

"Don't argue. Lock the door behind me and get up on that nightstand."

She held on to him, then whispered, "I love you."

He kissed her and grabbed a candlestick before opening the door. He left the room and instantly knew something was wrong because the light in the kitchen was off. He slipped down the hallway on bare feet, looking in the kitchen doorway for the agents. They weren't there.

The back door was open. Rob eased past the table and looked into the living room. Both agents were lying on the floor.

"Wanda, run! Wand—" Someone grabbed Rob from behind and threw him to the floor. He rolled, trying to escape, but hands grabbed his legs. As Rob tried to break free, a second man pounced on him and tried to pin his arms. He broke free of his grasp, swung the candlestick, and struck the man on the side of his head. The man fell over, and Rob struck him again, then scrambled out of his reach and got to his feet. He was immediately hit in the back with a metal kitchen chair and fell face down.

Someone jumped on top of him, but Rob quickly threw him off. The man tackled him again and pinned him by the arms, allowing his partner to pound Rob in the face.

Rob freed his arms and landed a hard right to his assailant's jaw, knocking him on top of the other. He scrambled away and almost reached the hallway when everything went black.

*   *   *

Rob felt a sharp pain to the side of his face, and then another.

"Esteban, enough. He is awake."

Rob struggled to open his swollen eyes. A man's face bobbed inches from his. The fog in his brain began to clear, and Rob realized he was in the bottom of a flat-bottomed aluminum boat in the middle of the bayou, and his hands and feet were tied.

"Where's my wife?"

"She is no longer your problem," the smaller of the two men said.

"What did you do to her?" Rob yelled. "If you hurt her, I'll kill you."

The man started to laugh. "There are two of us, gringo."

Rob tugged and pulled at his restraints, causing the boat to rock.

"César, make him stop," Esteban said, gripping the boat's sides. "I can't swim."

Rob felt the pressure of something hard pressed against his skull.

"Stop, or I will have to kill you."

"No, you won't. Carlos wants me alive so he can do it himself."

"That is true." César holstered his weapon. "But Esteban can make you wish you were dead. He is particularly good with a knife. Just ask the people back at the house. Oh, that is not possible. They are dead."

Fear gripped Rob. "Damn you," he growled between clenched teeth. "What did you do to my wife?"

"Soon you will see, gringo. Soon, you will see. Enough with the talking." César grabbed him by the arm and sat him up. "Gag him, Esteban. I need to get us further away from the house."

Rob thrashed from side to side to break free of the rag being forced into his mouth.

"Esteban, get out of the way. It should happen about--" Before he could finish, a blast of light lit up the sky, followed by an enormous fire.

Rob screamed behind the gag as embers and flaming debris splashed into the black waters of the bayou. He fought to free himself, but it was useless.

César laughed, but there was no humor in the sound. "It will take them weeks to find all the scattered body parts."

Rob lunged forward and was jerked back to the bottom of the boat. The sound of the two men laughing sickened him.

"Capturing you will make us wealthy men, gringo."

Rob said nothing. His eyes were fixed on the flames leaping into the air as the boat moved further down the bayou. By the time they reached a small landing, the red glow was dancing above the treetops, and the sound of fire trucks and police sirens pierced the silence of the night air.

"Stay with him," César ordered. "I will get the car."

"Hurry," Esteban said as he slapped his face and arms. "These bugs are eating me alive." Moments later, César returned and ordered Esteban to untie Rob's legs, and they pulled him from the boat. The moment his feet hit the dock he butted the shorter Mexican and lunged for the taller man, but a blow to the jaw with a gun sent him to the ground.

"Save your strength, gringo," César said. "You're going to need it." The men pulled him to his feet and shoved him into the car's back seat.

Rob twisted his body as much as he could to watch the red glow until it disappeared. He fell back against the seat and closed his eyes, reeling from despair.

CHAPTER THIRTY-SIX

They stopped at a darkened market on the outskirts of town and took Rob from the car to a pay phone on the side of the building. César removed his gag. "It will do you no good to yell for help because no one is around." He turned to the other man. "Guard him, Esteban, while I make the call."

Esteban took his knife from its sheath and pressed it to Rob's throat. "Behave yourself, or I will slice you open."

Rob spat fibers from his mouth. "Go ahead. I don't care anymore."

"Shut up," César said. "The boss is on the line." He pressed the phone to Rob's ear.

"Roberto, Roberto. It has been such a long time since we spoke."

"Not long enough."

"My brother is dead, Roberto. He died because of you."

"That's not true. He's dead because he followed you into your drug business."

"No. He is dead because you betrayed me." Carlos paused. "I was told your friend whimpered like a child. Perhaps you will too."

"You're insane, Carlos."

"That may be true, but I would rather be insane than be you, my friend. My mother will not have peace until you pay for her son's death."

"By the time this is over, she could be grieving for two sons, Carlos."

César punched Rob in his gut, and he fell to his knees.

"You must be special, gringo," Esteban said as he lifted Rob to his feet. "The boss has not left México since his brother's death."

"Shut up, Esteban, and take him to the car," César said as he hung up the phone.

Esteban shoved Rob into the car's back seat, and then got in beside him. Rob lost all track of time and location until they passed a giant illuminated billboard that read *Welcome to Galveston*.

César followed the coastline, passing shops and businesses until there was nothing but moonlight glistening over the vast expanse of the Gulf. A short time later, he slowed and pulled off the road.

Rob sat up and looked out the window. The full moon setting above the waterline made it possible to see a boat dock across from where they had parked. In the distance, silhouettes of beach homes suspended on pilings dotted the coastline. César turned off the headlights and engine before exiting and opening the back door. "Time to go, gringo."

Esteban pulled Rob from the car, and the two men took him to the dock. The boards creaked under their weight until they reached the end of the pier, where a speedboat was tied. Esteban shoved Rob off the dock into the boat, where he landed face down.

It took Rob a moment to realize he had fallen on something. César and Esteban were busy readying the boat, and Rob took the opportunity to turn to his side and wiggle until he could take hold of the object with his bound hands. It felt like a quart-size bottle. He ran his fingers over the plastic container and discovered it had a screw-on cap. He gripped the bottle tightly between his hands and rolled on his back to conceal it.

As the boat eased away from the dock, Esteban pulled Rob up and shoved him into the seat at the back of the craft. He secured Rob's feet with a rope and went to the front of the boat. César tested the motor's power, almost tossing Esteban backward.

Rob looked up and noticed that the stars were dimming, which meant daybreak was coming. He had to get free of the ropes before that happened. He ran his hands along the length of the bottle until he came to the cap and worked at it with his fingers until it came off.

Some of the contents splashed on his hands, and he rubbed his fingertips together. It certainly felt like motor oil.

Working the liquid into the bindings around his wrists, he kept a close watch on the two men at the front of the boat. It took time, but he was finally able to wiggle a hand free. He checked on the two men again before pouring the oil on the cord around his feet.

The boat took a big dip, causing water to spray over the vessel, and Rob quickly put the bottle and his hands behind his back as Esteban turned to look at him for a few seconds, then turned again to the front.

Rob watched the men as he worked the knot at his feet. When they were free, he looped the rope around his ankles and resumed his captive position.

Esteban pointed to something, and Rob shifted in the seat to get a better look. He saw a sprinkling of lights near the waterline. It had to be an oil rig.

Esteban seemed to get excited when he saw lights circling the night sky above the rig. The lights drifted down to the Gulf and disappeared, and Rob realized it was a seaplane. The speeding boat suddenly veered to the left of the oil rig platform as a beam of light from the oil rig flashed across the water. A searchlight. Esteban turned, and Rob thought he was looking at him until he started shouting in Spanish and pointing to the rear of the boat.

Rob turned, too, and saw several sets of lights coming in their direction. César pushed the throttle forward and the engine roared, splitting the waves with all the force the motor could provide. Rob looked back again. Whoever was following them was still getting closer. Rob glanced to the east and saw the first glow of dawn on the horizon.

César eased back on the throttle and approached the aircraft as the glow of dawn spread across the water. The door to the plane opened, and Rob saw Carlos sitting next to the pilot.

"We have him, El Cerebro! We have him!" Esteban shouted as he took hold of the plane's pontoon.

A series of horn blasts sounded.

"Get him on the plane!" Carlos shouted.

Rob rewrapped his wrists with the oil-soaked bindings and braced himself as César dragged Rob to the boat's side and pushed him up.

Another horn sounded, followed by a megaphoned voice "This is the United States Coast Guard! Stop your engines and prepare to be boarded!" Carlos unbuckled his seat belt and stepped out onto the plane's pontoon as César pushed Rob up.

Rob took several deep breaths, pulled his hands free, grabbed Carlos, and plunged into the Gulf. Carlos broke free of Rob's grasp as they sank beneath the dark water, and Rob swam to the surface looking for him. When he surfaced, he saw the Coast Guard vessel chasing the speeding boat and the plane taxiing across the water, preparing to get airborne again. Rob spun around and saw Carlos swimming toward the oil rig. He swam as fast as he could and grabbed Carlos from behind, wrapping his arms around his chest and pulling him under the water. Carlos clawed at Rob's face, arms, and body, as the two of them sunk deeper. Rob refused to let go of Carlos, dragging him down with all his might until finally, Carlos stopped moving. Rob felt the encrusted piling of the oil rig. He paused against it and released Carlos. Moments later, something large and scaly brushed against his leg.

CHAPTER THIRTY-SEVEN

People enjoying the sandy beaches of Galveston were shocked to see a man stagger from the water wearing nothing but boxer shorts.

Rob was too weary to care as he forced his tired legs across the scorching hot sand to the road's edge. Several souvenir shops and what looked to be a diner were on the other side, and he was about to cross when a helicopter overhead drew his attention. He turned to look at where it was going and saw that other helicopters were hovering over the water near in the direction of the oil rig. Rob stepped barefoot onto the hot asphalt and hurried across as a car sounded its horn and a young woman leaned out the rear window, whistled, and shouted, "Hunk-a, baby!"

Rob approached the diner and peered through the large window. There were a few customers, and an older man working behind the counter. When the bell jingled as he entered, every person in the room stopped and looked at him. After a moment, the man working the counter approached him.

"I've had more than my share of guys come in here after a hard night, but none that's looked as bad as you." He held up a hand. "Don't move. I'll be right back." The old man hurried away. When he returned, he gave Rob a shirt, a pair of pants, and a couple of dish towels.

"I know my clothes are too big, but it's better than walking around in your underwear."

"Thanks, Mister--"

"Sol. I own the place."

"Thanks, Sol. Where can I—"

Sol pointed to the door at the far end of the counter. "Wash up and I'll get you some coffee and something to eat. You look like you could use it."

Rob limped to the restroom. When he returned, he sat at the counter. Sol set a plate of scrambled eggs and bacon and cup of coffee in front of him. Rob's hands shook as he put the cup to his lips. He took a sip from the cup and looked down at the plate.

"Thanks."

Sol leaned forward on his elbows. "Normally when someone staggers in, it's booze, a woman, or both. But from the look of those cuts and bruises, I'm guessing it's something else." He paused a moment. "What happened to you?"

Rob's eyes dropped to the cup's black liquid, and he swallowed hard. "Let's just say I went through the worst night of my life."

Sol pointed toward the Gulf. "Does it have anything to do with all that commotion?"

"Not sure."

Sol reached back and got the coffee pot. "You got someone you can call?" he asked, topping up Rob's coffee.

Rob thought for a moment. "There's one."

"Then come around and use my phone."

"It's long-distance," he said as he got off the stool.

"That's okay."

Rob went to the phone and dialed. "I need to speak to Agent Tom Neal."

"One moment, please."

"Lady, don't put me on hold."

Another woman came on the line. "Sir, who gave you this number?"

"Neal did. Is he there?"

"I can't give out that information."

"Then tell him to come to—" Rob looked at Sol.

"Sol's Twenty-Four-Hour Diner on the west end of Seawall Boulevard, Galveston Island."

"Did you hear that?" Rob asked.

"I did, and what is your name and the phone number where he can call you?"

Rob read the number off the phone. "Tell Neal it's the kid. He'll know who I am." As Rob hung up, the bell over the door jingled, and a young couple walked in.

"Why don't you sit at my grandkid's table in the corner next to the window?" Sol said. "It's going to get busy in here pretty quick."

"Thanks." Rob went to the table and watched as more people entered. He looked out the window and saw police cars buzzing past, and more gathering on the beach. Images of Wanda flooded his thoughts, and he had to fight to hide his tears. Sol continued to check on him over the next few hours, but Rob had no interest in food.

The sun was setting on the Gulf when a black automobile turned in front of the diner and parked. Rob recognized Neal as soon as he got out. He stood looking out at the activity on the Gulf for a long moment before removing his jacket and tie and tossing them into the front seat of his vehicle. He entered the diner and approached the counter. Sol pointed at Rob, and Neal went to him, shaking his head.

"Damn, kid. I thought you were dead."

"Neal, Wanda's missing," he said with tears falling from his eyes. "There was an explosion, and I'm afraid she didn't—" He couldn't finish.

Neal reached out and squeezed his shoulder. "Let me see what I can find out." He went to the counter, said something to Sol, then went to the phone. Several minutes later, he started back, and Rob got to his feet.

"Sit down, kid. This will take a while. My office will contact my men and give them this number." Neal took the chair across the table from Rob.

"What took so long for you to get my call?"

"I was in Virginia when I heard about the explosion. I flew to Houston thinking you were dead. I can't tell you how glad I was to get your message." He glanced at the cuts, scrapes, and bruises on Rob's face and arms. "How many did it take to do that to you?"

"Two."

Neal looked out at all the activity on the Gulf. "Coast Guard says an oil rig reported a seaplane landing last night without lights or identification markings. The rig suspected it might be a drug drop and gave the location. Does your being here have anything to do with that?"

Rob shook his head. "There was no drug drop, Neal. The plane was there for me."

"They were taking you to Rojas?"

Rob shook his head. "Carlos came to get me himself."

"Damn," Neal said, leaning back in his chair. "He's probably in Mexico by now."

"The plane could be, but Carlos isn't."

Neal sprang forward. "Are you saying he's here?"

"Not here." Rob pointed toward the Gulf. "There."

"What kind of boat picked him up? I need to report it."

"No boat. He wasn't picked up."

"Then where is he?"

"Under the oil rig that called in the report."

"Wait a minute. That rig's a good five miles out in the Gulf. How did you get here?"

"I swam."

"You swam?"

Rob nodded.

"You must be part fish to swim that far." Neal paused a moment. "So, you were the one the rig crew said pulled another man out of the plane."

Rob nodded.

"If you made it here, Carlos could have too. I need to report this."

"Don't bother. There's nothing left of him by now."

"What are you talking about?"

"Alligator gar."

"What the heck is that?"

"It's a carnivorous fish with a long snout of sharp teeth. They gather under oil rig platforms to eat the garbage that gets tossed over.

Plus anything else that falls overboard." Rob took a deep breath. "I gave them Carlos."

Tom sat back for a long moment in silence. "This poses a problem, kid. Without his body and yours, the organization will think he's alive and come searching for both of you."

"Let them come. Nothing matters without Wanda."

The phone rang, and Rob jumped to his feet. He watched Sol answer, then set the receiver down and call out, "Mister, it's for you."

Rob's heart was pounding and he could barely breathe as he watched Neal talk on the phone. Rob searched Neal's face as he approached and stopped breathing when Neal placed his hand on his shoulder. "She's alive, kid. My men are with her now."

Rob dropped into the chair, covered his face, and wept. He was barely conscious of Neal's hand resting on his shoulder. After a moment, he looked up. "Was she hurt?"

"She apparently jumped out a bedroom window and crawled into a concrete culvert to hide before the explosion. She's at the hospital now being checked out."

"And the baby?"

Neal patted Rob's shoulder before he sat back down. "Relax, kid. I'm sure they are both fine."

"How can I relax? I can't let the organization near her again. Without Carlos, the organization will be in chaos. This is my chance to take down Diego and Alejandro."

"You aren't doing anything. Anger and hate are clouding your judgment."

"I have to get rid of them, Neal. It's the only way to protect my family."

"You will be protecting them by helping us. We need all the information you have before you forget it."

"That's never going to happen."

"Oh, it will. I see it all the time."

"It won't. Every bank, account number, contract, property document, face, name, and conversation I've had with them is locked in my head."

"That's not possible."

"For me, it is. I have a photographic memory."

Tom held his gaze for a moment. "So that's why the organization picked you to launder their money."

"And it's why Diego and Alejandro will keep hunting me until they kill me. I know all their secrets."

"I see your point."

Rob shook his head. "I need to see Wanda."

"That's not a good idea right now. Once the Bureau knows you survived the house explosion, they will take you in for processing, and you could be separated for months."

"They can't do that. I need to be with Wanda when our baby is born."

"Then you need to listen to me. For now, it's best that no one knows you're alive."

"What about the Bureau?"

"Especially the Bureau. Schneider is back in Virginia trying to persuade the director to return Wanda and your case to him."

"Neal, if Schneider takes over, he will send Wanda to jail."

"Trust me, kid. I'm not letting that happen." Neal stood, took two large bills from his wallet, and placed them on the table. "If you want to see her, come with me.

Rob got to his feet. "Then what are we waiting for? Let's get out of here."

*   *   *

Five months later

Rob stood inches from the glass partition as a nurse presented his beautiful, pink-cheeked baby girl.

"Amazing, aren't they?" a voice from behind him said.

Rob turned and saw Agent Neal grinning at him. "When did you arrive?"

"A few hours ago."

"If you're here to take me back for more debriefing, forget it. I'm staying here."

"That's what I told the director. He's agreed to give you some time with your family before you have to return. I came to congratulate you and ensure my people were covering you."

"Has word leaked that I'm alive?"

"As far as we know, the organization thinks you're dead."

"That can change, though. Those people are vicious."

"I know, kid. They killed my son."

Rob was speechless until a nurse called out to him. "Sir, we just moved your wife into room 308."

"Oh, thank you. I'll be right there."

Rob waited until the nurse was gone before turning to Neal. "When did that happen?"

"Two years before I met you." Neal looked away for a moment. "You remind me of him." He cleared his throat. "That's all I'm saying about it."

Rob saw the pain in Neal's eyes and changed the subject. "Are you going back to Virginia?"

"I will after I inspect your new home. I want to make sure it's secure before your wife and baby leave the hospital."

"The Bureau's relocating us?"

"It's time you and your family were out of a safe house. This is a special time, kid. Don't waste one minute of it."

"How will I let you know when we're released?"

Neal pushed the button for the elevator. "You won't. My people will handle it. Give Wanda my best." The doors opened, and Neal disappeared behind them.

Rob turned back to the window and took one more look at his baby girl before going to see her mother.

He entered Wanda's room, holding a bouquet of pink roses.

She smiled wearily. "They're beautiful. Thank you. Have you seen your daughter?"

He set the flowers on the windowsill near her bed. "She's perfect, sweetheart. She looks like you."

Wanda's smile faded. "Rob, are you positive we're safe? I'm terrified Carlos's people will find us."

He placed a gentle finger across her lips. "Haven't you been through enough today? We should be celebrating."

"How can I? We have a baby to protect."

Rob took her into his arms. "Sweetheart, the FBI has people here protecting us."

"But we had FBI protection when Carlos found us."

"I just spoke to Neal. He's moving us out of the safe house to a more secure location as soon as you and the baby are released from the hospital."

Before Wanda could respond, a nurse entered the room with their baby in her arms. "This little girl wants to see her parents." She placed the child in Wanda's arms. "I think it's time the three of you get acquainted," she said, leaving them.

Wanda kissed and spoke softly to their newborn infant as Rob took it all in, his heart expanding in his chest. He pushed Carlos and his organization from his thoughts and locked this incredible moment into his memory forever.

ACKNOWLEDGMENTS

Love and gratitude to my dear friends and beta readers. Thank you for suffering through all those early drafts. I couldn't have done this without you.

Marolyn Lampman

Maria West

Denise Rives

Suzanne Rankins

Dennis Owens

Kathline Salem

Joy Payton

Kathy Nobles

Jerry Bridwell

Sarah Thompson

Hsb Writers

Sherry Maysonave

And editor Pam Johnson for taking me through all the first edits of this book.

ABOUT THE AUTHOR

Donna Joppie was born with an insatiable desire to create. This desire has dominated most of her life in many forms. Painting, interior design, photography, but none have been as rewarding and fulfilling as her love for writing.

The Memory Trap was a finalist in the Thriller, Action, Suspense category of the 2016 Writers League of Texas Manuscript Contest for her unfinished edition.

Donna was born into a large family and raised in South Louisiana. She has traveled the world, but she and her husband Rick chose the beautiful hill country of Texas as home.